NO WAY BACK

ALSO BY J. B. TURNER

Jon Reznick Series

Hard Road
Hard Kill
Hard Wired
Hard Way
Hard Fall
Hard Hit
Hard Shot
Hard Target
Hard Vengeance

American Ghost Series

Rogue
Reckoning
Requiem

J.B. TURNER

NO WAY BACK

This is a work of fiction. Names, characters, organizations, places, events, and incidents are either products of the author's imagination or are used fictitiously. Any resemblance to actual persons, living or dead, or actual events is purely coincidental.

Published by Thomas & Mercer, Seattle

www.apub.com

ISBN-13: 9781542030052
ISBN-10: 1542030056

Cover design by @blacksheep-uk.com

Printed in the United States of America

To my mother

She felt her body being dragged through woods. The necrotic aroma of leaves. Bone-dry earth. Scorched grass. Branches scraping her skin. She realized she was breathing faster. And faster. Then she sensed she was in water. The Potomac. Cold water. Paralyzed with fear, she tried to open her eyes, but try as she might, she couldn't. She attempted to scream. But no sound came, like in a bad dream.

The screams echoed only in her head. She wanted her husband to hear her. The cold, dark water began to wash over her skin. Her body began to shake. She tried to struggle. Her mind implored her to move. To lash out. To fight. But there was nothing. She couldn't move. She floated.

The voice whispered in her head. Time for a long sleep. Don't be afraid.

She somehow opened her eyes one last time.

The man wore a mask, assessing her; his eyes were cold, wide, and demonic. A whiff of strong cologne. She wanted to panic. Her body slipped under. Gulps of water. Lungs ready to burst. Throat compressed. Choking.

He was holding her down.

She tried to move her head but couldn't. Frozen. Her mind willed her to move again. Then a dark screen slid over her eyes. Like a black curtain.

Her lungs filled up. No air left.

The man's hands pressed down onto her chest.

She looked up, saw tears in his eyes and slivers of silvery moonlight above the water.

One

Jack McNeal held up the photo of the swollen, bloodied face of the boy. "He was unconscious when they brought him in. Broken jaw. Detached retina. Lacerations. Psychological trauma. You got anything to say?"

The cop sat curled into himself, shaking, his hands trembling in his lap. His attorney took copious notes. The cop said quietly, "I had a blackout. I can't remember."

McNeal put down the photo. His colleague, Sergeant Aisha Williams, shifted in her seat as she scribbled new questions on NYPD Internal Affairs–headed notepaper.

"Don't give me that bullshit," McNeal spat out. "You were drunk. Blind drunk. Your wife told us where you had been drinking. She'd been calling you. You didn't want to come home. But she insisted, didn't she?"

"She never lets up. She never gives me a break."

"So, you reached your breaking point?"

The cop glanced at his attorney, who didn't look back. "We all have our breaking point," he muttered.

"She told me that you were having money worries. You were spending a lot of money on liquor. Gambling at the track. And, to top it all off, with your new lady friend. A fellow cop—a married cop, like yourself."

"That's got nothing to do with this."

"It doesn't?"

"I haven't been myself. I can't remember what I did yesterday."

McNeal gazed at the photo of the boy's battered face. "I'm not buying it. I think it's bullshit. You're an animal. How very convenient that you can't remember what happened."

"It's true. I can't." The cop's attorney scribbled on the legal pad, his face like stone. "I have episodes."

McNeal's stomach knotted with fury, gnawing away at him. "Three fucking witnesses! Your wife, your sister-in-law, and your twelve-year-old son, Steve. You beat your son to within an inch of his life. The surgeon said it was the worst case of child battery he'd seen."

The cop shrugged as his gaze wandered around the windowless interview room.

"You sent him to the hospital. You are responsible. How does that make you feel?"

The cop blanched. "I've got a problem. I know that."

"Damn right you've got a fucking problem. You call yourself a father?"

"I said I can't fucking remember!"

Williams intervened for the first time. "You can't remember or won't remember. Which is it?"

The cop closed his eyes for a brief moment.

"Let me jog your memory," McNeal said. "You grabbed little Steve by the hair, and you smashed his face through a glass door, driving shards of glass into his eyes."

The cop scrunched up his face, not wanting to hear any more.

"He was motionless. Instead of calling an ambulance, you punched his mother, pushed your sister-in-law to the ground, and lifted up your semiconscious son before proceeding to pummel him with your fists until he blacked out, breaking his jaw. A child. Your son."

The cop shook his head.

McNeal held the picture up to the cop's face. "This is what you did. We have witnesses."

"I can't remember."

"Can't remember . . . Yeah, right. I'll tell you someone who does remember: your son. Know what he said to me?"

The cop shook his head.

"*I just wanted my dad to stop beating my mom.* A child confronted you. Your son. He showed courage. Character. And yet still you sit there, saying you can't remember. Let me tell you this: I will personally make it my mission to ensure not only that you lose your job, but that you go to prison. Think you're a tough guy, huh?"

The cop shook his head.

"You like throwing your weight around? You think you'd like to do the same to me?"

The cop remained silent.

"You're not a cop. You're not a man. You're a fucking coward. A psychopath. An alcoholic. And a bastard. Your son should have been safe in his home. Safe with his father. It's your fucking job to keep him safe. This bullshit that you can't remember a thing . . . I'm not buying it. No one is buying it. Your little game is over. You're done. You're a disgrace to the uniform. To the badge."

The cop blinked away tears.

McNeal fixed his glare on the cop. He suppressed an urge to grab the fucker by the neck and beat the living daylights out of him. "We're done for today."

When the interview had finished and the guy and his attorney left the building, McNeal headed back to his desk and slumped down in his seat. His gaze fixed on the TV. A Fox News reporter stood outside the White House. "The President just returned from a private memorial service for the wife of an old friend, Henry Graff. He has no further engagements today."

McNeal picked up the remote and turned off the TV. His thoughts turned to the boy terrorized by his cop father. He had read the reports of the boy's bravery. It took some guts to stand up to such a monster.

He had long since become desensitized to the stuff he heard. He found that was the best way to deal with it. He had a three-month backlog of cases: alcoholic cops, psychotic cops, womanizing cops, bad cops, good cops who had gone bad, veteran detectives watching porn instead of surveillance videos, cops illegally accessing the cell phone numbers of informants, cops punching out children on the subway, cops stomping on panhandlers . . . on and on. Most New York cops were good, hardworking, decent people. McNeal dealt with the small percentage of dregs. That's what he did. That's all he did.

Aisha walked slowly up to McNeal's desk, resting her manicured honey-brown hand on his computer monitor. "A quick word, Jack?"

"Sure."

"You need to ease up on the gas. You were going at him pretty hard."

"Maybe."

Williams grimaced. "Definitely. I think you crossed the line. More than once."

McNeal sat and pondered. It was true. He had crossed a line in the interview.

"Just try and ease up in the future. I'm just saying."

"I hear you."

"I don't want you getting in trouble, Jack. Shit like that ain't worth it."

McNeal smiled. "What can I say?"

Williams shook her head and smiled. "Take it easy next time."

Aisha had only recently transferred to Internal Affairs from Robbery. McNeal knew she was right. His gaze lingered on the pile of manila folders and files on his desk. It had to be months of work before him. She turned and headed back to her desk.

Lieutenant Dave Franzen waddled into view, munching on a doughnut and carrying a coffee. "Buckley was looking for you earlier."

"What did he want?"

"Don't know. Was just asking where you were."

McNeal shrugged. "I was here, interviewing. Where the hell is he? It's been days since I've seen him."

"He's around sometimes. I hear he was interviewed by the *New York Times* last week."

McNeal groaned. "Swear to God, he'd be a great politician."

"You know how he is."

McNeal shook his head. He knew only too well what Assistant Chief Bob Buckley, head of the NYPD Internal Affairs Bureau, was like. He had reported to him for four years. He was a good guy. A good detective. But in the last year, Buckley's appearances at Internal Affairs on Hudson Street, over on Manhattan's West Side, seemed to grow few and far between. It seemed to the team that Buckley enjoyed spending increasing amounts of time in the Commissioner's office. He reveled in talking with journalists, on and off the record. Chatting with the mayor. He also appeared more and more on TV.

McNeal understood why he was doing it. Buckley said that he wanted the Internal Affairs Bureau to have a higher profile in the city. It would attract more resources. More favorable headlines. That was all probably true. Buckley was also leading a "reorientation" of the Internal Affairs Bureau. He seemed to be talking more about the Internal Affairs Bureau "becoming a force for good."

It grated on McNeal and the other officers in the Bureau. McNeal always thought the point of the Internal Affairs Bureau was really simple: establish criminality among officers alleged to have committed crimes and then punish them, whether by disciplining them or firing them.

McNeal didn't have any problem reaching out to minorities to attract the best candidates to work in the Internal Affairs Bureau. None at all. He wanted the best investigators. Who could argue with that? But McNeal and other officers, some he would call old-school cops, believed Buckley was also using his agenda for his own political aims. It was clear that was the purpose of the "reorientation." It was all about currying favor. His face was known throughout the city, more than any of his predecessors.

The *New York Post* and *New York Times* had both speculated that Buckley was a favorite to become the next commissioner. It seemed like every week he was having lunch with the mayor at Cipriani Downtown, hanging around city hall, or pressing the flesh at business breakfasts and luncheons with "influencers." Which was all fine. But it seemed to be taking precedence over the record number of cases, cutbacks, and low-level disgruntlement in the ranks of Internal Affairs.

McNeal looked at Franzen enviously. "So, when are you headed down to Florida, Dave?"

"Three weeks, three days. Can't wait."

Franzen and his wife, Nicola, an ICU nurse, were both retiring to Boca Raton. They had already sold their house in Queens and were renting a property in Brooklyn. "You're not going to miss us?"

"You kidding? Twenty years, ten in Internal Affairs, is enough for any man."

"What about the weather? You're going to miss that for sure, right?"

Franzen laughed. "Yeah, right. My car wouldn't start this morning. Had to call a tow truck."

McNeal's cell phone rang, and he winced. He looked over at the phone and checked the caller ID. "Speak of the devil. Have to take this."

"You headed for a drink after work?"

"Not tonight. I'm saving myself for your retirement party."

Franzen laughed. "You better show up, man."

"Scout's honor."

"Catch you later."

McNeal picked up his cell phone.

"Jack, how did it go with that animal?" The voice of Bob Buckley.

McNeal leaned back in his seat. "Says he can't remember."

"Bullshit."

"I know. But we've got him where we want him. Where are you now?"

"Commissioner's office."

McNeal smiled. "Tell him from me that we need more resources."

"I know, Jack. But I can't go rushing in, demanding the earth. It's all politics."

"That's all I keep hearing. We need some help down here. You saw my backlog?"

"I'm working on it. You remember your appointment this afternoon?"

McNeal closed his eyes for a moment. He had forgotten all about it.

"Did you hear what I said?"

"Gimme a break, Bob. I've got a mountain of paperwork to get through on this case. I'm not going to allow this slimeball's attorney to get this fucker off on a technicality."

"Paperwork will still be there in the morning. This appointment is important."

McNeal resented having to take an hour out of his day just because his boss "insisted."

"Jack, do you hear me?"

"I don't understand why I have to go. It's bullshit. I need to do my job."

"We've had this discussion before. You need to go."

"And if I don't?"

"It's nonnegotiable. Don't be late."

Two

It was nearly dark.

Jack McNeal walked along East Tenth Street, cold rain slashing at his face. He headed toward a classic prewar building at the corner of University Place, prime Greenwich Village. It was home to a smattering of wealthy New Yorkers. An A-list actor, a record producer who had worked on a Rolling Stones album back in the day, a sci-fi author, a celebrity chef, the ex-wife of a billionaire hedge fund exec, an entertainment attorney who represented some hip-hop guys, and a few other newsworthy celebrities. The building dated from 1928, but it had been redeveloped in 2009 to stunning, high-end specifications. A world-famous interior designer had been flown in from Marseille to oversee the transformation. It boasted a twenty-four-hour doorman to go with ultra-tight security. It reeked of money. And privilege.

McNeal didn't give a shit about any of that. He would much rather be doing what he was paid to do.

He signed in at the desk, showed his ID, and the doorman escorted him to the elevator.

McNeal rode alone to the ninth floor. He walked along a carpeted corridor. The apartment he was looking for sat at the end.

He checked his watch. He was one minute late. He knocked and the door opened.

The woman wore black. "Nice to meet you, Jack," she said. "Belinda Katz."

McNeal shook her hand and followed her down a hallway. He couldn't help admiring the lacquered herringbone flooring. He considered how much per square yard that had set her back.

He was shown into a huge drawing room. A few large lamps added extra warmth.

She motioned for him to sit in a dark-brown leather armchair. "Glad you could make it."

Jack McNeal slumped down. His gaze wandered around the room. It was painted white, with large pieces of modern art adorning the walls. A floor-to-ceiling bookshelf held everything from Freud to books on Eastern philosophy. Outside, rain lashed against the window.

The woman sat down in an Eames chair opposite him and put on her glasses. She began flicking through some papers on her lap before looking up and smiling. Her nails were painted dark red, matching her lipstick. "So, let's try and ease ourselves into this, Jack," she said. "Firstly, I don't come cheap."

McNeal smiled at the quip.

"But that's not your problem. Bob Buckley is a good friend of mine."

"Lucky you."

Katz gave a grim smirk. "He's not to everyone's taste, I know."

"He's fine. Intense. But fine."

"Okay. Let's get started. You have been sent as a referral. Do you have any idea why you're here or what led to this referral, Jack?"

"I was hoping you could answer that."

Katz scribbled some notes. "People who care about you say you have serious issues."

McNeal readjusted his weight. He wasn't comfortable talking about himself. "Most people I work with have serious issues. Actually, most people I know have serious issues. It's an occupational hazard."

"I understand," she said. "It is a highly stressful job."

McNeal said nothing.

"I can imagine Internal Affairs gets its fair share of complex and difficult cases."

"It is what it is. Some weeks are better than others. And that affects mood and behavior."

"I want to explore that, if you don't mind."

McNeal sighed. "I don't mean to be rude, but why exactly am I here?"

"There's been some cause for concern. People are worried about you."

McNeal went quiet.

"It has been noticed by a few of your colleagues, and your boss, that you don't seem yourself. Really, really not yourself. And you haven't for quite some time."

"What the hell does that mean?"

The psychologist smiled. "It's okay to be defensive. These colleagues of yours are concerned that you appear, as they put it, increasingly isolated. And they say that's been noticeable over the last six months." She flicked through her papers again. "They also mentioned increased hostility. Anger issues. Does this sound like something you're familiar with?"

McNeal leaned forward in his seat.

"I was reading your file. And I believe I might be able to help you."

"No disrespect, but I just want to do my job and get on with my life."

Katz nodded and pursed her lips. "I would like to talk about something that happened five years ago, Jack."

McNeal's insides tightened.

"Would you like to talk about that?"

"Not really."

"I deal with a lot of cops, and it's invariably the same. There are signs of acute stress. The drinking. The blackouts. Infringements of NYPD rules. Obsessiveness with work. Guilt over what happened. And sometimes, we're talking about people having suicidal thoughts. Bottling it all up is not the way to go."

"That's not me."

"Isn't it?" The psychologist's gaze lingered on him longer than was comfortable. "Jack, you're a human being like all of us. It's important we explore these feelings."

"What if I don't want to explore those feelings? What about that?"

The psychologist scribbled some notes. "I've met a lot of people like you, Jack. But most want to work with me."

"Nothing personal, but I just want to be left alone. To get on with my job—a job I love."

"Look, this is our first session. I understand why you might want to keep things to yourself. Men are more likely to be a closed book. I get it. But ultimately, the feelings you have, the dark feelings, will need to be explored. It's going to take time. I want to help you get through this."

"Get through what?"

"The pain you're holding in. The guilt over what happened that night five years ago."

McNeal sighed. His gaze wandered across the artworks on the wall. "No disrespect, but you don't know the first thing about me."

"I believe I do."

McNeal bowed his head.

"Some cops say the job grinds them down. The things they see. You were a detective for eight years before you started in Internal Affairs. You must have seen all kinds of deaths. Murders. It is a lot to deal with. It all builds up."

McNeal was silent.

"What happened five years ago has haunted you. I can see that. Tell me about your wife. How was she affected by it?"

McNeal had wondered when she was going to get around to that. "I don't want to talk about it."

The psychologist fixed her steely gaze on him. "Tell me what happened five years ago. I need to hear it from you. I believe you were off-duty."

"I'd rather you didn't talk about that."

"Okay, so why don't you talk about it? How about we start with that night. What happened?"

Jack closed his eyes.

The psychologist leaned forward. "You need to resolve these issues, Jack, once and for all. I'm here to help you."

Jack stared at her.

"You are compelled by Assistant Chief Buckley, head of the Internal Affairs Bureau, to attend these sessions. I can help you, but you need to open up."

Jack turned toward the rain-streaked window to see darkness finally falling over the city.

The psychologist leaned forward and handed him her card. "I can see this is going to be difficult for you. So, if it's okay with you, I'm going to cut this session short. You can take some space and time to think about what I'm saying." She pointed to the card in Jack's hands. "Call me at that number, whenever you want, day or night. Maybe face-to-face doesn't feel right for you."

Jack sat in silence, memorizing her name and number.

"You need to do this, Jack. It would make it a lot easier if you allowed me into your world."

"What if I'm not ready to do that?"

"Then I'm afraid," she said, a tone of foreboding seeping into her voice, "you'll have to deal with the fallout down the road. And it might come at a terrible price."

Three

It was nearly midnight when the phone rang.

McNeal ignored it as he stared down through his rain-streaked apartment windows onto West Third Street, gun in hand. It was a Glock 17. The latest model. He'd tested it at the NYPD firing range at Rodman's Neck in the Bronx. West Third was bathed in the red neon light from the window of a tattoo parlor. A motorbike pulled up outside. McNeal watched as rainwater poured down a curbside storm drain like rivulets of blood.

The radio played low, a Springsteen song from the *Nebraska* album. Down below, a cab sped past, spraying water onto girls leaving a bar. A few high-pitched screams. Then laughter.

McNeal felt empty. He contemplated heading out for a drink. A few beers. A scotch. A few shots of tequila. The session with the psychologist had brought back a lot of bad memories he had consigned to the darkest recesses of his mind.

The phone stopped ringing. He sighed and turned off the music. He put down his gun on the dresser beside the photo of his son. His flesh and blood. A picture of innocence.

McNeal allowed the silence to smother him for a few minutes. His emptiness returned. The terrible emptiness. The pain he carried. Five long years his son had been dead.

His mind flashed back to that stifling, dark night in a Staten Island backyard. He closed his eyes, and he was there again . . .

He faced his partner, Juan Gomez, who had a gun pointed at Caroline. In his other hand, Gomez held a half-empty bottle of vodka. Gomez wanted to die. He wanted Jack to kill him. He wanted suicide by cop. He saw it clearly. His partner had cracked. The high-pitched sound of screaming all around. The smell of smoke. He shouted at Gomez to put down the gun. Gomez sobbed. His partner waved the gun and aimed it at a wall. A gunshot rang out. Then Patrick collapsed, blood pouring from his neck. Ricochet bullet. Pandemonium. Suddenly Gomez was inconsolable and turned the gun toward McNeal. His pal. His partner.

The sound of more gunshots. Gomez was down. The bottle smashed. Blood congealed around his dead partner's head. The screaming returned. Sirens in the distance. McNeal stood alone, looking down at his dead son. He cradled him in his arms. Stroked his blood-soaked hair.

Slow motion as Caroline began to shriek.

The phone rang again, snapping McNeal out of his dark thoughts from five years ago.

"Yeah. McNeal."

"Jack, sorry for calling at this hour." It was Bob Buckley. "Listen, we got a problem."

McNeal closed his eyes. "Do you know what time it is?"

"I know what goddamn time it is. I just got woken up myself. Some guys want to talk to you."

"What guys?"

"They were kinda cagey. They just said they wanted to talk."

McNeal wondered if this was blowback after his internal memo. His concerns focused on priorities. He had highlighted Buckley's obsession with plugging up media leaks, the most common being officers emailing photos of crime scenes to reporters. These offenses showed terrible judgment and should be investigated. But McNeal thought the Bureau's paranoia and relentless focus, combined with Buckley's political ambitions, had come at the expense of the crimes committed by members of the NYPD—serious crimes, including an officer in the Bronx who alleged her partner had raped her and blackmailed her over her opioid addiction. "Is this from the Commissioner's office? Is that what this is all about?"

"No, Jack. That's coming, don't worry. That's a separate matter. And we're going to have to talk about it."

McNeal sighed.

"They want to talk to you in the office. Right now."

"The office? At this time? Who the hell are *they*? Feds?"

"I asked them. They're not from the FBI. They just asked me to get hold of you within the hour. They wouldn't give further details."

"Are they cops?"

"These guys aren't cops."

"Did you ask them?"

"Yeah, I asked them."

"And they wouldn't say where they were from?"

"Correct."

"They didn't identify themselves?"

"Correct."

"Bob, tell them I'll talk to them tomorrow."

"Not an option."

McNeal tried to stifle a yawn. It had been a long day. "What do you mean it's not an option?"

"I mean these guys weren't fooling around. I've got a bad feeling about this. You need to come in."

Four

It took McNeal half an hour to get showered, shaved, and changed into a fresh shirt and suit. He took a cab across to Hudson Yards on the West Side. He rode the elevator to the third floor and fixed himself a coffee.

"Hey, Jack, you working late?"

McNeal looked up and saw Lieutenant Dave Franzen carrying a report, drinking coffee out of a Styrofoam cup. "Got some visitors."

"At this time? Who?"

"No idea. Got a call from Buckley."

"Christ. Commissioner's office coming to bust your balls?"

"I don't think so."

"So, who the hell turns up at this time of night?"

McNeal knew whoever it was, it was not going to be good news.

"No idea. I'll keep you posted."

Thirty minutes later, McNeal watched two men wearing raincoats dash into the building. His instincts told him that these people were from the government. Franzen, eating a doughnut, escorted the men through the offices. He pointed them to McNeal's desk.

The men approached, taking off their coats.

"Jack McNeal?" the heavyset man said.

"Yeah."

The guy flashed a Diplomatic Security Service ID badge. He shook McNeal's hand, as did his colleague. "We've got some questions, if you don't mind."

McNeal shrugged. "At this time of night? Must be serious."

"It is. We'd prefer to talk in private."

McNeal brought them to an empty conference room adjacent to the control room. Diplomatic Security Service specialized in protecting diplomats. It was the federal law enforcement and security arm of the State Department. They also investigated visa and passport fraud. Was this in connection to a case he was working on? Had a diplomat or his family had a run-in with a cop under investigation? In all his years on the force, he'd had no dealings with them.

He flicked on the lights as the two men pulled up a seat each. McNeal remained standing. "So, what's this all about?"

The heavyset guy nodded as his mustached colleague settled into his seat. "Appreciate your time, coming in at this hour." His voice was a whisper, as if he was worried about being overheard. "We've had a very busy day. Sorry we couldn't give you a heads-up about this."

McNeal looked at his watch. "You guys want to get to the point? I've been up since five yesterday morning."

The thickset Diplomatic Security guy stared at him. "Join the club. Jack, you're a difficult man to track down. We have your address as Westport, Connecticut. We headed up there earlier."

"Yeah, I've got a house there. It's on the market."

The agent grimaced. "Explains a lot. So, where are you living?"

"Got a small apartment in the Village. If you don't mind, I'd appreciate it if you got to the point. Lot of stuff going on here at the moment."

"What sort of stuff?" The sentence hung in the air like an insinuation.

"Court stuff, emails, internal investigations. It's been crazy here for a few months. No letup. Backlogs like you wouldn't believe."

The agent nodded as his colleague just stared. "I get it. Not enough hours in the day, right?"

"Precisely."

"When was the last time you spoke to your wife, Jack?"

McNeal took a few moments to let the question sink in. "My wife? Is she okay?"

"When was the last time you spoke to your wife?"

"What the hell kind of a question is that?"

"It's a simple question, Jack."

McNeal's ulcer began to burn. "I'm sorry, I don't understand. You're talking about my wife, Caroline McNeal?"

"Caroline McNeal, that's right. Can you answer the question, Jack?"

"As soon as you tell me why you want to know that."

The heavyset guy sighed. "Let me spell it out for you. You know how this works, Jack. We just want you to answer the question. When was the last time you spoke to your wife?"

"What happened? Stop fucking around."

"Your wife has access to various buildings on Capitol Hill. Government buildings. Doesn't she?"

McNeal pulled up a chair and sat down across from them.

"She has what we call a hard pass," the agent explained.

"Okay."

"Access-all-areas type of thing."

"She's a political journalist. Sure. What's this all about? Are we talking leaks? She messed up protocol for her card? Is that what you want to find out?"

The mustached man sighed. "Jack, this isn't easy."

"Spit it out."

"Would it surprise you to learn that Caroline hasn't been to work for the past five days?"

Jack took a few moments to think about that. That didn't sound like his wife. "Seriously?"

"Not like her, I assume."

McNeal detected a cold tone in the question. "Is she sick? Maybe she's on vacation?"

"You don't know?"

"No, I don't."

The agent rubbed his mustache and leaned forward, hands clasped. "That's a bit strange. You're her husband, and you don't know where she is."

McNeal's mind began to race, imagining that something had happened to Caroline. Despite their separation, her disappearing for any length of time without telling him wasn't like her at all.

"She works in DC, and you work in New York. But you're married, right?"

"We're separated. Have been for over a year."

The heavyset man scribbled down some notes on a legal pad. "Just so you know, we're treating this as a missing person case. Possession of a White House hard pass is strictly monitored and regulated."

"I get that."

"She's not at work. She's not at her place in Georgetown."

McNeal's stomach tightened.

"We'd like you to come with us, Jack."

"What the hell for?"

"Some people want to speak to you."

"About what?"

"About your missing wife."

Five

In the dead of night, the SUV headed across the Manhattan Bridge to downtown Brooklyn.

McNeal sat in the back with the two guys from Diplomatic Security. His ulcer burned. He popped a couple of Zantac washed down with a bottle of water the driver gave him.

"You okay?" the Diplomatic Security agent to his right said.

"No, I'm not okay. You're not telling me the whole story."

"This is a sensitive case. I can't say much. I'm sorry."

McNeal knew deep down in his bones that something had happened to his wife. The hard pass was not what this was about. It had to be the Feds. But why were they taking him to Brooklyn and not Lower Manhattan? The FBI were in Federal Plaza, close to Tribeca. On and on the questions mounted.

A few minutes later, the SUV edged through downtown Brooklyn, then turned into an underground parking garage.

"Jack, let's move."

McNeal followed the two Diplomatic Security guys to the elevator. They rode it in silence to the sixteenth floor of an office block. The bulkier agent showed him into an interview room.

Two men in suits sat behind a paper-strewn desk, waiting for him.

McNeal pulled up a seat without asking. “You mind telling me what the hell is going on? You cops?”

The older guy sighed. “Appreciate you seeing us at such short notice. Tom Clarkson, Secret Service. This is my colleague, Norman Finks.”

“Secret Service? You got ID?”

The men produced their IDs before putting them back in their wallets.

Clarkson leafed through a few papers before he fixed his gaze on McNeal. “I apologize for approaching you in this manner.”

“You mean using Diplomatic Security?”

“Precisely. That was a way to speak to you without arousing more fundamental concerns about our involvement. I hope you understand.”

McNeal nodded.

“Jack, earlier today, we, with help from Diplomatic Security, searched your wife’s house.”

McNeal could only hear the beating of his heart in Clarkson’s pauses.

“Her employer was concerned. She hadn’t turned up for work in days. Diplomatic Security were concerned about your wife’s hard pass. We didn’t find that pass there.”

“You want to just back the fuck up for a few moments? My wife doesn’t turn up for work. Her employer is worried. You guys are alerted. And you do a check? Wouldn’t that be a matter for DC police?”

Finks leaned forward and smiled. “You’re absolutely right, Jack. Ordinarily that’s what would have happened. Maybe FBI, I guess, in the extreme. But, you see, this is no ordinary case. Your wife is presumed missing.”

“Okay . . . What else?”

"Her cell phone isn't responding. She seems to have vanished off the face of the earth."

McNeal's head swam as if he was daydreaming. A silence stretched between them for a few awkward moments as he wondered what had happened to Caroline. He sat completely still. They stared at him, as if trying to ascertain what he knew. "Have you tried the hospitals?"

"We have. Nothing. We were hoping you could help us."

"Why would you think that?"

"You're married to her."

"We separated nearly eighteen months ago."

Finks scribbled down some notes. "I understand. So, when was the last time you spoke to her?"

McNeal shook a thought from his head. "If what you're saying is true, I don't quite understand the involvement of the Secret Service for a missing woman. That makes no sense. If it was the wife of the President or Vice President, I would understand."

"We have our reasons."

"I see. You mind explaining?"

Clarkson rubbed his eyes. "Not at the moment. Getting back to the question. When was the last time you spoke to your wife?"

"Five, maybe six days ago. I don't know exactly."

"What did you talk about?"

"Am I under arrest? Do I need a lawyer?"

"No, you're not under arrest. And if you want a lawyer, you're free to call any lawyer you want. But if you could answer the question, it would save us all a lot of time."

McNeal's brain felt foggy. "What was the question again?"

"The last time you spoke to her. What did you talk about?"

"The house."

Finks scribbled, flicking through some papers. "The house in Westport?"

"We're selling it. I live close to my work."

"Which explains why no one answered the door in Westport. Where are you living now?"

"I moved into a one-bedroom apartment at 121 West Third Street. Second floor walk-up."

Finks noted the address. "Let's get back to your wife. She had access to government buildings, senators, the White House press briefing room."

"That's not the reason you're involved, is it?"

"It is part of the reason."

"Why are you really here?"

Finks sighed. "Your wife is a prominent Washington journalist, right?"

McNeal nodded.

"When we searched your wife's house, there was no sign of forced entry. We have evidence that suggests she had three laptops. None were there. She also had several cell phones; iPads; hundreds of notepads with details of meetings, longtime confidential sources, and White House briefings. All of it, gone. So, what happened to it? Did you or someone you know take all of it?"

"Absolutely not."

"Jack, I want to speak frankly. Her disappearance and the missing notes and electronic equipment alarms us. Her sources include senators and congresspeople. She has details of off-the-record conversations with government employees. Some high-level. This might be a serious security breach by someone she knew, or it might not. It might just be a woman who decided it was time to move on with her life and not tell anyone until she's good and ready. But it might not. And it's a concern. So, we have to keep an open mind."

"That makes sense."

"She may also have a reason to want to disappear."

McNeal bristled at the tone of the conversation. The insinuation that she wanted to escape him forever hung in the air. He didn't believe that. "And what might that be?"

"I don't know. You tell me. Maybe she was just fed up. Maybe she just wanted to get away from it all."

"Caroline wasn't like that."

"Maybe you'd grown farther apart than you realized. Maybe she had changed."

"I get where you're going with this line of questioning."

Finks held his gaze. "Maybe she doesn't keep you up to date with everything she does."

"We might have been separated, but we spoke. We were open like that."

"Did she confide in you?"

"Yeah. Everything."

"Did she tell you about a prowler?"

"What?"

"Caroline had apparently confided in her coworker, a fellow journalist, about a prowler around her property in the days leading up to her disappearance. Are you sure she didn't mention that to you?"

"No. I didn't know about it. Was it reported to the police?"

Finks shook his head. "We're still checking, but we haven't found a report."

"Caroline never mentioned anything like this to me. I would have remembered it."

"Is that unusual?"

"Is what unusual?"

"Caroline not mentioning stuff like that to you. I would've thought a wife, even if separated from her husband, might want to let him know if there was a prowler around. Would she have mentioned something like that to you? You did say she confided in you. Everything. But it appears she didn't confide in you about this. Why do you think that is?"

McNeal tilted his head back and exhaled.

Finks stared at McNeal. "Your separation was amicable?"

McNeal sensed a frostiness in the tone of voice. "Separation is never easy."

"Was it her idea? The separation, I mean."

McNeal knew what they were doing. They were painting him as the angry husband who didn't want his wife to leave.

"She wanted more space, that kind of thing? How did that make you feel?"

McNeal sighed. "It's a personal thing. People grow apart, I guess."

"So, you're saying she grew apart from you?"

"People change. What can I say?"

"Jack, you're a rising star with Internal Affairs. I've read your file. You were investigated by Internal Affairs five years ago, after you killed your partner."

"I was cleared. A bullet from my partner's gun ricocheted and killed my son."

"And you in turn gunned your partner down. That's a lot to deal with. You have a college degree. You applied to join Internal Affairs. Why?"

McNeal steepled his hands. It was a question he had answered more than once in his life. "My partner should never have remained a cop so long. I believe strongly after what happened that the NYPD shouldn't have people like that in its ranks."

"The file said that you are, to put it nicely, obsessive about your work. I've heard that you seem to have become more withdrawn and had been referred to a clinical psychologist who specializes in PTSD, grief, and anger issues."

McNeal sat in silence.

"It's clear that you're struggling."

"You don't know the first thing about me."

"They say you don't let things go. You're obsessive."

"You keep on saying that."

"Is that what happened here? You couldn't—or wouldn't—let her go?"

McNeal took a deep breath to keep these men from getting under his skin. "My job is to investigate allegations of NYPD corruption and criminality. I do so without fear or favor. I care about the investigations. I care that we get resolution. Bad cops need to be outed. I don't apologize for that."

"Maybe you've taken that same devotion and obsession with your job into your private life. Maybe you didn't want to let Caroline go. Is that what this is about?"

McNeal shook his head, nursing his fury. It was like they were picking at a raw wound.

"I spoke to a few of your more senior colleagues earlier today. They said you're unyielding. You don't like some aspects of the Internal Affairs culture. They say you don't believe they're rigorous enough investigating dirty cops. You believe they're complacent. And you've brought this up time and time again."

"What exactly has that got to do with my wife's disappearance?"

"I think it tells us something about your personality traits. Your mindset."

"Are we getting into behavioral science now?"

"A very senior officer talked to me about confrontations you've had with several other Internal Affairs staff. Said you're on edge a lot of the time. More so since your wife left you."

"I care about my work. My private life is just that. Private."

Finks added, "The officer said he overheard a heated telephone conversation between you and your wife."

McNeal could see the questions growing more pointed. “Am under suspicion?”

Finks stared at him long and hard. “We’re just trying to get to the bottom of this. My ex-wife is tough to deal with. I get it. They push you and push you, until you can’t fucking take it anymore. I get it. Trust me.”

“She’s not my ex-wife. Caroline is my wife.”

“You’re separated, though,” Finks pointed out.

McNeal nodded.

“Let’s get back to this stalker. Maybe she was targeted.”

“By who?”

“You tell me. Have you ever visited her at her home in Washington?”

McNeal shook his head. “I know what you’re getting at.”

“You do?”

“You think I’m her stalker?”

“I never said that.”

“You didn’t have to. Just for the record, no. I never stalked her.”

“Were you invited to her place in DC?”

“Yes, I was.”

“Did you have a spare key?”

“No, I did not.”

“Did you visit her there, Jack?”

McNeal drummed his fingers on the desk. “No.”

“Why not?”

“I didn’t see the point. My wife didn’t want to get back together. She wanted to remain friends.”

“You wanted to get back together?”

“Very much. But it wasn’t meant to be.”

“I can imagine that might have caused some tension between you.”

McNeal shrugged.

"But you still remained friends?"

"We were cordial on the phone."

"What did you talk about?"

"Again, mostly about selling our home in Westport. It's in both our names."

Finks pinched the bridge of his nose. "So, I'm just trying to wrap my head around the chain of events. You said she left you?"

"Yes, Caroline was the one who left."

"Did she leave you for another man?"

"Not as far as I know."

"How do you know for sure? You don't, do you?"

McNeal waited out the silence.

"She's a driven person, right? A lot of power lunches with politicians. Interesting people. Power brokers, that kind of thing. I'm guessing a lowly Internal Affairs guy in New York must seem pretty ordinary by comparison."

McNeal leaned back in his seat. "Good try."

"Does she have many male friends, Jack?"

"She knows a lot of people, as do I. Men and women. It's called life. Work. You meet people."

"Wonder if that's what's happened."

"You're reaching."

"Am I?"

"She's a workaholic, same as me. Her work comes first."

"How did that make you feel?"

McNeal rubbed his eyes. "You think I'm involved in this, don't you?"

"We're just trying to establish the whereabouts of your wife, Jack."

"You're trying to establish motivation. I get it. But spare me the phony line of questioning."

"Jack, we're going to need to check your cell phone records. You know the drill. Do we have your permission to scan those?"

"No, you don't have permission. I have sensitive information and numbers on my cell phone and laptop."

"In your West Third Street apartment?"

"Yeah."

Finks handed McNeal a search warrant.

"Are you kidding me? You had this the whole time?"

"We want to get to the truth. That's all. So, we—just so you know—we'll be accessing your cell phone records too."

"You believe I'm involved in her disappearance, don't you?"

"We're just trying to establish the facts, Jack."

McNeal leaned back in his seat. "You're trying to set me up."

"That's not the case."

Finks looked at his watch. "What do you say we have a breather. I'll bring you some coffee. Wait here."

Six

The breather lasted three hours, long enough for the Secret Service to gain access to his tiny Greenwich Village apartment as well as his home in Westport and find whatever the hell they thought they would find.

Finks returned with a coffee just after five a.m.

McNeal sat sullenly, staring at a wall.

"Black okay?"

"Fine, thanks. You find anything?"

Finks slumped in a seat opposite. "We're not enjoying this any more than you."

McNeal nodded.

"We'll give you a list of the items we removed."

McNeal gulped some hot coffee. "It's not a problem."

"My colleague, who you spoke to earlier, is speaking with our superiors in DC. Just so you know, forensics have now copied all the data from your electronic devices found here in New York and in Westport. They'll be analyzing everything over the next day or two, including your cell phone records. You know the drill."

"Could take a while."

Finks nodded. "Probably."

McNeal rubbed his hands over his face, trying to wake himself up. It was like a bad dream. "I don't understand Caroline's disappearance. It's so out of character. What's freaking me out is her valuables—her cell phone, laptop, and notebooks, all taken."

Finks leaned back in his seat. "I'm guessing there's a possibility she might've just wanted some space from her high-pressure job. Maybe disappear for a while. Catch up on some reading. Writing. Can you think of any place where she might have gone? A retreat, that kind of thing? Second home?"

McNeal racked his brain. He remembered a place her family owned. "She has a place in Catoctin Mountain Park. If she needed peace and quiet or had a deadline for a book, she'd head there."

"Where's that?"

"Not far from Camp David. Her father had a cabin there. I don't have the address."

Finks scribbled in his notepad. "The parents are dead, I believe."

McNeal nodded.

"So, she has no living family or relatives?"

"None. Apart from me. She was an only child."

"I appreciate the heads-up about the cabin."

"Don't know if Caroline uses it much these days."

Finks stared at McNeal. "I've got a sensitive question to raise with you. And I apologize if it sounds uncaring. Harsh, even."

"Shoot."

"So far, we've taken notes but have no taped recording. None of this is on the record. We thought it important to win your trust in difficult circumstances."

McNeal had thought it strange they hadn't recorded their talk. He let it slide. "What's on your mind?"

"We checked your estranged wife's finances. We found her will at her house in Georgetown. It leaves everything in her estate to one person."

McNeal shrugged. "No idea."

"The sole beneficiary. You."

"What's your point?"

"My point is, she has three and a half million dollars in her bank account from the sales of her last two books and also stocks and shares valued at fifteen million dollars in today's prices, inherited from her father. It means you're rich."

McNeal saw where this was headed. "You think because I would benefit financially that I'm somehow responsible for her disappearance?"

"Just laying out the facts. You know as well as I do, Jack, that's a solid motive. You have a lot to gain."

"She's my wife! I loved her."

"Your estranged wife. You said it yourself. She left you."

"You're building a case against me."

"You want an attorney?"

"First things first. I want to know that my wife has been found, safe and well. Christ, I'm worried sick."

"Like I said, we're keeping it as low-key as we can. From our side as well as yours. It'd be like a feeding frenzy in the press if any of this got out."

"Has the FBI been informed of this investigation?"

"We're leading on this. That's all I know."

"What about DC police? Surely they need to be informed."

"They will be."

Alarm bells went off in McNeal's head. "Wait a minute. Are you saying the DC police and the FBI don't know my wife is missing?"

"I'm saying we're leading on this."

"Surely it's standard protocol for the local cops and the Feds to be involved."

"There are national security concerns. We don't want every cop telling Fox News and CNN that a prominent DC journalist has gone missing. We'll be talking with the FBI. Eventually."

"Why the hell aren't you talking with them now?"

"It's complicated."

"Bullshit."

Finks's cell phone began to vibrate on the desk, stopping the exchange in its tracks. "I thought I said I wasn't to be disturbed?" He went quiet for a few moments. "When?" A pause. "Are we sure?" Finks ended the call and sighed, fixing his gaze on McNeal. "We're headed to DC, Jack."

"Why?"

"There's been a development."

"What kind of development?"

"I can't say any more."

As the Gulfstream took off for DC, McNeal sat alone at a table. He knew in his bones his wife was gone. He just knew. But no one would tell him anything.

An SUV picked them up at Reagan. McNeal sat in the back with one of the Secret Service guys. "You've found her, haven't you?"

Finks sat up front, leafing through papers, clearing his throat.

"I need to know. Have you found her? Is that why we flew down here?"

Finks turned around. "We're on our way to the hospital, Jack."

McNeal knew what that meant. He swallowed back bile as they headed into the city. He began to steel himself. As a cop he'd seen more dead bodies than most. But being up close to a corpse, the smell of death in one's nostrils, erodes something within a person: The compassion. The humanity.

He withdrew, more adrift. Alone. A reminder of his own mortality. Maybe a reminder of the past.

He closed his eyes. Mile after mile, getting closer to seeing his wife. The only woman he had ever loved. He wished he had been there for her. How had it come to this? Maybe he should have worked harder on their relationship. Maybe he should have taken her up on her offer to visit DC. He didn't know why he hadn't. Maybe he was just like his father—a stubborn, grouchy old man. A man who nursed regrets and grievances, real or imagined. A working-class cop who returned each night to the warmth of a family home. His mother had sacrificed her career as a nurse to look after her husband, her family, and the house. Money was always tight. But they had each other. The family unit always came first.

McNeal's mind raced through all these irrational, pointless factors as he passed a sign for the hospital. He had made similar trips as a detective with other people's wives and husbands to the morgue. He always remembered the deathly silence of the journey.

The SUV pulled up at the hospital's underground parking garage.

"This is us, Jack." Finks snapped McNeal out of his morbid thoughts.

McNeal got out of the vehicle and followed Finks and two Secret Service agents, taking the elevator down to the basement, through a door marked Medical Examiner.

McNeal had been in dozens of such facilities over the years. It was always the same. A mixture of dread and sadness. His stomach clenched as he was ushered down a corridor that smelled of bleach. He was shown to a viewing area. Through the glass, a gurney with a sheet over it, a body underneath. *No! Tell me no.*

Finks ordered, "Pull back the cover to just under the chin."

The technician on the other side of the glass drew back the sheet.

McNeal stared at his wife's gray face. Her dirty, mousy-brown hair had fragments of leaves embedded in the strands. Her eyes were shut. Her mouth turned down.

"Can you identify this person, Jack?" Finks asked.

McNeal tried to gather his thoughts. He pressed his face to the glass.

"Jack?"

He felt his throat tighten. He pressed his hand to the glass. He didn't know why. He wanted to touch her. "It's my wife, Caroline McNeal."

"I'm so sorry."

McNeal could not look at anything else but her lifeless body. He sensed he was about to break down. Being in the morgue triggered powerful memories. His mind flashed to images of his dead son. He felt as if his heart had been ripped out at its roots. A terrible emptiness opened up within him. He wanted to tell her all the things he hadn't over the years. How much he loved her. How much he needed her. How much he admired her. But it wasn't in his nature. Now it was too late. "How did she die?"

"I'm not prepared to answer that."

Tears clouded his vision, spilling down his face. "How did my wife die?"

Finks sighed. "She was found floating in the Potomac. I'm so sorry."

Jack McNeal stared at his dead wife. He felt light-headed. Time seemed to stop. Even until the last moment, when the cover was lifted back off of her face, he clung to hope. He prayed it was someone else. A big mistake. But as he stared at her lifeless body, her twisted neck, her beautiful face like gray wax, he felt his body go into shock.

He didn't want to believe it was her. He struggled to comprehend that she was really gone from his life—this time for good. He felt dislocation, as if it was happening to someone else.

McNeal pressed his forehead against the glass. He closed his eyes as he fell to his knees, weeping, unashamed, at her loss. He thought of everything they had. The love. The years together. The terrible sadness they shared. And then the estrangement.

He never imagined this was how it would end for her. For them.

"Caroline! I'm so sorry!"

McNeal was sorry he hadn't been there for her. He couldn't imagine his wife taking her precious life. Never in a million years. He questioned if he could have done more. Caroline always said he was closed off emotionally. It was true. The death of their son had had a profound impact on them both.

He had dealt with it by retreating into his work. Stoic, like his father. He drank heavily. Caroline wanted to talk about it. He didn't. He never did.

After their son's shocking death, they had hugged and cried for a time. But then McNeal had locked himself back into his world. She had reached out to him. She had talked to a therapist. Then she began a gradual retreat into her own world. The world of politicians, DC, Capitol Hill, and the media. She didn't come home as often. Eventually, she didn't come home at all.

Finks helped McNeal away from the glass partition. "Come on, Jack. It's time to go."

Seven

A burnt-orange sun peeked over the horizon, bathing the historic monuments of downtown Washington, DC, in a tangerine light.

Henry Graff was already pounding the cinder path between the Capitol and Lincoln Memorial. It was the way he started each and every day. Athletic gear on, sport sunglasses shielding his eyes from shards of harsh sunlight. He needed the shot of adrenaline and the endorphins to kick in. It was what he lived for. It calmed him, this four-point-three mile run around the National Mall.

He passed the Korean War Veterans Memorial. The main memorial a triangle. He always stopped for a few moments at the monument, which was carved in black granite. It was a war his father had fought in and returned from. A man. A general of men. A leader.

Graff possessed the same fanatical interest in physical fitness his father had. He exercised hard. He worked hard. He abhorred slovenly behavior. The fat Americans who would soon be waddling around such sacred ground enraged him. They didn't care for the country like he cared for the country. They cared where their next jumbo-sized meal was coming from. Dumb fuckers, the lot of them. An embarrassment to the nation. A nation he himself had fought for. War was a family tradition.

He had joined the Rangers straight out of West Point, served his country. All corners of the globe. Black ops. And he would continue to serve his country until the day he died. Just like his own son, still over in Iraq. That was a place Graff had grown to loathe. The dust. The filth. The 128-degree heat. Maddening. Sickening.

Graff was born lucky. He was an American. A sacred birthright. The land of liberty. He took a deep breath in the sultry early-morning air. Another day in the capital city of the free world. He was blessed. America was blessed.

Graff finished his run, checking his heart rate on his Fitbit. Perfect. He strolled back to his car, parked a block from the Smithsonian. It was only a short drive across the Potomac to his twenty-fourth-floor penthouse in Arlington with its floor-to-ceiling views of the monuments. Every day he was alive, he was privileged to appreciate their magnificence. They represented his values: Patriotism. Exceptionalism. Stoicism. Honor.

He gulped down some chilled Evian, quenching his thirst. He fixed himself the same breakfast he had every morning—freshly squeezed orange juice, black coffee, and muesli—to get his sugar levels back up.

Graff felt his mood begin to lift as the endorphins raised his spirits. He showered, shaved, brushed his teeth, and put on his favorite navy suit, starched white shirt, pale-blue tie, and expensive black leather oxfords. He fixed his gold cuff links. He checked himself out in a full-length mirror in the hall.

Ready.

Graff climbed the stairs to his home study on the upper level of the duplex and sat down behind his desk, panoramic views of the monuments framing him. A soft orange tinge washed over the granite and marble, bounced off of the reflecting pool.

He settled into his chair, his gaze wandering around his study. Black-and-white framed photos on his wall. A photo of him as a boy with his father, taken on the steps of the Lincoln Memorial. A photo of him and the President. He had known the President for years. A close friend. A photo of him and his wife on their wedding day. Before it had all gone wrong. Somewhere along the way, whatever love they'd had for each other had eroded. It had pained him to begin with. In the end, he was just glad to be rid of her. The constant bickering, her liberal friends who held the country in contempt, her drinking, her pills, and her barely disguised hatred for him. It had taken time—years and years. He had begun to loathe her presence. Eventually, she was gone. It was just as well. He took a good long look.

Beside the wedding photo was a black-and-white photograph, taken by a photographer from *Time*, of Graff wearing a *perahan tunban,* the traditional shirt and pants outfit, and standing beside an Afghan elder smoking opium from a pipe. He didn't recognize himself. He had trekked alone for three days before the day it had been taken, ingratiating himself with the villagers he knew would be loyal to the Taliban. But he only needed the tiniest pieces of information. Part of a jigsaw puzzle. He would show them a photo. Had they seen this man? This was a very bad man, he would say. The bad man hated children. And Graff wanted to make sure this man was brought to justice. That, along with gold, usually did the trick.

He reflected on the three photos. The things that mattered most to him, all encapsulated in those three photos. Family. Blood ties. Country.

The sound of his cell phone ringing snapped him out of his reverie. He had been expecting a call.

Graff picked up. "Hope it's good news."

"Nico sends his love."

The coded phrase he had been waiting for. He had been waiting for days. Finally, Caroline McNeal was dead.

Eight

It was late morning when McNeal, traumatized and exhausted, was driven to Dulles and caught a flight back up to New York. He took a cab to the Village and looked over his small apartment. The place didn't look as if the Secret Service, or anyone for that matter, had crawled all over it.

He locked up, got in his car, and drove away from Manhattan, all the way back home to Westport, Connecticut. He desperately wanted to be alone. He needed time. But maybe more than anything, he wanted space. Open space. A place to hide. A place to contemplate. A place to grieve. He felt as if part of him had died. A tiny piece of his heart. He hadn't stopped loving her. Ever. And he never would.

But now, his mood spiraling, he needed a sanctuary.

McNeal pulled up the gravel driveway, taking in the colonial house overlooking Compo Beach, with its For Sale sign outside. The rain fell hard, trickling down the windows. The house had sat empty for over a week.

He locked the door behind him, stepped over the pile of mail on the welcome mat, and slumped on the sofa in the living room of his beautiful house. A house his wife had bought the moment she had set eyes on it. He could never abide the commute from

Westport. But they had both loved the home. The town. He loved it for the sense of calm, away from the intensity of Manhattan and his work in Internal Affairs.

The place where his wife had returned on Friday evenings after her working week in Washington. The place where he had sat and waited for her to come back from her trips abroad. And eventually, the home to which she had never returned.

He sat in silence as the rain lashed Long Island Sound. He gazed at pictures of Caroline and him on their honeymoon in Hawaii, photos of them before seeing a show on Broadway. Photos taken on a European vacation to Sorrento. Photos from their wedding day—Caroline looked into his eyes, her smile dazzling. Photos of them with her colleagues from the *Post*. Reminders of their past together.

One of his favorite pictures was of Caroline and Patrick stacking rocks on Compo Beach. She said it was meditative. Patrick spent hours balancing rocks as they watched him in rapt amazement. Their only child. The only son.

McNeal's mind flashed back to a time before Patrick was born. A peaceful vacation down in the Lower Keys. Little Duck Key. Sugarloaf Key. The sound of birds flapping their wings against the water. The stillness. The almighty stillness and quiet. He lay on tiny, deserted beaches with Caroline, alone with his thoughts, at peace with the world.

Stopping for beers in little shacks by the road. Lying on more deserted beaches. Clouds hanging low, like you could touch them.

McNeal was cocooned in warm memories. He turned on the TV and watched an old video. The footage of Caroline and Patrick on Compo Beach. She cradled him in her arms as he slept, rocking him back and forth. She began to sing softly, soothing him. More footage of Patrick's fifth birthday party. She carried a cake, candles on top.

He watched, heart breaking into a million pieces.

The two people he loved more than any others. He felt a terrible emptiness opening up inside him. A chasm. His mood was darkening. He felt tears on his face. "I'm so sorry."

McNeal's head reeled. He needed fresh air. He turned off the TV. He put on a Berghaus overcoat and headed out into the driving rain. He walked down to the wet sand of Compo Beach. The smell of salt water in the air. Clean air. He walked down to the water's edge and gazed out over the gray waters of Long Island Sound. They were as murky as the whole bizarre series of events engulfing him.

The questions mounted in his head. What had happened? Had she taken her own life? Was he responsible in some way because he hadn't wanted to visit her since their separation?

The more he thought about it all, the crazier he felt. Nothing made sense. Caroline was not the sort of person who would kill herself. Never. Perhaps it was an accident. Was that it? Why were electronic devices missing from her house in Georgetown? Was that a coincidence? Was it connected to her death? Maybe she had an apartment he didn't know about. Had she taken all her stuff to a friend's house?

The questions kept piling up. Pressing down on him, like tons of concrete blocks ready to crush him.

He was still a person of interest. The Secret Service and the Diplomatic Security had said as much. They had confiscated his passport. They told him their investigation was well underway. And they were following a definite line of inquiry. At least that's what they told him.

His interest was piqued upon hearing that there had been a prowler around his wife's house. His experience as a cop told him that the perpetrator was usually someone who knew the victim.

Maybe she had started dating. The guy was crazy. A psychopath obsessed with Caroline. Who would want to harm his wife?

Around and around, he tortured himself with all the permutations. Lines of inquiry that he, as a detective, would pursue. He needed to know more, a lot more, about the circumstances of her death. He couldn't rest until he knew for sure what happened and why. She was still his wife. Death might have parted them, but his love for her endured. That would only die when he had shuffled off his mortal coil. When he finally turned to dust.

He closed his eyes as the rain lashed his face.

Caroline had wanted to be buried in Westport. McNeal had contacted the funeral home on the journey up to Connecticut. They had the details. And they expected the funeral to be next week. He never imagined he would have to bury his wife.

McNeal couldn't imagine a future without her. Estranged or not, he missed her. There would be no more children. He wanted children. They had lost a child. But McNeal didn't want to think about that. The agony of their loss five years earlier had torn them apart.

That had been the main bone of contention between them. He had wanted them to try for another child after Patrick's death. He couldn't imagine not having children. Caroline said she was too old. But the truth was, events from five years earlier had destroyed her hopes, then his.

As a detective he had seen his fair share of hellish scenes. Murders. Stabbings. Mutilations. Twisted, bloodied corpses of jumpers from high buildings. In his role at Internal Affairs, he had investigated a catalogue of criminality, both minor and serious, committed by bad cops. Wives beaten to a pulp. Children locking themselves in bathrooms to hide from their crazy cop fathers. Kickbacks. Mob links. On and on. But his wife's death had resurrected the only feelings he truly wanted to forget. A heartache torn open five years earlier. The two people he loved more than anything in the world were dead.

McNeal walked away from the water. He stopped occasionally as he headed along the beach, tilting his head back. He loved the cold wind and rain. He walked and walked as far as the beach would take him.

He was drenched to the skin. Cold and shivering. He walked the beach. It felt like hours.

It was nearly dark when he turned and headed back home.

In the distance, through the gathering gloom, McNeal thought he saw something. He could hear shouting. Walking toward him were two figures. He stood and watched as the two figures got closer.

McNeal felt his throat tighten. He realized who it was. It was his flesh and blood. His family.

His brother, Peter, and his father, Daniel.

Nine

The three of them hugged, crying, before winding their way back up the beach toward the salt-blasted colonial.

"Christ, son," his father said. "I'm so sorry."

McNeal locked the door behind them. "I know, Dad."

Jack's father hugged him tight. It wasn't like his father. He couldn't remember the last time his father had gotten so emotional. Probably after the loss of Molly, Jack's beloved mother.

"I wish I could do something to make it go away."

He felt his father's tears on his cheek.

"God rest her soul."

McNeal was glad to have his father and brother with him. He thought he had wanted to be alone, but it felt good to have someone there. People he could trust. People he could confide in and show his true feelings to.

McNeal got some towels, and they dried off in front of the gas fireplace. He fixed three single malts. They each knocked them back in one gulp.

He refilled the glasses as they warmed up in the living room that looked out over the water. McNeal slumped in an armchair. His brother and father sat on the sofa opposite.

He looked across at his father, who started crying again.

"Dad, it's tough. I know. But I'll get through this. We all will."

His father shook his head. "What the hell happened? Peter said she was found floating in the Potomac? Is that true?"

"That's what I've been told. I don't know the circumstances. They think she might have killed herself."

His father shook his head. "Not a fucking chance. I knew Caroline. I loved her like a daughter. She was a smart girl. I'm not buying it! Not for a second!"

Peter put an arm around their father.

"I'm so sorry, son." His father shook his head. "I don't want to overstep. But it's true we loved her. She was a beautiful woman. I know you and Caroline weren't together . . . but still, she was the daughter I never had. She was a nice person. A good person."

McNeal nodded and bowed his head.

Peter sipped his single malt. "Christ, I don't know what to say, Jack."

"There's nothing to say. I appreciate you both being here. It means a lot."

Peter rubbed his eyes. "I wondered . . ."

McNeal shrugged.

"I wondered if you've watched any news."

"News? My wife's dead. Why the hell would I be interested in that?"

Peter sighed. "Jack, I'm sorry to be the one to tell you . . . but they were saying on Fox . . ."

"What? Were they talking about my wife?"

"A few channels are talking about the story. They're all saying the same thing. They said she had been seriously depressed, and everything pointed to a suicide."

McNeal stared at the amber glow from the gas fire. "She's barely dead, and they're already raking over her life. Disgusting."

"She never seemed down," his father said. "Even when you were going through difficulties. She wasn't the type."

"Dad, she was devastated after we lost Patrick. We both were."

"I know. But she was tough. I find it hard to believe she would just check out on life. Not the lovely girl I knew."

McNeal felt the warmth from the fire as it bathed the cavernous room in an ethereal glow. "It's not easy getting over the loss of a child. He was her only son. I don't know. Maybe she was more upset about the separation than I thought. She was good at holding in her feelings. But I know what you mean. She was tough. I'm struggling to accept that she might have killed herself."

Peter looked around the living room. "Hard to believe she's gone. I mean, gone forever."

McNeal nodded.

"No matter what, Jack," Peter said, "I'll try and help you. I mean, with the funeral arrangements. You know, that kind of stuff."

"Funeral home has all the details. They're liaising with the medical examiner in DC, and we'll have to wait until her body gets released. Toxicology tests and everything. Might take a while. It'll show . . . well, you know, if she had taken an overdose."

"What are you going to do?" Peter said.

"Like now?"

"No, I mean after the funeral."

McNeal sighed and took a sip of his scotch. "Get back to work, that's what."

Peter nodded. "I understand. It's just that you might want to take some more time off to get over this."

"I'll never get over this. But I'll need to work to keep my mind busy. Christ . . . I don't know."

His father smiled through his tears.

McNeal continued, "Caroline . . . she's gone. But even though we were separated, she left everything to me. So, I don't *have* to work."

His father bowed his head. "God rest her soul," he repeated.

McNeal felt sick. Money had never meant much to him. As long as he had enough for his family to live a comfortable life, enjoy the occasional vacation, have plenty of food on the table, that was enough. More than enough.

Peter said, "Jack, I understand what you're thinking. But she wanted you to have it."

"I know she did. But how do you think this makes me feel? How do you think this looks?"

"What do you mean?" Peter asked.

"Last night I was interviewed shortly before I learned her body had been found. I was then taken down to the morgue. The Secret Service guys think I'm involved."

McNeal's father said, "Secret Service? What the hell does this have to do with them?"

"Security pass she had gave her access to the White House press briefing room. Her house was missing laptops and cell phones. Those had a lot of classified numbers in the administration."

"Seriously, they think you're involved?" Peter said.

"That's what they said. Well, that's what they insinuated. That's what it looks like. I get the money. You understand now?"

"You said cell phones, laptops are missing?" Peter continued.

McNeal nodded.

"I know I don't have to tell you, Jack, but that, on the surface, looks like a robbery. There were sensitive documents on her computer, right?"

"Right. But the news is reporting she was depressed, took some pills, and then drowned herself. That doesn't add up."

Peter nodded. "The question is, what would missing notebooks or her laptop have to do with her killing herself? Did she destroy them before she killed herself? I'm not buying it."

McNeal's father stared at him. "I don't understand why the Secret Service seem to be taking the lead on this. Why not the Feds? That would make sense. The DC police, right?"

Jack stood up, glass in hand. "None of it adds up."

"You don't believe the official line?"

"Not a word of it."

"So, what're you going to do about it?" his father asked.

"Find out what really happened. No matter what."

Ten

The days leading up to the funeral began to take a toll. McNeal couldn't sleep. He sat in silence for hours at a time and stared at the walls. He was slipping into a deep depression and didn't want to shave or wash. He locked himself away. He read the newspaper headlines about his late wife. They cut deep. He felt as if she was being violated.

The more he read, the more withdrawn he became. His wife was being called an introvert by unidentified colleagues. That definitely wasn't his wife. Not the woman he knew. She was gregarious. Fun. Definitely outgoing.

McNeal reflected on his wife's illustrious career. The stories she had broken, the people she had interviewed—it would now all be obscured by these rumors. She would be defined and remembered by her death. A suicide.

Stories made the rounds on social media that she was not a team player in the newsroom. She was indeed a lone wolf. He knew that better than anyone. She didn't wait to get a story and develop it. She found stories, sniffing them out. She wasn't part of a collective. She hunted down stories. And she was amazing at it.

There was no dignity in death. Some people on Twitter were alking about her drinking. Her violent outbursts. Her sullenness. All these rumors were attributed to former colleagues or people who claimed to be friends. It was like a parallel universe. Who the hell was saying all this?

His one and only consolation was that, as per Caroline's wishes, her funeral would be a private family affair.

Suddenly, his cell phone rang. McNeal didn't recognize the caller ID. "Yeah, who's this?"

"Jack McNeal?" drawled a man's voice.

"Yes."

"My name is Charles Garrett. I was your wife's lawyer in DC. I'm the head of estates and planning."

"It's not the best time, Charles."

"I'll be quick. It's very important."

McNeal sighed. "Fine."

"First, I'm so very sorry for your loss, Mr. McNeal. Caroline was a client of mine for several years. A lovely woman and, as you know, a brilliant journalist. So sad."

McNeal cleared his throat. "Thank you."

"We have sent your late wife's papers. They were kept by us in a safe. She wanted you to have them."

"Her papers? I don't know what the legal position is on this. We were separated."

"You were still married at the time of her death. I am the executor of the will, and I can say that her estate in its entirety is passed over to you, less our modest fee, which will be shown on your statement which you will receive within the next thirty days."

McNeal sat down. It confirmed what Finks had already told him. "Go on."

"I spoke to Caroline extensively about her wishes, making sure she knew the implications. And she was very, very clear. You were to receive everything. It's a lot of money. A lot of assets. I will be in touch about that. But in the meantime, I just wanted you to know that the documents should arrive the day after tomorrow. They're being couriered securely."

McNeal sat in contemplation. He thought of his wife meeting with Garrett at his office in DC, talking over her business. He felt an unbearable sadness seep once again into his heart. It was almost too much to bear. Even though they were separated, she had gifted him a fortune. But he didn't want it. He wanted her. That's all he wanted. His wife.

"I'm assuming you must have a few questions for me."

"I'm just trying to wrap my head around this. It's a lot to take in. When did you last speak to her?"

"Ten days ago."

"That recently?"

"Correct. Just before she died. She sent in private papers, a copy of the will, and photographs. She said it was important, and just for you."

"How did she seem?"

"I'm not qualified to give an assessment of her physical or mental condition."

"I never said you were. I'm just asking, was she compos mentis?"

"I'm her lawyer, not her doctor."

McNeal felt slightly empty, knowing for certain now he was going to inherit his dead wife's estate. He had never craved material things.

"It's usually the men who go first," Garrett added. "I mean who die first. I expected to go before my wife. But she died three years ago. Quite unexpectedly."

"I'm sorry to hear that."

"A word to the wise, Mr. McNeal. Take time to mourn. Take time to remember the good times. Time is indeed a great healer."

McNeal closed his eyes, tears streaming down his face.

"Day or night, don't hesitate to contact me if you need any help or guidance on this."

"Thanks."

"Try not to worry about the legal side of things. We'll sort all that out."

Eleven

The sky was slate gray on the day of Caroline's funeral. Dark clouds rolled in off Long Island Sound. McNeal stood by the graveside at a cemetery outside Westport. He was flanked by his brother, Peter, and his father, bearing witness to her passing. The wreaths of flowers around the graveside rustled in the wind, the handwritten cards flapping noisily. The minister spoke of not having known Caroline, though he had read her work. And he had spoken with her husband, Jack, who knew her best.

McNeal gazed down at the empty grave.

"She was a tenacious woman, principled and driven," the minister said. "A woman so deeply loved by her husband, Jack. So deeply loved. Words were her tools, and she deployed them expertly. She was smart. Highly educated and very well-read. But she wore her learning lightly. She will be sorely missed."

McNeal felt his throat tighten. He bowed his head as the coffin was lowered into the grave.

"She is now at peace, lying in the arms of her heavenly father. May God rest her soul."

McNeal stared at the highly polished coffin. His father, a man not known for shows of emotion, began to sob again, which cut right through McNeal. He stood solemnly by his wife's grave. He always tried hard not to show raw emotion. His own father had taught him that as a boy. But now his father was the one who wept at his breaking point.

He stood and waited in silence. He wanted to say a final goodbye. In private.

Peter and his father, as if sensing that, hugged him before they walked slowly from the graveside.

The minister stepped forward and shook McNeal's hand. "In this time of darkness, Jack, please remember the Lord is watching over us all."

McNeal nodded. "I hope so."

The minister drifted slowly away from the graveside, finally leaving him alone with his thoughts.

McNeal stood for what seemed like an eternity. Off in the distance he could see two gravediggers waiting for him to depart. They stood beside some trees on the edge of the cemetery. He bent down, picked up some dirt, and threw it down onto her coffin. "Caroline, until we meet again. I wish I could have been there for you. I just want you to know that I love you, and I haven't stopped loving you. Maybe sometime soon, who knows when, I'll see you again."

He stared down at the lumps of earth on the coffin, his heart feeling as if it had been ripped out by its roots.

"I just want you to know that."

A few hours later, the McNeals returned to the sanctuary of the Westport house. Jack's sister-in-law, Muriel, had told Peter she'd stay there with their three children while the others were at the cemetery.

Muriel fussed around, fixing drinks and food.

McNeal read the cards from friends and colleagues, past and present. And there was even one from Bob Buckley expressing his deep sorrow.

McNeal was touched. His boss was tough. He hadn't expected that.

When Muriel had fed the kids and everyone had a drink in their hand, she took herself and the kids out of the house and across to the beach. It was like she instinctively knew the men wanted to be by themselves.

Peter leaned forward, glass of beer in hand. "I don't know if and when I should talk about this. Maybe it's not the best time."

"What is it?" Jack said.

"I hope you don't mind me speaking my piece, Jack."

"Spit it out. We're family."

"It's been more than a week, and still we don't have a rational explanation. We've got an official narrative. The chain of events. She was depressed. She took the pills. Then she took her life. But did she? I feel as if . . . something doesn't feel right. I can't imagine her taking drugs. I can't imagine her walking into the Potomac."

Jack felt the same. He wasn't surprised Peter had raised the issue. None of it made sense. The shocking nature of Caroline's death. The widespread press coverage. "It's a lot to take in."

"I just don't get it," Peter said.

"There were drugs in her system."

"I'm not buying it. I've got a feeling about this. In my bones."

McNeal nodded.

"I can't quite explain it."

"You don't want to explain because it might upset me?"

Peter bowed his head. "That's right."

Their father fixed his gaze on Jack. "Maybe it was a tragic accident. That's what they're saying. It was a cry for help. But what are you saying, Jack? What do you think happened to Caroline?

I don't know about you, but I'm still struggling to accept that she would take her own life. I don't believe she walked into the water and killed herself."

McNeal took a small sip of the scotch and sighed. The liquor warmed his belly. "Sometimes we think we know people. I thought I knew her. But maybe I didn't know her as well as I thought I did. She was away a lot. There was distance between us a lot of the time. She was hit hard by Patrick's death. That's a lot to deal with."

"Caroline always struck me as a straightforward kind of girl, if you know what I mean."

Peter nodded his agreement.

Their father went on, "I think it's a stretch, a major league stretch, to believe she killed herself. What do you think?"

"I don't know. I wish I knew. What do we know for sure? All we know is she was found floating in the Potomac. She was an avid jogger. She said she regularly jogged the trails that go past the Potomac. Maybe she fell in. I don't know."

Peter said, "Jack, you know how it works. I know you're Internal Affairs now, and you know how I feel about that, but you were a cop once. A detective. Where are the DC police in this? Why haven't they been speaking to you? Why the Secret Service? It's like a lockdown situation. Everything is need to know. It's weird."

McNeal sighed, not wanting to drag his family into the whole sad saga. "All I've been told is that the Secret Service are leading on this. I assume they have their reasons."

"Like what?"

McNeal stared at his headstrong brother longer than he wished to.

Peter flushed, embarrassed. "Jack, I love you, I didn't mean any disrespect. Not at this time. Not ever. But why would the Secret Service be so prominently involved in this?"

"Well, for starters, the Diplomatic Security guys are involved because of her hard pass. Secret Service is there because her laptop were stolen."

"Jack, listen to me. This is all very, very bizarre."

"I know it is. I know how it looks. Better than anyone."

Jack's father said, "You know how long I was a cop?"

"A long time."

"Too goddamn long. Forty years. Who serves forty years these days? No one. They wait until twenty and they're done. But I'm telling you this, and I don't have the fancy degree you've got, but I can tell you something is not right here. The way it came about. You being interviewed. Taken in the middle of the night to speak to the Secret Service officer in Brooklyn? You, as a suspect? I mean, what the hell?"

"I know exactly how this looks. I feel the same."

"Question is, son, what are you going to do about it? As a family, we need answers. You need answers."

McNeal agreed with both his father and brother. He knew something was wrong. The whole thing felt wrong. It was the nature of her death, the secrecy, the air of unreality. He sensed shadowy forces were at work. It was almost as if the chain of events had been carefully choreographed. But maybe he was just dwelling on the tragic and unforeseeable death of his beloved wife. Was he seeing things that weren't there, magnifying heartfelt loss in an attempt to understand the shocking nature of events? Was that it? "I'll get answers. But in my own time. I'm still pretty raw."

"I know you are," Peter said. "Listen, I know a guy down in DC. He might be able to find out more."

"What are you saying?"

"I know people."

"Not now. It's important we don't let our emotions, which are running high, carry us away."

"I don't mean do anything illegal."

"You know what I do, Peter. I can't overstep, not in my line of work. I need to operate strictly according to rules, jurisdiction, and the law."

His father said, "I understand, son. I think Peter just wants to help you. You know we'd do anything for you. We all loved Caroline."

McNeal smelled the distinct peaty aroma of the rare scotch in the tumbler. It brought back memories of a trip to the highlands of Scotland. A few trips to distilleries. The Isle of Skye. It was like a lifetime ago. The rain in their faces. The low clouds hanging around the Cuillin, an otherworldly mountain range. It was there, in a small cottage they had rented, where Patrick was conceived.

Peter said, "So, what do you suggest? That we just sit back and accept that we don't know how your wife died?"

Jack slammed his hand down hard on the side of the armchair. "That's enough! What is wrong with you?"

"What's wrong with me? What the hell are you talking about? I'm just asking if we should just accept this bullshit version of events."

"I'm accepting nothing. But I do things my way."

"I'm out of line. Sorry. I had no right to say that."

"You don't have to apologize. I'm having trouble accepting that Caroline would kill herself. But you need to understand, Peter, as it stands, the official version may be suicide, but make no mistake, I'm in the picture. I'm now in their crosshairs. Do you fucking understand that?"

"I understand it, sure," Peter said. "But it's bullshit. You didn't kill her."

"I know that!"

Peter averted his gaze.

"That's not how the Secret Service will view this. And I'm sure the cops will be here, asking me questions before long. The motive is clear. The money. That's motive for you."

"That's a crock of shit, Jack," Peter said. "I can help you. I know people. I know we have different ways of doing things."

"I believe in justice. So do you. But that means doing things the right way. I'm not a vigilante."

"I never said you were."

"I work strictly according to the law. I will get answers. But I'll do it by the book. It's the only way. To do anything else would tarnish Caroline's memory."

"I just don't want you to shut me out."

Jack nodded. "I won't."

"I'll always be here for you. You're a stubborn bastard, but you're my brother. We're family, right?"

"Right."

"So, I've got your back. No matter what."

Twelve

It was just past midnight and McNeal sat in his living room alone, gun by his side. His brother and father were both sound asleep upstairs. He picked up the Glock 17. A torrent of thoughts and ideas raged around his head. He ran his thumb along the barrel of the gun. Suddenly, his cell phone vibrated on the wooden coffee table.

He put down the gun and picked up the phone.

"Yeah, who's this?" he said.

"I'm sorry to call so late." A woman's voice. "Is this Jack McNeal?"

McNeal was wary, assuming it was a journalist sniffing around for a story. An interview. "Who's this?"

"My name is Anna Seligman."

"Who are you?"

"First, I just wanted to express my sincere condolences. I knew your wife."

McNeal sat upright. He wondered if she was a college friend of Caroline's. Maybe she had even worked with her at the *Post*. "How did you know Caroline?"

"I was her psychologist."

"I didn't know she was seeing a psychologist."

"I've been meaning to talk to you but never managed to get around to it."

"How did you get this number?"

"This is the emergency number Caroline listed when she became my patient. I've been going through her file all day."

McNeal cleared his throat. "It's very late, Dr. Seligman . . ."

"I can call you tomorrow morning if it's easier."

Jack stifled a yawn. "What do you want?"

"Well, your wife had been seeing me for nearly two years. She had signed a release form in case of her death so that what she had discussed with me could be passed on to you, her husband."

"We were estranged."

"I know that, Mr. McNeal. But as it stands, my files on what we talked about can be shared with you. She was adamant that this information be passed on."

"I don't mean to be rude, but I don't really see the point in my knowing her personal feelings about me, herself, or us. No disrespect."

"That's perfectly understandable, Mr. McNeal. However, I believe some concerns she had might be of interest."

McNeal slowly got to his feet and began to pace the room. "What sort of concerns?"

"Personal safety concerns. Can I speak frankly?"

"Of course."

"Caroline was frightened. She was becoming more paranoid. It concerned me."

"Paranoid? That doesn't sound like my wife."

"I agree. It wasn't like Caroline. She talked mostly about the loss of your son. But also the disintegration of your marriage, which she regretted."

"I didn't know that."

"She regretted it very much. Thought she had been hasty. And she was greatly bothered by the hurt she had caused."

McNeal closed his eyes. "I didn't know that."

"I know it's not easy to hear in light of what happened."

"You mentioned that she was becoming paranoid. Did she say what she feared? What exactly was making her paranoid?"

"Over the last few months, before her death, she talked about people following her."

McNeal's mind flashed back to the conversation with Finks of the Secret Service. Caroline had mentioned a prowler around her home. "Following her?"

"One man. Always the same man. That's what she said. Numerous times. I have notes, all typed up, which give more details about the times and places it occurred."

"I'd like to see those."

"Of course. She also talked about her work as a journalist. She told me, and this is what I wanted to tell you, that she had unearthed some highly sensitive information."

"What kind of information?"

"I'd rather not speak over the phone. But I can get that information to you. It was regarding a story she had been working on for the last year. She grew obsessed with it. It meant a lot to her. She said she wasn't sleeping. It was causing her anxiety. I have all the notes in my office."

McNeal's senses were on high alert. "Could you send them to me?"

"I could courier them. I'll try and send them to you by the end of the week."

McNeal wondered what he should do now. He didn't want this lead to go cold. "Listen, I could head down to DC the day after tomorrow. It might take five or six hours to get down there, driving. But we can meet up. I need to know more. How does that sound?"

"That sounds fine. I can meet with you in the afternoon at the Willard. I'm speaking at a conference there. How is four o'clock?"

"That works for me. I'll see you in the lobby. How will I recognize you?"

"I'll find you. I already know what you look like. Caroline showed me a picture. She kept it in her wallet at all times."

Thirteen

Dawn's first light flickered through the wooden blinds as Andrew Forbes sat at his desk in the White House, checking emails on his cell phone. He shared a small office with the personal secretary to the President, right outside the Oval Office. He was waiting for the President to stop by, as he always did. Forbes was usually the first person to greet the President in the morning and often the last to go home at night.

He leaned back in his seat, wondering what the big guy would want today. Invariably it was just a chat. It might be about baseball, Wall Street, or more small talk, filling a few minutes before a national security briefing. The President liked small talk. Andrew and the President played golf together at home and abroad. But he also liked gossip. The juicier the better.

Forbes was a constant presence for the President. He was always on call. He got along with everybody. It might be the chief executive of a Fortune 500 company or a cleaner in the White House. He had time for everyone.

Each and every time, he would be with the President at meetings, always there in case the President wanted something.

He knew the President loved movies. The President's favorite director was John Ford. Westerns—good guy, bad guy. They often watched movies at night over a beer.

The President was fascinated by Hollywood. He lapped it all up. The big guy pretended to hate all the liberal actors with their focus on identity politics and actresses and their virtue signaling. But he was dazzled by them.

Forbes, on the other hand, like his father, loathed each and every one of them with a passion. Handing out food parcels to Syrian refugees with photographers in tow, fundraising for transgenderism in the Third World, advocating for women's rights in Vietnam, setting up tax-deductible charitable foundations to fund outreach programs for Sub-Saharan Africa, promoting literacy programs for women wearing blue burqas in rural Afghanistan, actresses and singers with white savior complexes adopting photogenic orphans from Darfur, establishing global human rights advocacy centers, creating toy giveaways for destitute children in Cambodia, being photographed posing arm-in-arm beside rainbow-painted pedestrians outside the United Nations, building schools for orphan girls in Rwanda, flying to Davos on private jets as UN goodwill ambassadors and giving primetime speeches on global responsibility, calling for foreign intervention under the guise of UN humanitarian work, hiring ghostwriters to pen *New Yorker* essays calling for foreign intervention to "defend our values at home and across the Middle East," and hosting glittering charity dinners in Beverly Hills for starving Haitians, all before they fled back to their gated communities in Pacific Palisades, Bel Air, or Malibu. Virtually none of the wretched fuckers who talked about *giving back* were interested in *giving back* to America's poor. A handful did, to be fair. But most of Hollywood's waxed and surgically enhanced, plastic, globally aware liberal elites didn't give a fuck about Americans down on their luck. They were embarrassed by real Americans.

Their arrogance was astounding. Tone deaf, they just didn't get it. They all had child-like messiah complexes, wanting to show the world how good they were.

The more he saw of them, the more Hollywood elites made him want to leave America. It was a pitiful sight, liberals wanting to ram their diluted Marxism down everyone's throats. Global citizens. What the hell was that? What about the forgotten in their own backyard, the people who had lost their jobs and houses and had to live in their cars? The men and women, Black and white, who suffered year after year? Who endured real hardships? No actor came to their aid. Occasionally they pulled up to a South Central soup kitchen with a camera crew. The white savior to the rescue! But whatever the rights and wrongs of those narcissistic fuckers, the President was fascinated and beholden to the glitter in some ways. He enjoyed when they turned up at the White House. Column inches. Prime time minutes on chat shows. That's how he saw it. And he was right. He leveraged whichever stars wanted to back his policies. Invariably country stars with amphetamine habits. Sometimes a whacked-out hip-hop multimillionaire who objected to paying his taxes rolled up in his new designer range of leisurewear. It was a win-win for everyone.

Forbes was privilege personified. He knew it. But he sure as hell didn't apologize for it, unlike the squeamish liberals. Why the fuck should he? He was not embarrassed to have made it. Like his father, he was a libertarian. His father had worked his way up from a dirt-poor coal mining town in West Virginia to build a fortune. It was the American Dream.

Forbes cultivated useful friendships. He was only twenty-seven. But he already knew a ton of people, mostly through his father's extensive contacts in business, which were cultivated over forty years. He knew everyone who was anyone. Powerful industrialists, venture capitalists, tech start-up kids, billionaire philanthropists, NBA stars who needed to invest their money—his father knew them all. In turn, over the years, Forbes had grown to know the same people.

He ate in fashionable Washington restaurants. He hung out in the Hamptons. He skied in Switzerland. He vacationed in the Bahamas. He understood offshore tax havens like the back of his hand. But in the last eighteen months, Forbes had only one job: the President's body man.

If the President needed his suit mended, he would take care of that. The President needed a pal to watch *Monday Night Football*, he was there. The President needed cotton swabs for his ears, he had that covered. Dental floss, mouthwash, nasal spray. Gum. Advil. Coke. Not the small C variety. Vitamin pills. But he also provided steroids and amphetamines if he needed a pick-me-up. That was their little secret, among others.

The body man carried it all.

Forbes leaned farther back in his seat. Pain shot through his right knee, and he winced. The injury was the result of a snowboarding accident in Gstaad the previous winter. He popped a couple of oxycodone tablets, washed down with his morning coffee. Thirty minutes later, the pain began to slowly subside. He felt better. Calmer. Way more relaxed.

Forbes stared at his cell phone, waiting for the call. He checked his watch. It was 5:45 a.m. The West Wing was wide-awake, with the sound of the President shouting at an advisor. A few moments later, the President walked in, shutting the day quietly behind him. Forbes got to his feet. "Mr. President, how are you this morning? Can I get you some coffee?"

"Not now. You saw our latest polling numbers?"

"Highest ever, I believe."

"Economic growth. Jobs. They've never seen numbers like it."

Forbes smiled. He loved the President's positivity and bound-ss optimism.

"Tell me, how do I look in this suit, Andrew? They say it's got nice cut. But what do you think?"

Forbes thought it was a badly cut, off-the-rack suit that didn't onvey the power of the President or flatter his body shape. He had alked to the President before about his need to get a proper tailored uit. "Honest answer, Mr. President?"

"Of course."

"Get a new tailor. My father uses a guy from Savile Row. He lies in once a year. Very picky about his clientele. I'm sure I can get im access to you whenever you want, at a time of your choosing."

"This is an expensive suit I'm wearing," he said.

"It's not bespoke, sir. Do you want me to make a call?"

"This guy is good?"

"Prince Charles gets his suits from this guy."

"Seriously?"

"Oh yeah. My father gets two brand-new suits every year, made o measure. A pure wool suit and a lighter suit for the summer nonths. But only from this guy. This guy will rock your world."

The President stared at Forbes's suit. "What are you wearing?"

"A bespoke Huntsman suit. I got measured up in London last ummer."

"I must be paying you too much, Andrew."

Forbes laughed. "Leave it to me. I'll make a call."

"I want a dozen fantastic suits. Great suits. All weathers. And ome shoes."

"We'll get the best."

"I think even the Iranians seem to be getting better dressed hese days."

Forbes laughed again. "Not for long."

"Good work, Andrew."

The cell phone began to vibrate on his desk.

"You better get that," the President said.

"Will do, sir."

The President patted him on the back. "Tell your dad I asked for him. See if he wants to play a round at St. Andrews in a couple weeks. I'll be at a NATO summit in Edinburgh."

"Thank you, Mr. President. I'll pass that on."

The President slammed the door shut.

Forbes picked up his cell phone and answered. "Yeah?"

"We have a problem."

Forbes took a few moments to choose his words carefully. "What kind of problem?"

"The cop . . . the husband of the dead journalist?"

"I'm listening."

"The cop got a call. From his late wife's therapist. He's headed down there."

"He's headed to DC?"

"It's problematic. The therapist was privy to the journalist's innermost thoughts."

"So, what are we going to do?"

"Don't worry. We already have a plan in place. I'm hopeful the problem will be resolved very soon. I'll be in touch."

Fourteen

It was late afternoon when the FedEx truck pulled up outside Jack's Westport home.

He signed for the large package and hauled it into the house. Inside was a cardboard box full of Caroline's belongings, including her house keys, and papers sent by her lawyer in DC.

McNeal put down the box and cracked open a couple of cold beers for him and Peter. Their father had left early to head back to the familiarity of his old haunts on Staten Island.

Jack ordered Chinese for two, and they ate at the kitchen table. He was happy to have some company.

"I'm sorry, Jack," Peter said, scooping up some fried rice. "I've been thinking about what you said last night."

"And?"

"Maybe you're right. Maybe we should be cautious."

"Thanks. It's a lot to take in. I need time. I need space."

"I understand."

After the brothers finished their food, Peter cracked open another couple of cold beers. Jack carefully unpacked Caroline's papers, which included a copy of her will.

"What the hell is this?" Peter asked.

Jack told Peter about the telephone conversation with Garrett, the executor of Caroline's will.

"God bless her," Peter said.

McNeal laid out all the photos and legal papers on the living room table. Methodically. Photos of their wedding. Extensive typewritten notes from her diary that she had passed to her lawyer.

He began to work his way through it all. He skimmed through the sometimes painful insights into his late wife's mindset. She talked of "being watched" and being "under surveillance."

He read on, determined to find out what had happened to her.

Jack sipped his beer as he leafed through the typewritten notes. He highlighted in red pen a passage where Caroline had talked about cars following her. The sound of clicking on her home phone. A mysterious prowler outside her home in the weeks before her death.

"I don't know if she contacted the police about this. I'd like to know if this was followed up. If she even reported it. The Secret Service knew about this."

Peter shook his head, obviously struggling to wrap his mind around it all.

The more he read the notes, the more depressed Jack got. He knew his wife—or at least he thought he did. She had been a rational person. She wasn't superstitious. She wasn't easily spooked. She was tough. Independent-minded. But something had been troubling her. Deeply. She wasn't imagining it.

Jack spent hours plowing his way through the typewritten diary. He perused the letters from him that she had kept. Personal letters from friends she had received, and a couple of CDs. One was Jackson Browne. He knew she liked him. But Lady Gaga? She didn't like her music at all.

The last item on the table was a thumb drive.

Peter leaned back in his seat, gulped some more beer. "Wonder what's on it."

Jack shrugged. He went up to his study and brought down his laptop. He inserted the thumb drive. The screen came alive. A homemade video of Caroline appeared, smiling, tears streaming down her face, filmed in what looked like her kitchen.

Peter patted him on the back. "I'm so sorry, Jack."

Jack sighed as his throat tightened, seeing his late wife. "Hey, honey," he said, without thinking.

Caroline smiled back at him, wiping away tears, speaking from beyond the grave. "Jack, if you're watching this, it means I'm dead, darling. This is so difficult. I don't know who I can trust. But I do know I can trust you. I always could. You were always the one I could turn to."

Jack stared at the screen.

"I want you to know," she said, brushing her brown hair from her glassy eyes, "I believe people are trying to kill me. I wanted you to know that. Maybe I should have told you sooner. But I guess it's too late now. I know you're a good man, Jack. I always did."

Jack closed his eyes.

"You're a cop, Jack. So, I know how you think. I know how you feel about things. And you're probably wondering why I didn't go to the cops. The truth is, I did. I reported this. I believe they spoke to someone. They didn't give me a name. The thing is, I'm scared. And I want you to know what I know. There's so much I want to talk about. I want you to know that I bitterly regret leaving you. I hope you can find it in yourself to forgive me one day. You know my happiest day? It was the day I married you. Don't forget that. I remember that day. Hottest day of the year. Pouring rain the day before and the day after. But for our wedding, it was flawless. Do you remember that day, Jack? I'm sure you do."

Jack tasted his salty tears and shook his head.

"I feel so unsafe. I'm afraid. You know me, Jack. I'm a fighter. But I know something is wrong. I know you're probably wondering what this is all about. It's a long story. I think it has to do with a story I'm working on. All the information, my notes from the story, are on a disc."

Jack immediately thought of the Lady Gaga CD. He smiled as Peter wrapped his huge arm tight around his shoulders.

"I trust you, Jack. I know you'll find out not just who killed me, but also who killed the woman whose story I was investigating. Her name was Sophie Meyer. It wasn't a sanctioned story by the *Post*. They didn't want to touch it. This is my work. I wanted to write a book about it. But I guess that wasn't to be."

Jack reached out and touched the screen. "I love you, darling."

"Jack, do what you can." She dabbed her eyes. "I believe I'm being watched. One man. There might be others. I'm worried. Really worried. I thought I was imagining it. But I'm not. I just think . . . I don't know what's going to happen to me. So, I'm making this recording for you to know that I believe this man is going to kill me. I have no proof of that. But I think it's because of my investigation. The woman was a socialite, Sophie Meyer. Magazine covers, you might remember."

Jack remembered reading about the story in the *New York Post*.

"I believe her husband was involved in her death. I don't know how. But I believe he had some part in it. His name is Henry Graff."

The name crashed through Jack's head. His mind flashed back to the brief Fox News clip he had seen back in the Internal Affairs office in New York. He remembered that the President had attended a private memorial service on the third anniversary of her death. And they specifically mentioned it was to commemorate the late wife of Henry Graff, an old friend of the President. He paused the footage and told Peter. "I remember that name, son of a bitch!"

Peter wrote it down.

"He's a friend of the President," Jack said.

"I swear to God. This is not good."

"The clip didn't mention the name Sophie Meyer, as far as I can remember. But they definitely said Henry Graff. The same woman Caroline is talking about."

"And he was married to this socialite, Meyer?"

"That's what she's saying."

"That's fucked up."

Jack gathered his thoughts and resumed the footage.

"You're probably wondering what made me look into her death. Well, journalists talk to people. Off the record. And something about the nature of this woman's death—she overdosed—and her connections to a host of powerful people in Washington . . . I thought that was too convenient. She took a lot of secrets with her to the grave. It looked like a typical overdose. But why now? Had she gotten careless? And so, I started digging into it. I was greeted by a wall of silence to begin with. I was warned by people not to pursue this. That freaked me out. But it also made me more determined to find out what really happened. I believe the same people who killed her will come for me. I don't have any proof of that. But the man who is following me might be one of them. Why did they kill her? The woman who died knew too much. Maybe I know too much. Henry Graff is the key."

Jack sighed. "Oh Jesus, Caroline."

"I hope you take the necessary action with all this information. I want people to be held accountable. It's probably too much for one person to investigate. I would hope the FBI would be interested. But I've come up against numerous brick walls since I started this investigation."

Jack closed his eyes tight. The sound of her voice was breaking his heart. It reminded him of the day of their wedding. The clarity of her speech. The lightness. It made him feel good remembering it.

"I miss you so much, Jack. I don't blame you for not wanting to get involved after Patrick died. I understand now. I understand the terrible hurt you must have gone through. I know you felt guilty. I don't blame you at all. When Patrick died . . . I know part of you died. I tried to reach out to you. But you had retreated into yourself. I can see that now. I was harsh on you. I did blame you. I was wrong. I don't blame you. I only loved two people in my life. You and Patrick. That's all there ever was."

Jack bowed his head and began to sob.

"I just wanted you to know that I'm very scared. I wish you were here with me. I wanted to talk to you about it. I just never got around to it. I was afraid if I called you, *they* would know. It would lead them to you. And I didn't want that. But I just wanted you to know all of this in case something happens to me. Until we meet again, Jack. Love you."

Then the screen went blank.

Fifteen

McNeal gripped the table, losing his grasp on reality. This was getting weirder and darker. The same thoughts had run through him five years ago. The night all the trouble began. Now this had opened up all the hurt and anger he had suppressed. He could feel it building. Slowly.

"You okay to do this?" Peter asked.

Jack grabbed them another couple of cold beers. "She wanted me to know what she knew. So, I need to see it."

"I'm just trying to protect you. I don't want you going off the rails."

Jack took a long gulp of Schlitz. He wondered what the hell he was going to find on the goddamn CD. "Let's do this."

"You sure?"

"Do it."

Peter handed the CD to Jack, who slid it into the side of the laptop. Dozens of Word documents appeared on the screen. He scanned the file names. He printed them all out. Together, Jack and his brother read the contents as the time ticked away.

Slowly a story fell into place . . .

Caroline had been privately investigating the death of a Washington, DC, socialite, Sophie Meyer, the daughter of a wealthy blue blood East Coast family. Meyer had died three years earlier. Found by her cleaner at her DC home, sprawled on the floor of her bedroom, pills strewn over her body.

Jack googled the name Sophie Meyer and countless articles appeared. It showed her at museum openings, *Vanity Fair* parties, the Met Gala, White House parties, film premieres—anywhere people with money and influence gathered. He didn't see any pictures of her with her husband, Henry Graff. None at all.

Meyer partying in DC, New York, London, the Hamptons, Milan, the Bahamas, Hong Kong, and everywhere in between. You throw a glamorous party, and she would be there. Dressed impeccably. Powerful connections. Her grandfather had been good friends with a Rockefeller. Her father was one of America's first billionaires.

"Am I reading this right?" Peter asked. "Maybe I'm fucked up by all this. But this Sophie Meyer woman was found dead of an overdose at her home in Washington, DC, and Caroline is found floating in the Potomac, also in DC? Two separate women? And your late wife was investigating this woman's death? That's a red flag if ever there was one."

Jack scrolled to the next article. "The official version says Sophie Meyer was manically depressed; was addicted to cocaine, amphetamines, barbiturates; had a complicated social life; and had sleeping pills and four other drugs in her system when she died."

Jack considered. He wondered out loud what the chances were that the woman investigating another woman's suspicious death would wind up dead too, in suspicious circumstances. The same city. But this was about way more than probability. It was about what Sophie Meyer knew and about what Caroline McNeal knew.

Peter shook his head. "It's bullshit, Jack. I'm calling it the way I see it."

"I don't know." Jack closed the files. He stared at the screen. He scanned the files before realizing there was one more he hadn't seen. It was called *Encrypted for JM*. He clicked it, and the computer prompted him for a six-digit code.

"What the hell is it?" Peter said. "Damn. A fucking code. I can never remember my passwords and goddamn codes."

Jack held up his hand to calm down his brother. "Let's work this out. Let's take our time. Caroline downloaded this to a CD, along with all the other documents about Sophie Meyer."

"Is it her date of birth?"

Jack tried that, but it came back *Password incorrect.*

"Damn."

Jack's mind was racing. "Hang on, in the video. What was the thing that stuck in my head?" He clicked his fingers, trying to remember. "Yeah. 'The day I married you.' That's what she said."

Peter grinned. "That was a good day. The day after Independence Day, right?"

Jack entered 070508. The document opened, decrypting before his eyes. A handful of official-looking documents. Pentagon-letterhead notepaper. Partially redacted.

Peter whistled as he read the documents. "Okay . . . What the fuck?"

Jack began to read. Slowly he began to understand. A combination of classified Pentagon intelligence documents and classified diplomatic cables. The latter had been sent to the State Department but leaked by a whistleblower to WikiLeaks. The documents showed conversations about why Sophie Meyer was a liability. A national security advisor had done an assessment showing Meyer as a serious and credible risk to the United States. But what the documents also contained were clandestine options to deal with her. "These are Department of Defense and State Department documents."

Peter sat quietly, reading another document. "I don't like this."

"How did Caroline get her hands on this?"

Peter got up, beer bottle in hand, and began to pace the room. "This is fucked up. I don't like it. I don't like it at all."

Jack took about an hour to read the half-dozen special access Pentagon memos relating to Sophie Meyer. Redacted names discussing options on the table to neutralize the threat. The wording was ominous. The documents were dated three months before Meyer died. He scanned the rest until he came to the final two documents. They were autopsies carried out by two separate medical examiners. An official version showing Meyer died by a drug overdose. A simple suicide. And a second version which showed suspicious needle marks on the neck. There was no mention of the needle marks in the first autopsy report.

He showed his brother the autopsy reports. "Read that," he said. "What do you make of that?"

Peter leaned over his brother's shoulder and scanned. "Motherfucker."

"This is something that Caroline either unearthed or a source in the Department of Defense passed to her."

"What do you think, Jack?"

Jack's mind raced. He wanted to watch the video of his wife again. And again. He wanted to listen to her talk. He wanted to not only hear her voice but also listen closely to what she was saying.

"So, what should we do?"

"We need to do the right thing. We need to take what we have to the FBI."

Peter stared at him. "Do you trust them?"

"I don't know."

"This seems to indicate that someone, maybe someone close to Sophie Meyer's family, ordered a private autopsy. Maybe they didn't believe the official version."

Jack nodded.

"It points to foul play. A cover-up. Call it whatever you want. The needle marks."

"I don't think this is the full story. Not by a long shot. I say we ake what we have to the Feds, eventually. But let's wait and see if ve find out anything else."

Peter nodded. "Probably our best bet under the circumstances. Do you think these documents got Caroline killed?"

Jack stared at the two autopsies on the screen. "I wish to God knew."

Sixteen

The following day, after a long drive south from Westport, McNea sat in the lobby of the Willard hotel in Washington, DC, nursing a soda, anxiously waiting to meet up with Anna Seligman. His cel phone rang.

"Jack, it's Anna." Her voice sounded strained.

"Hey, everything okay?"

"I'm so sorry. I had to leave the conference early."

"So, you're not at the hotel? Nothing serious, I hope."

"Listen, I won't be able to make it. I've got a major problem."

"Are you kidding me?"

"Unfortunately not. I've had a break-in at my office. Files are missing. It's very serious."

"It's not a problem for me to head on over and continue our conversation there."

"That won't be possible right now."

"Just give me a few minutes of your time. I drove a long way today just to speak to you."

"I'm sorry for wasting your time. The place is crazy."

"What happened?"

"I came back to my office about an hour ago. My talk finished early, and I wanted to pick up Caroline's files and a few other things. When I got here, I realized that a batch of maybe forty files had been stolen, along with a laptop and an iPad. It must've happened when I was giving the lecture."

"And the police are there?"

"They're here now. I'm really sorry."

"What about cloud backup?"

Seligman groaned. "I just checked my Dropbox. I always back up my files to the cloud, securely. I checked on my cell phone. All my online files were accessed four hours ago, exactly when I was giving the talk. They're all gone. Years of work, including Caroline's notes. It's a major data breach. A friend of mine, an IT guy, said I might have inadvertently downloaded ransomware that wiped out these files."

McNeal's mind raced ahead. He could see as clear as day that something was very wrong. It pointed to a targeted robbery. His gut reaction told him Seligman was telling the truth. "That must've been very upsetting for you," he said.

"Awful. I feel sick."

"If your IT guy thinks it is ransomware, did you receive any demands? You know, hand over ten thousand bucks and we'll restore your files?"

"Nothing like that. If this gets out, my business will be ruined by this."

McNeal groaned. "Are you sure I can't briefly stop by?"

"I asked the police if I could speak to you. I showed them on my calendar that we have an appointment. They told me it wasn't possible. I'm so sorry."

"I understand. Look, I appreciate you reaching out."

Seligman was quiet for a few moments. "Do you mind me speaking frankly, Jack?"

"No."

"I'm not one for conspiracy theories . . ."

"Neither am I."

"However, I was wondering if there could be any connection between Caroline's death and the files going missing. It's a very strange coincidence."

"It crossed my mind as well."

"This makes me very uneasy."

"I know exactly how you feel. I used to deal with robberies in Manhattan. You feel like you've been violated."

"I also feel like the confidentiality of my patients has been breached. Anyway, I'm sorry I can't help you further. And sorry you traveled all this way."

Caroline had divulged sensitive information to her psychologist. Someone wanted to know what it was. McNeal stood and started back toward his car. "Thanks for your time. I'll let you get back to talking with the police."

"If the files are returned or found, I'll be sure to let you know."

Seventeen

McNeal was emotionally drained. It had been a long and fruitless drive down to DC. He wondered if he should just stay overnight at the Willard and drive back home in the morning.

The psychologist might have been able to provide a greater insight into Caroline's mindset before her death. In the blink of an eye, McNeal was back to square one. He weighed the pros and cons of the drive. He could see no point in enduring a five-hour trip up I-95 now. Better to get refreshed and head off when he was rested.

McNeal reserved a room for the night. He ordered a burger and a cold beer from room service as he watched the news. He showered and put on the hotel's white monogrammed robe. He wondered what his next move should be. He contemplated just forgetting about the whole thing. But there were already too many unanswered questions. Too many strange occurrences. Maybe Caroline was being followed. Maybe not. And then, on top of everything else, Caroline's files were missing from her therapist's office after a break-in.

It was all too much to believe. It didn't make sense.

McNeal called his brother. "I need to talk."

Peter sighed. "What's on your mind? You at home?"

"I'm down in DC."

"What?"

"I had to meet up with someone."

"Why didn't you let me know? I could have come with you."

"I don't need someone to hold my fucking hand."

"I never said you did. I'm here to help. I want to do what I can."

"You have a family to look after."

"I'm serious. Is there something I need to know about?"

McNeal took a few minutes to tell Peter about the call from Seligman, the sudden cancellation of the meeting after a break-in, and someone remotely accessing the Dropbox files before deleting them. "So, after learning about Caroline's death, and that she was investigating Sophie Meyer's death, this all points to the same thing."

Peter was quiet for a few moments, as if contemplating everything he'd just been told.

"I think Caroline knew too much. Whatever she had unearthed about Sophie Meyer and the nature of her death got her killed. That's what I think."

"You can't prove it."

"Maybe not. But I'm not buying that Caroline's death was a suicide."

"I never believed that for one fucking moment. We're on the same page for sure. She knew something, Jack."

"The psychologist I was supposed to speak to alluded to an investigation Caroline was working on. It must've been related to the documents we saw. But all the notes the psychologist took from the sessions are gone. Everything."

"Let me make a few calls."

McNeal shifted the phone to his other ear. "Not yet. I want to establish some facts before I decide what I'm going to do. I'm still a person of interest, and if I start contacting cops, informally,

Feds or whoever, they might think I'm trying to interfere in their investigation."

"That's bullshit."

"It's a fact. Now listen, I'm going to try and figure out how I'm going to approach this. You know how I work. It's methodical, right?"

"Jack, I can't just sit here after what happened. I need to get involved. Christ, I want to help you."

"I know you do. Peter, listen to me. What happened is a tragedy. I'm still reeling from it all. But I'm no closer to establishing what happened. The psychologist who saw Caroline mentioned she was paranoid."

"You think that sounds like her?"

"No, it doesn't. But I'm looking at this from an investigator's point of view. I'm playing devil's advocate. Maybe she was on medication. I just don't know. Maybe . . . I don't know, maybe the fact is I didn't know my own wife."

Peter got quiet, then lashed out, "This was no fucking accident. Listen, I understand you've got a fancy degree. We're proud of you. You're the smart one. But sometimes playing by the rules gets you nowhere."

McNeal knew from firsthand experience at the Internal Affairs Bureau that there was something to what Peter was saying. He had run up against the bureaucracy and powers that be before. The Internal Affairs Bureau had tried-and-tested ways of doing things. He had lost count of the number of bad cops he had investigated who were put on dismissal probation. It meant if they kept their noses clean for a year, everything was forgotten. There were scores and scores of cases like that. The system sometimes worked. Usually it was imperfect, and that was being diplomatic. He had fired off numerous emails and internal memos about the lack of rigor. A rigged system. He was told that he was a first-rate officer, but he had to understand that this was the way things were done. Despite his best efforts, he kept coming up against a brick wall.

Peter took a deep breath. "You know what I mean, Jack. If we don't try and get to the truth of this, we'll never find out what really happened."

"I'll find out, alright. I'm just going to do it my way and in my own time."

Eighteen

Henry Graff spotted her. The woman was pretending to take photographs of the monuments at night. She was wearing sensible shoes, a white shirt, jeans, and a white Yankees cap. She was standing close to the Lincoln Memorial, bathed in its eerie light. He approached her, and she didn't acknowledge him. He brushed past her, and her eyes fixed on his.

Graff walked on slowly. He turned and slowed further to make sure she was following close behind. He stopped for a few moments until they were finally walking together.

"Nice evening for it," he said.

"What took you so long?" She aimed her camera behind her. A nice bit of countersurveillance.

"Recalcitrant staff. Pain in the ass."

She shook her head. "I've told you before, you employ too many people. Let me deal with whatever it is you need dealing with. And I mean everything. You need to delegate more. Outsource more."

"I already do. I don't know, maybe I'm too loyal."

"You're soft, Henry. That's what your problem is."

"That's not what you said last month in Jakarta."

Feinstein smiled. "Hah!"

He had known ex-CIA special operations analyst Karen Feinstein for the best part of fifteen years. They had been intimate for the last ten. She lived in New York, he in Arlington. He needed his space. But he could always rely on her and her firm, Fein Solutions. He had relied on them for years.

She was smart, tough, and about the only person on earth he really trusted. She didn't sugarcoat things. If there was bad news, she didn't shirk from giving it to him straight. He liked that about her. And she had a ruthlessness about her that he found alluring. A coldness. Some people viewed her as standoffish. But not Graff. He viewed her as a rational person who didn't get swayed by emotions. And that made her, in his eyes, the perfect hire.

"First up," Graff said, "I'm assuming I don't have to frisk you."

"You can if you want." She stared straight ahead as they walked.

"No cell phones. No devices of any kind. Those are the rules."

Feinstein smiled. "So, do you want to frisk me? You haven't done that for a few weeks."

"I trust you."

"And I trust you."

"Good. Enough pleasantries," Graff said. "I thought it was all signed and sealed, this Caroline McNeal business."

"It was. It is. But there are . . . loose ends. I thought it important to let you know."

"I don't like loose ends when I pay you such exorbitant fees."

Feinstein glanced over her shoulder, as if sensing someone watching her. She waited until a Lycra-clad jogger ran past. "Can't be too careful."

"Tell me about the loose ends."

"We managed to retrieve all the information from Caroline McNeal's psychologist. We got everything off the cloud, and an operative secured entry to her office after we remotely disabled an internal surveillance system. That's the good news."

"Tell me about the loose ends, Karen."

"I was getting to that. The loose ends are that the psychologist, Anna Seligman, reached out to Jack McNeal."

"I'm assuming you factored into our calculations that Jack McNeal, as a cop, albeit with Internal Affairs, might investigate the death of his wife. You've got to expect some trouble farther down the line."

"We did. But this psychologist is way out of left field. We knew Caroline McNeal had a therapist. But we didn't think that might be a problem."

"We are where we are. These things happen. I get it. Did you manage to get a trace on the call, backdated?"

"A former colleague of mine ran a dummy test; it's like a parallel operation."

"I'm not interested in how you got to the conclusion. I'm interested in the conclusion."

Feinstein stopped as her gaze fixed on the Korean War Memorial. "He's in town."

"McNeal is in town? Now?"

"We'll deal with this. It's under control."

"Tell me more about him."

"He's highly intelligent. Diligent. Doesn't attract attention. Manages his investigations with a cool detachment."

"So, what happened?"

"What happened is Seligman told Jack McNeal that she had been looking over the transcripts, and she talked about how Caroline McNeal had been paranoid. Thought she was being watched. Followed."

Graff contemplated how that might work in their favor. "That might feed into the official narrative we want to cultivate that Caroline McNeal was depressed."

"It does. The problem is, because he has headed down to DC to meet up with this psychologist, he is now aware of the break-in."

"How?"

"She called him to tell him."

"I need this sorted out."

"What do you want?"

"I want you to neutralize the threat. I don't want *him* neutralized. Just the threat he poses."

"That's what I intend to do. I'll get a couple of my operatives to put in some calls. I know exactly what we can do."

"What's that?"

"Does Jack McNeal want people to know he is a person of interest for his wife's death? How would his fellow detectives in Internal Affairs, maybe cops in the NYPD, react if they heard rumors about that? McNeal's reputation would be trashed. And his name would be worthless. Can you see how this could play into our hands?"

"You really are a danger to society, Karen."

"I like to think so."

"Can we get a roving bug on his personal cell phone to find out what he's saying and who he's saying it to?"

"I've already tried. He took out the battery. Like I said, he's intelligent. I suspect he might also be using another cell phone."

"So, electronic surveillance is problematic. Can we get eyes on him?"

"I don't think so. He's not going to be chatting about important stuff when people are around. The good news is that all written references to Caroline McNeal's phobias and fears of being followed are all gone. Wiped clean. Shredded."

"Every copy?"

"Bleached electronically, overwritten, data scrubbed. The works."

Graff turned and headed back toward the Lincoln Memorial, passing dozens of nighttime tourists mingling, admiring the alabaster stone. He waited until Feinstein was in step before he spoke. "He's not a stupid man."

"Clearly not."

"While it's possible for a person to commit suicide, or appear to commit suicide, for there to also be a break-in at the office of the therapist his late wife was seeing strains credulity. He'll know there's more to this."

"Maybe he will. Maybe he won't."

"What's your gut reaction?"

Feinstein considered before speaking. "If Jack McNeal's past and personal psychological profile and reports are anything to go by, he won't get involved much further. He's reserved. His brother's a hothead. But Jack appears to be the polar opposite. He doesn't make spontaneous decisions."

Graff wondered if Feinstein was underestimating the threat Jack McNeal could pose.

"I think he'll rationalize that his wife got involved in something, maybe a relationship. It turned toxic, and she took her own life. With regards to the break-in, there were forty-three separate files taken, including Caroline McNeal's. So, Jack might think this was just a random break-in. Dumb luck, that kind of thing."

"I don't think he'll buy that."

Feinstein's gaze wandered around the floodlit monuments for a few fleeting moments. "Then we may have a problem on our hands."

Nineteen

It was late the following morning, after McNeal had packed his bags for the long journey back to Connecticut, when he decided to call his closest friend in Internal Affairs, Dave Franzen. He wanted an update on his latest case.

"Hi, Dave. Sorry to bother you. You got a minute?"

"Jack, I just wanted to say how sorry I am. Nicola and myself, all the people in Internal Affairs . . . we are all devastated for you. I know how much you've gone through in the past. If there's anything I can do, just ask."

"Appreciate that, Dave. Means a lot. I'm sorry I couldn't make it to the bar."

"You didn't miss anything. We got drunk, we watched football, and we argued about Buckley."

"Some things never change."

"How are you holding up?"

"I'll be okay. It's been hard. But we keep on going, right?"

Franzen sighed. "I don't know what to say . . . Is there anything I can do for you?"

"I'm just looking for an update on the cop who knocked his kid unconscious."

"Don't worry about that. We've got this."

"I know. But I just want to make sure that we're on top of that one."

"You need to switch off, Jack."

"I know."

"Gimme a minute and I'll pull up the file. Let me see . . . So, I had his attorney on the phone yesterday. The guy is pleading guilty, is full of remorse, undergoing counselling for alcohol addiction—you know, the usual bullshit. And we're going to fire his ass."

"So, we got him?"

"Damn right. He'll be off the force."

"What about his pension?"

"We're going to try and take it, but the attorney threatened to sue us if we do."

"What did Buckley say?"

"Not much. Here's the thing . . . Guess where Buckley was when I caught up with him last night?"

"Mayor's office?"

"The *New York Times*."

"Last night? He turned up there?"

"Late. It's not what it looked like."

"What do you mean?"

"Buckley went there for a reason."

"Spit it out."

Franzen sighed. "I don't know if I should tell you this."

"Tell me what?"

"A young reporter on the *Times* called me and Buckley for an off-the-record chat just after lunch."

"Chat about what?"

"To see if you had been contacted by the Secret Service in relation to the death of your wife."

McNeal took a few moments to process the information. "How did they know about that?"

"That's what Buckley was trying to find out. He was speaking to one of the editors. He headed right up there. It appears they got an anonymous tip-off saying the reporter should pursue this angle and that the Secret Service had been in touch with you about the death of your wife."

"Dave, I really appreciate that information."

"It didn't come from me. You want the name of the reporter?"

"No. I'm assuming they just received the tip-off and were pursuing the angle. But it's good to know."

"How you holding up?"

"I just need some time and space to get everything straight."

"If there's anything you need, don't hesitate to call. Day or night."

"You got it."

McNeal hung up and went numb. He wondered if this was someone's way of turning the spotlight on him. He assumed it might have been part of an operation to put psychological pressure on him. He wondered how long it would be until a story appeared in the *New York Times*. And if it hit the *Times*, the *Post* and the rest of the papers and media would be clambering all over the story.

He imagined a feeding frenzy. The rogue cop. The bad cop. The cop who once killed his partner. The distraught New York cop who killed his wife for leaving him.

He began to imagine all these scenarios playing out.

The more he thought about it, the more he realized the scale of the threat that Caroline had been facing. Insidious, subversive ways to destroy him without actually pulling the trigger. He didn't know who he could trust. He was in the middle of a waking nightmare. He felt himself getting sucked deeper into a quagmire, a shadowy world of invisible people pulling the strings.

The phone on the bedside table rang, snapping him out of his thoughts.

"Hi, Mr. McNeal. This is the front desk. We have a call for you."

"Who from?"

"A Mr. Finks. He didn't say where he was calling from."

"Put him through."

A couple of seconds passed. "Mr. McNeal, I didn't realize you were in Washington," the Secret Service agent said.

"I didn't realize it was widely known."

"I just wanted you to know that we just got the toxicology report back from the medical examiner. I'm pleased—relieved, even—to say that you are no longer a person of interest. The toxicology points clearly to an overdose."

"What kind of overdose?"

"I don't have the full report in front of me. I read barbiturates, cannabis, and alcohol. And some ketamine. A lethal combination."

"Caroline took ketamine? That's a goddamn horse tranquilizer. Are you seriously saying she took these drugs and just walked into the Potomac?"

"No one can know the exact manner of her death."

"What do the DC police say about it? What are their conclusions?"

"Same as us. They've ruled it a suicide."

Twenty

It was dark when Andrew Forbes left his apartment in DC, a bag slung over his shoulder and one in his hand. He had a rare night off. But this was a special appointment.

He had been instructed to take a few countersurveillance measures. He had to cover his tracks. The first part of the measures was walking to the nearby Sofitel. He jittered, excited at what was to come, but it was also good to take some time out from the hothouse atmosphere of the White House, attending to the President's every whim.

He loved the big guy. He would do anything for him. But at times, even Forbes's good humor and patience were stretched to the limit by the President's foibles.

Forbes had been up late the previous night and into the early hours. He'd had to listen to every gripe under the sun. Poor-quality air-conditioning at the White House, the grass was a strange shade of green on the North Lawn, Air Force One always seemed to run out of cashews. He made a mental note of the complaints and random observations, not knowing whether to laugh out loud or cry. On and on, a catalogue of pettiness. Are there too many Hispanic Secret Service agents on duty in the West Wing? Did the pilot of Air Force One fly in Vietnam? Would Yankee Stadium be big enough for one of his rallies in New York? Would the Rolling Stones allow him to take the stage before a gig in New Jersey? Does anyone know if Mick Jagger is a communist? Where the hell is my wife?

Forbes did what a good body man did. He listened. He nodded. He agreed. He said he'd try and find out from someone who might know. Would you like some more candy, Mr. President?

At times it seemed as if the President had consumed speedballs, he was so fucking wired. Did the big guy ever sleep? He had too much energy. It was unnatural.

Tonight, Forbes got away from all that. At least for a while. A time to catch up on something he knew was vitally important. A side project of his.

Forbes arrived at the plush Sofitel and checked in under his middle name, Charles. He needed to ensure he left no trail. It struck him as odd when someone carried his bags for him. He was usually the one doing the lifting for others.

Forbes's overnight bags were taken to his room. He showered and changed into a button-down shirt, jeans, and sneakers. He checked himself in the mirror. He looked like any college kid. His cheeks were puffier than when he had started his job. Not as much basketball. More sitting on long plane rides and sitting at his desk, waiting for the President to call him. He needed to start working out more.

He opened the room's safe and put his cell phone inside, careful to lock it securely before keying in a four-digit code. Satisfied he wouldn't be tracked, Forbes headed through the lobby and to Lafayette Square, mingling with the tourists.

The second stage of the countersurveillance measures was underway.

He walked to the nearest Metro and took a train to Foggy Bottom. Then he walked a couple hundred yards to a run-down luggage storage locker. He tapped in the five-digit code and reached inside. He pulled out a backpack and slung it over his shoulder. He took a train back to his room at the Sofitel and opened up the backpack, took out a brand-new iPhone.

He started it up.

A message pinged on the screen.

Call this number.

A few moments later, a cell phone number appeared on the screen.

Forbes pressed the number and was connected right away.

An electronically distorted voice answered. "Thanks for calling."

"This cell I'm using is secure?"

"One hundred percent, Andrew. Sorry to be the bearer of bad news, but I believe we have a problem."

"Meaning?"

"Meaning people are beginning to ask questions. Questions about the two women. And we now have a cop, the husband of Caroline McNeal, asking questions. Do you follow what I'm saying?"

Forbes had assumed it was all taken care of. "Are you serious?"

"We're fine. But we need to make a decision."

"What kind of decision?"

"The cop's name is Jack McNeal. He knows something. He's been in touch with his late wife's psychologist. He's a problem. We need to face this."

"I can't believe what I'm hearing. This is ridiculous."

"He also received a FedEx delivery from his late wife's lawyer."

"I see."

"We need to get a plan in place."

"What kind of plan?"

"We need to think about how we can neutralize Jack McNeal."

Forbes cringed, as if his head was about to explode. "Hang on, we're getting off course. We haven't discussed this. That wasn't part of the plan."

"Plans change."

"Since when?"

"Since now."

Forbes wondered what the hell he had gotten himself into. He thought it would all be taken care of, and that would be that.

"Are you still there?"

"What do you propose?"

"You're the client."

"I understand. What would you recommend?"

"We need to find out what he knows first. And then we make our move. We can't have any more fallout from this."

"What if he goes to the cops? Other cops. The Feds? What if he goes to the media?"

"I've got a plan in place for that."

Forbes opened the minibar and took out a small bottle of whiskey. He unscrewed the top and gulped down the contents. A burning in his stomach. Blood rushing to his head. "You need to make this go away, or I swear to God, we're all going to prison. Do you hear me?"

"Loud and clear. Leave it to me."

"Do whatever you have to do."

Twenty-One

The following morning in Westport, Jack McNeal and his brother sat drinking coffee in the kitchen. They mulled one more time over the explosive documents Caroline had unearthed but also considered the news of the break-in and theft of files from Seligman's practice in Washington. They weighed it all up, knowing that Jack was no longer a person of interest.

"We need to do the right thing," Jack said. "We need to focus. But we need to keep within the law at all times."

Peter sighed.

"Agreed?"

"Sure."

Then they began to explore what their next step would be.

Eventually, they both agreed. They needed to inform the FBI as soon as they could.

The brothers left the house just after 8:30 and were in Bridgeport a half hour later.

McNeal checked his rearview mirror as he pulled up outside the FBI satellite office in downtown Bridgeport. A motorbike came into view for a few seconds. Then it disappeared from sight.

"How you feeling?" Peter asked.

"I don't know whether I'm coming or going. But I know this is the right way to respond to this. It's measured. It's legal. It's the right thing to do."

"You trust this guy?"

"Ryan Bone?"

"Bone, yeah."

"I think so . . . We worked together on an anticorruption joint task force thing when he worked in Manhattan. I haven't seen him for three years. But he seemed pretty solid, down to earth."

"Name rings a bell."

"He's from Staten Island."

"Yeah?" Peter grinned. "New Yorkers. Goddamn everywhere. I can't escape them even if I want to."

"They colonize every place they go."

McNeal turned off the engine. He picked up a large manila envelope containing some of the documents he had been given by Caroline's lawyer. He and his brother headed inside. They rode the elevator to the third floor and were buzzed into suite 306.

Bone was a huge guy, clean-shaven, dark suit. He shook both their hands and showed them into an interview room. "Nice to see you again, Jack." He shut the door behind him.

"You too. This is my brother, Peter. He's on the force."

"Nice to meet you, Peter. So, how can I help you guys today?" he said. "Pull up a seat. Take the weight off."

Jack sat down first as Peter pulled up a seat from the far end of the room. "Appreciate you seeing us, Ryan."

"How is Internal Affairs these days?"

"Busy. Real busy."

Ryan scribbled a few points on a legal pad. "I'm sorry about your wife. Very sad. I heard through the grapevine."

Jack nodded. "Appreciate that."

"She was a journalist, right?"

Jack nodded. "So, how's life in the FBI?"

Ryan shrugged. "What can I say? It has its moments. Anyway, how can I help?"

McNeal took a few minutes to explain the background. The deaths of both his wife and Sophie Meyer. "The whole thing, Ryan, is crazy."

Ryan took notes.

"Peter and I have been talking about something Caroline's lawyer passed on to me."

"Show me what you've got."

Jack handed over photocopies of several of the files from the CD. "This is what we have. It relates to my late wife's investigation into the death of Sophie Meyer a few years back. But it's just a taste, to give you a flavor of what this is all about."

Ryan scribbled some more notes before he leafed through the papers in the folder. He took a good ten minutes reading the information. "I can see this is something worth taking a very close look at. I know just the person."

"You'll make sure they get it?"

"I will send this down to DC myself, and I'll ensure that not only is it given priority but that I get back to you as soon as I can."

McNeal went quiet for a few moments.

"My wife was convinced she was being followed. Then she was found floating in the Potomac. She was investigating the death of Sophie Meyer, who was found overdosed three years earlier, also in Washington. I also watched a video of my late wife on the flash drive. It mentioned the name Henry Graff. Graff was Sophie Meyer's husband. I believe he's an old friend of the President. So, you can see why I'm bringing you such information. It's very sensitive."

Ryan nodded respectfully, slowly leafing through the papers again.

"I understand these are classified papers. Pentagon, top secret. No idea how Caroline got those. But there seem to be names of other key individuals who have been redacted."

"I think you did the right thing bringing this to our attention." Ryan scribbled down more information. "What do you believe happened? You're a cop, after all."

"I'm Internal Affairs. My brother is the cop. But we both think it's highly suspicious. To say the least. And that it warrants further investigation."

Peter stared at Ryan. "You're from Staten Island, Jack was saying?"

"Grew up there."

"Whereabouts?"

"Travis, on the West Shore."

Peter nodded. "New Dorp, on the East Shore."

Ryan nodded. "I know where you are. Giacomo's, right? Best pizza on the island."

Peter smiled. "You know it. Look, something is clearly amiss here. We want to be up-front. We're not looking for a favor. We're doing things by the book. Nothing to hide. I can see you're a stand-up guy. We all grew up in the same neighborhood, right? We just want you to open an investigation into this. Perhaps you might want to pass it on to the DC police after the FBI have checked it out."

"I can't make any promises. You understand that, right?"

Jack leaned forward. "As Peter explained, we don't want favors. We just want the FBI to investigate this. We thought about handing this over to the police. But this is clearly a sensitive issue. Perhaps with national security considerations."

"You made the right call, Jack."

"Just so you know, too, I was previously a person of interest. Diplomatic Security visited the Internal Affairs Bureau in

Manhattan. Then the Secret Service in Brooklyn wanted to talk to me."

Ryan added that to his notes. "That is interesting."

"I've been cleared. At least that's what the Secret Service said. Agent Finks."

Ryan sighed. "I'm assuming because your wife worked on Capitol Hill, she knew people there, hence the involvement of the Secret Service?"

"Right. Diplomatic Security couldn't find her hard pass. She attended White House press briefings, that kind of thing. She was a political journalist."

Ryan nodded. "Appreciate the heads-up. Makes sense. You got a cell number I can call you on?"

Jack handed over his Internal Affairs business card. "Day or night, call the cell phone number."

"I'll get back to you in a couple of days and hopefully give you a preliminary update of what's happening."

Peter stared at Ryan, long and hard. "We're trusting you to do the right thing. Just make sure you do."

Twenty-Two

The rain lashed off the eighty-seventh-floor windows as Henry Graff stared out over Manhattan's West Side. He had grown up in New York, privileged. But he never felt at home here.

The way the poor and wealthy mingled so freely. It unnerved him. Wealth could inoculate a man from the poverty and disease, though all too often the two worlds collided on the streets of New York. A simple walk down Fifth Avenue, and you could encounter a knife-carrying gangbanger who wanted your watch, drugged-out panhandlers, and mental patients who had been discharged from the hospital.

It was enough to keep any sane person on edge.

Graff could never relax in the city. A lot of people enjoyed the manic buzz, the constant noise, the relentless assault on the senses. He, on the other hand, loathed the appalling madness of New York. The sounds of jazz, hip-hop, and rock music blaring from cabs, buildings, bodegas, and headphones; the cacophony of traffic; the air pollution; the construction workers drilling holes in the fucking roads morning, noon, and night. If all that wasn't enough, there were people from New Jersey! If talking loudly, brashly, and fast was an Olympic sport, people from New Jersey would win the gold. Then there was the weather. One hundred degrees, stifling humidity, choking on car fumes. In the winter, ankle-deep slush. The list went on and on. It never stopped.

"Why in God's name did you want to set up shop here, Karen?" Graff chided. He turned around and looked at Karen Feinstein, who sat beside her desk, tapping away at her computer.

Feinstein smiled. "What is it with you and New York? How can you hate New York? How is that even possible?"

"It's dirty. The weather's terrible. It smells of piss and garbage in summer. There are socialists and communists everywhere. You want me to go on?"

"What do you even know about New York?"

"I know enough. I lived here once."

"When? Growing up at that townhouse on East Sixty-Third? Gimme a break."

"I was fortunate, I know. But this city makes me want to scream."

"Know why you feel uncomfortable here?"

"Why?"

"Do you really want me to tell you?"

"Are you trying to psychoanalyze me?"

"There are people from the Third World here. Is that what it is? People from Guatemala, Honduras, Puerto Rico. Am I wrong?"

Graff sighed and shook his head. "It doesn't look like anywhere else in America. That's what it is. Maybe Los Angeles without the smog. It doesn't think like anywhere else in America either. It doesn't even smell like America. Heartland America."

"What does America smell like?"

"The prairies of Iowa. The small towns of Virginia. The open spaces. New York doesn't smell like that."

"Henry, what the hell are you talking about?"

"I'm talking about this degenerate city."

"Seriously, Henry, you need to get out more. It's the twenty-first century."

"Diversity and fuck knows what else they're throwing at us. And still they come. Hordes of them. It's the fucking gateway to this country. If they can get here, they can disappear."

"Or work. Or wait tables. Tend bars. Pick up the trash. And save and go to college. The American Dream, right?"

"Are you kidding me? Picking up the trash? I wish they would. It's filthy. Do you know what I saw on Fifth Avenue earlier?"

"A panhandler?"

"A fucking rat! On Fifth Avenue! It's ridiculous."

Feinstein laughed. "It's New York. Deal with it."

"I don't want to deal with it."

"Look, I have several clients in the city. It's a great place. When was the last time you rode the subway?"

"The subway? I'd rather be dead than set foot on the subway. The amount of coughing, spluttering, screaming crazies, germs—and people who shit themselves in public? Seriously?"

Feinstein pointed to the seat opposite her desk. "You want to up your medication? Anyway, the demographics of New York are the least of our problems. Which is why you're here, right? I know you're worried about the unexpected intervention of Caroline McNeal's husband. And I know you want it resolved. We will resolve it. But we have another problem on that front."

Graff slumped down in the seat, crossing his legs. He had a feeling it was going to be bad news.

Feinstein handed him a black-and-white photo showing two men. "This was taken earlier today outside the FBI's Bridgeport satellite office in Connecticut."

Graff scrutinized the photo, recognizing Jack McNeal from a file he already had on the man. "The taller one. That's Jack, right?"

Feinstein nodded. "The burly guy? His brother, Peter. Bit of a handful by all accounts. Not averse to roughhouse tactics. Iraq veteran. Not the type to run from a fight."

"This is getting away from us, Karen."

"I have a team on this. We are dealing with it."

"So, what did the McNeals tell the Feds?"

"We have the transcripts, which I'll send over to you. We also have the documents the Fed helpfully scanned, so we have what they have. He sent it securely to FBI headquarters. We accessed it via the cloud."

"What exactly do they have?"

"It's not good, Henry. Somehow, classified Pentagon documents mentioning Meyer's name have been passed on. Caroline McNeal secured these memos, strictly classified and top secret, and squirreled them away. Jack has come into possession of them. We understand they were sent FedEx by Caroline's attorney."

"You think she's been holding on to documents for safekeeping in case something happened to her?"

"Exactly. And now Jack has them, told his brother, and headed out to the FBI."

Graff contemplated the situation. "Okay, this is your area of expertise. You've got free rein. What do we do?"

"I've reached out to a source close to the director through a back channel, an old Pentagon pal of mine. We're going to work it like that."

"What's the name of the Fed they contacted?"

"Special Agent Ryan Bone. Former NYPD cop. He's bright. Very capable. Similar background to McNeal's. He's from Staten Island too."

Graff smiled. "I can see an opening here. I mean, Jack McNeal is in possession of classified material? Was it stolen?"

Feinstein nodded. "I'm already two steps ahead of you. There are serious issues McNeal could face. We can frame it that Jack has classified government documents, and he passed them to a government employee. It would be a federal offense under the Espionage Act. Secondly, we will insist the FBI return all the 'national security' documents in their possession to the Department of Defense staffer who drew up the details. The name I have is Thomas C. Ridell. I know him. What would this achieve? The evidence would point to McNeal committing a serious crime, but, crucially, the stolen documents would not be published or distributed."

"Excellent."

"Thirdly, we want Ridell to ensure that all outstanding copies, be they electronic or paper files, are deleted or burned. Everything. Fourthly, we're going to be putting pressure on the FBI to put Jack McNeal and his brother at the center of this."

"Political contacts?"

"Intelligence committee chairs. They love having Swiss bank accounts."

"I'll bet they do."

"So, Jack McNeal and his brother were forwarding this classified information. Did they steal it? That's our angle. That's just the beginning. I'm in the process of dealing with Special Agent Bone."

Graff shuddered, an incredible sense of foreboding washing over him. "This needs to end."

"We'll reach our goal. This is going to be a multipronged approach. Jack McNeal and his brother don't know what's about to hit them."

"I get the sense that things are fraying. The plan is fragmenting."

"That's why you have people like me on speed dial. I deal with this sort of mess all the time."

"This seems different. It's turning into a monster. And I'm worried this monster is going to consume us all."

Twenty-Three

Three days passed, and McNeal had still not heard back from Ryan Bone. He called Peter, who was home in New Jersey.

"I expected to hear from him by now," Jack said.

"You know how it is. Backload of cases. Probably waiting to hear back from DC."

"I guess."

"Why don't you give him a call?"

McNeal didn't want to appear to be interfering with an FBI investigation. "I don't want to, you know, throw my weight around. It's early yet."

"You're not interfering. You're just asking if he has any news on the material you passed to them."

McNeal wondered if he shouldn't just let Bone get back to him. But, at the same time, he wanted answers. His wife was dead. He had passed on documents that he thought pointed to doubts about the suspicious death of Sophie Meyer.

Peter prodded. "This isn't some little bodega robbery."

"Yeah, I guess."

"Way more important than that. I say give him a call, Jack. He's a stand-up guy. Staten Island boy."

"Think I'll do that."

"And get back to me as soon as you hear something."

"Got it."

McNeal ended the call to his brother and called Special Agent Bone's office number. Jack looked out the window as he stood in his kitchen. There wasn't a soul on Compo Beach. No dog walkers. Nothing.

Clouds hung low in the sky.

The phone rang five times before it was finally answered.

"Special Agent Woods. How can I help?"

"I'm sorry, I was looking to speak to Special Agent Ryan Bone."

"Ryan?"

"Yeah, Special Agent Ryan Bone. Spoke to him three days ago."

"He no longer works here."

McNeal was taken aback. "You know where I can reach him?"

"I believe he's in DC. That's all we're authorized to share at this time. Can I take a message?"

"No. I've got his cell number."

McNeal ended the conversation. Ryan hadn't mentioned he was being transferred down to Washington. But then again, maybe the news was not something he had been able to share.

He called Bone's cell number. It rang seven times before it was finally answered.

"Special Agent Ryan Bone speaking."

"Hey, Ryan. It's Jack McNeal."

A pause. "Jack . . . right. I'm sorry I haven't gotten back to you."

"I was wondering if there was an update on those documents."

"I'm not at liberty to talk about that."

McNeal thought his tone sounded defensive. "I just wanted to follow up. That's it."

"We're disseminating the information. I've passed it on."

"Okay, I appreciate that. So, who have you passed this information on to? Within the FBI?"

"We've got a couple of guys looking at this. But it'll take some time."

McNeal exhaled, deflated by the standoffish response. "Do you mind me asking who is responsible for what I've passed to you, so I know who to contact?"

"I can't say."

"Ryan, am I missing something? . . . I sense you're not telling me the full story."

"We have ways of doing things."

"Sure, I understand that. But what's happening? You've been transferred down to headquarters since our visit? That seems pretty sudden."

"I can't talk about operational matters. I'm really tied up now with a case. I appreciate you reaching out."

"All I want to know is who is dealing with this."

"I've said enough. We'll be in touch."

The line went dead.

Twenty-Four

McNeal called his brother right away.

"He's being leaned on," Peter determined. "He said he was sending it to headquarters. And now he's suddenly working at the Hoover Building. It's bullshit. I'm telling you, the fix is in. Something is seriously wrong. What do you think?"

"The whole thing seemed off. Didn't sound like Ryan. Not the Ryan I knew. The conversation was stilted."

Peter was quiet for a few moments. "So, what now? We're back to square one."

"Maybe. We now know the FBI has the information in their possession. That's a step forward."

"It doesn't feel like a step forward."

"Let's see what the Feds say."

"I wouldn't hold out too much hope on that front. The Feds will smother that. It'll never see the light of day."

"Maybe."

"Jack, you know what they're like. It's all political agendas these days. Beyond that, they answer to no one."

"I'll find out, one way or the other."

"Maybe we should consider taking what we have to the cops in DC? Maybe they can help?"

"I'm not sure passing around classified information to DC police is the way forward. I think we need to be careful how we approach this. Technically, this is in the hands of the FBI."

"Nothing will come of it, I guarantee it."

"I know a guy in DC. A cop. He's a good guy. He might be able to help."

"You want me to come with you?"

"No, I've got this. I think it's important that we're discreet."

"So, this cop. He's someone you can rely on?"

"He's someone I've worked with. Sam Daniels—you remember him?"

"Big Sam? He's solid."

"If anyone can help me, it'll be him."

McNeal packed an overnight bag and a hard-sided, lockable case with his gun inside. He drove south from Westport to DC and checked into his hotel in Georgetown.

He took a hot shower and changed. Gun holstered, concealed from sight.

McNeal walked the short distance to Martin's Tavern. He found Sam Daniels in the same booth where JFK had apparently written the first draft of his inaugural speech. Daniels, an ex-colleague at Internal Affairs, nursed a beer. He stood up and hugged McNeal tight. "Jack, so sorry about Caroline. We're all really broken up about it."

McNeal slid into the seat opposite. It felt good to catch up again with Sam. "I appreciate that."

Daniels ordered two more beers. "If there's anything I can do, I will. We loved Caroline." The beers arrived. Daniels waited until the server was out of earshot before he spoke. "I can only imagine what you're going through."

"I have good days and bad days. It'll take time."

"Of course it will. Just glad to see you, albeit under such terrible circumstances."

"Are you okay to talk?"

Daniels chugged some beer. "It's me, Jack. What do you mean? What do you want to know?"

"It goes without saying, Sam, that if I disclose any details on the investigation I'm talking about . . . I have to trust you. This is strictest confidence."

"Got it. Are you looking for something in connection with the NYPD or Internal Affairs business?"

"Absolutely not."

Daniels cleared his throat. "So, we're good. Just shooting the breeze. Cop to cop, right?"

McNeal took a couple of gulps of the beer. "Big change, New York to DC, I'd imagine."

"Whole different scene, let me tell you."

"How long you been down here now?"

"DC? Couple years."

"How you finding it?"

"I love it. The weather is insane. Way too hot in the summer. Like a fucking steam bath."

"How are Kate and the girls?"

"They're good. They're at the age when they're talking back, but it's pretty routine."

McNeal nodded and smiled. He began to think of children. The highs and terrible lows. He stared into his beer, contemplating how he was going to explain the background of the story.

"Jack, look at me. You okay, man? You seem a bit detached. I'm assuming this has hit you real hard."

"It's brought a lot of other stuff to the surface."

"You mean Patrick?"

McNeal nodded. "It's always with me. I can't get over him. The loss, I mean."

"Nobody gets over losing a child."

McNeal gulped some beer.

"Tell me why you're down here. I'll see if I can help. I can't promise anything, but I'll do whatever I can. How does that sound?"

Slowly, deliberately, McNeal revealed to his oldest friend, a guy he'd graduated with from the academy, what had happened.

Daniels listened closely, occasionally sipping his beer. He nodded a few times.

"You know DC better than me. I don't know what Caroline got into. It appears the death of this socialite, Sophie Meyer, is propelling the whole thing."

"Agreed. I read about Caroline's death in the papers, the same as everyone else. But it didn't mention anything about an investigation into Sophie Meyer."

"This appears to be a carefully orchestrated cover-up. A conspiracy."

Daniels stared into his glass of beer. "Jack, you don't usually talk like this. You sure you're not conflating events?"

"No, I'm not. Something is fucked up here. And I don't know what it is."

Daniels leaned in closer, staring at him across the booth. His voice was a whisper. "Listen to me. I have no idea what happened. But I know a lot about Sophie Meyer. What exactly do you know or what have you heard about her?"

"I googled her. She's a socialite. Very well known."

"You have no idea how *well known* she is."

"What do you mean?"

"Sophie Meyer was a player."

"Party girl?"

"Oh yeah. She had a very, very colorful lifestyle."

"How colorful?"

"For starters, and this is not just idle gossip, she was wildly promiscuous."

"What else?"

"She was unbalanced, according to people who worked the case. It happened a few months after I moved here. But she was a piece of work, let me tell you."

"The official version is she overdosed at her home."

"Meyer knew a lot of interesting people. You saw the *Vanity Fair* party pictures, the photos from Hamptons summer events, polo matches, all that stuff?"

"Yeah, I saw that. And I thought . . . well, actually, I thought, hanging around with that crowd—fast-living, wealthy, money no object—I thought drugs."

"Yeah, dead on the money with that. Meyer went through the best part of two hundred thousand dollars of blow a year. At least from what I've heard."

"I saw the autopsy. The official autopsy. It mentioned drugs, cocaine, in her system."

"Wouldn't surprise me."

"Here's the thing, Sam. My wife—I mean my late wife—her autopsy showed she had barbiturates, booze, etc. in her blood when she was fished out of the Potomac."

"Caroline? Bullshit. Come on, are you kidding me?"

McNeal shook his head. "That's what it says."

"Caroline was no drug user. She was clean."

"Super clean. Fit. Very together. She enjoyed a glass of wine. That was it."

Daniels said, "Drugs don't fit her profile. Not one bit."

"You see why I have concerns about the death of my wife and how it ties to Meyer?"

Daniels nodded.

"Here's another interesting little fact to chew over. I went to the FBI in Bridgeport and met with Ryan Bone. Then I get told he got transferred to the Hoover Building three days after meeting with me. Something is seriously up. He gave me his card. He clearly didn't think he was headed anywhere anytime soon."

"What are you saying?"

"I think he passed on what he had, and he got called in. Maybe I'm not reading this right, but it's strange. Then when I called him, he tells me someone else is dealing with it."

"That by itself doesn't necessarily point to a conspiracy. But taken together with the other things you mentioned, it appears, like you say, troubling, to say the least."

McNeal took a sip of his beer. "What are you thinking?"

Daniels was quiet for a few moments, contemplating.

"You know something, don't you? Whatever it is, tell me. I'm asking as a friend."

"We go way back, Jack. I'm devastated for you."

"I've got the rest of my life to grieve. I want answers. I want to know more about Sophie Meyer. She's the key to this, I know it. If you know something, something more than you've already said, you gotta tell me."

"Want a piece of advice?"

"Sure."

"You need to be very, very careful."

"You want to explain why?"

"Jack, you know how it is. Listen to me closely. Meyer's husband is known to DC police. He was a person of interest three years ago."

"Henry Graff, right?"

"Be careful with him."

"What do you know about him?"

"Henry Graff is connected. He works for himself. Runs a shadowy security consultancy out in Arlington. A lot of government contracts. Pentagon. Homeland Security."

McNeal drank the rest of his beer. "You think Graff had his wife killed?"

"No one could prove a thing. But he's a cold bastard. My advice? Steer clear of this guy."

"I get it."

"You don't know the big picture. There's a lot of things to consider. The case against Graff got dropped. He knows a lot of people. But so did Sophie."

"What kind of people?"

"Sophie Meyer had powerful friends. Very powerful friends—friends in high places."

"Who exactly?"

Daniels again leaned in close before he whispered. "She's been around. A lot. She had many lovers. Powerful men."

McNeal could see exactly what Daniels was getting at. Her powerful friends could also have had her killed. "You got any names?"

"In this town, Sophie Meyer was an open secret. She was a druggie basket case. She'd fuck anyone. The richer and more powerful, the better. She kept diaries of all those men. Oligarchs, tech billionaires, hedge fund cokeheads, diplomats, UN secretary general, Hollywood actors."

"You think one of her lovers got her killed?"

"Honestly? I don't know. No one ever will."

Twenty-Five

The conversation with Sam Daniels played in a loop in Jack McNeal's racing mind. He got back to his hotel room and called his brother. Peter, although temperamentally more charged than Jack, had always been a useful sounding board.

When he'd finished outlining what Daniels had said, Peter was quiet. Jack prodded him along, adding, "By the way, I meant to ask earlier, how's Dad holding up?"

"Not great. He's taking Caroline's death hard. It's not like him. Nothing seems to rouse him. He's really down about it."

"We'll get through this. Try and keep his spirits up."

"I'll do my best. He said to give you the number of an old friend of his. Might be able to help in some way with Caroline's death. He knows a lot of people."

"You talking about O'Brien?"

"That's the guy. Down in Florida. You got a pen handy?"

"Sure." Jack scribbled down the number. He let the silence stretch until it became uncomfortable. "You still there, Peter?"

A long sigh. "Jack, I'm worried about you."

"I'm fine. I'll just ask O'Brien some questions. Nothing illegal in that."

"I don't know. I can see how this is going to go."

"And how's that?"

"The investigation is going to drag you down. I'm worried about that aspect."

"Put that aside. What are you thinking?"

"What am I thinking? The whole thing is fucked up. I've said it before, and I'll say it again: This is a mess. And it seems to be getting murkier and darker the more we learn. I don't like it. I think you need to consider pulling out."

McNeal was surprised that his brother would advocate such a move.

"I've got a bad feeling about this."

McNeal wondered if his brother wasn't being unnecessarily cautious. Peter's instincts were usually to get his head down and plow forward when things got tough. "I can't walk away from this. My wife is dead. I've gone to the Feds. I've reached out to a cop I trust. Whoever killed Sophie Meyer may have been involved in Caroline's death. Maybe the people Meyer hung around with. She clearly knew too much, and it got her killed. Maybe it was her husband. He was a person of interest, Henry Graff. But the DC police investigation didn't go anywhere."

"What else do we know about him?"

"Enough to put him on my radar. But I'm going to need to do a lot more digging on him. Doesn't seem like you to get cold feet."

Peter stammered, "No one's getting cold feet. Don't fucking say that. But I just have a bad, bad feeling about this. I feel like you're being dragged, bit by bit, into something no one understands, least of all you. There are shadowy elements at work here. I'm talking intelligence agencies, you know what I'm saying?"

Jack knew exactly what he was saying.

"Maybe you need to back off, turn around, and head back home."

Jack realized Peter's response was the correct one. It was a calibrated response, not to mention the legal and smart response. It was also the response of a family man with responsibilities. Jack understood that. But the truth of the matter was, Jack was seriously conflicted. On the other hand, his default position was one of caution. He would always stay within the law. But something deep within Jack was gnawing away at him. Was he just going to walk away? Was turning the other cheek the right thing to do here?

No. The right thing to do—the only thing to do—was to find out the truth. Could he really just forget everything that had happened? Was he going to rely on the FBI to find the truth and bring the culprits to justice? There had been no justice for Sophie Meyer. Why the hell would there be for Caroline McNeal?

McNeal's rational mind began to kick in. He needed to think of his job. He would be fired if it was revealed he was pursuing a lone-wolf investigation. He could also face charges. The humiliation. Was that how his career and life would be defined?

All his life he'd played by the book. Adhered to the letter of the law. That was his way. But something, he didn't know what, had pulled him into a deadly quagmire. Maybe it was love, maybe loyalty to his wife, maybe vengeance—whatever it was, it burned inside Jack McNeal.

He felt it in the very depths of his soul. The love, the rage, and the terrible sadness that had been reignited. It had lain dormant for five long years. The death of his son, Patrick. The son he grieved. The pain and guilt. The self-imposed isolation. But recently, the sense of desolation and the suicidal thoughts, something he had tried to keep at bay, had crept back into his psyche.

Tears spilled down his face. He had never felt more alone. The memory from that darkest night years earlier began to play out. His mind flashed images of Patrick's last moments.

His thoughts switched back to his investigation. He sensed this was not the end but the beginning of the end.

He knew if he headed down the path of natural justice, it would end in tears. Blood. And death.

Peter cleared his throat and snapped Jack's attention back to the call. "You've gone real quiet on me."

"I don't know. The smart thing to do would be to just forget it all. But here's the thing: I can't. I can't let this go. Imagine if it was your wife, how would you feel?"

Peter sighed. "Point taken."

"I need to pursue this. I *have* to pursue this."

"You're going to talk to Graff, aren't you?"

Jack nodded. "That's exactly what I'm going to do."

Twenty-Six

McNeal read the number scrawled on the piece of paper. He considered whether his father passing on the number was his way of prodding him to reach out and ask for help. Before he spoke to Graff, he needed to find out more about the man, and if anyone could find out about Henry Graff, it was someone like O'Brien.

Finn O'Brien was ex-NYPD. He had set up a successful private investigation firm in Boca Raton. He provided surveillance for ex-wives to help secure higher divorce settlements, background checks on government employees, bankruptcies, credit ratings . . . you name it, he did it. He was tough. Inscrutable. He had a ton of contacts in law enforcement and various New York and Florida Mafia hoods he was friendly with.

McNeal took a deep breath and dialed the number. It rang three times before it was picked up.

"O'Brien Investigations," a voice answered, then the man cleared his throat. Finn was still a big smoker. From what his father had told him, Finn was also an even bigger drinker, especially after his wife died a decade earlier.

"Mr. O'Brien, my name is Jack McNeal. Hope you don't mind me bothering you."

"Danny's son?"

"That's right. I'm the eldest of Daniel's children."

O'Brien began to cough, which merged into a throaty laugh. "Christ almighty. I'll be damned. How nice to hear your voice. I haven't heard from your father for months. To what do I owe this pleasure?"

McNeal sighed. "Bottom line? I need some help."

"The NYPD Internal Affairs Bureau needs my help?"

"This is personal. Off the books, so to speak."

"I get you. Tell me, how's your dad?"

"You know how he is. Pain in the ass."

O'Brien let out a hacking cough and laughed hard. "He was always that. He's a good man. He was always there for me when I joined the force. I'll never forget that. Is he still living on Staten Island?"

"They'll have to take him out in a box. He'll never move."

"Florida. That's where it's at. You can't move for fucking New Yorkers. You can tell they're New Yorkers because they talk louder than anyone else!"

McNeal laughed. "It's true."

"Fucking right it's true. Big-mouthed sons of bitches. But hey, we are what we are, right?"

"Absolutely right."

"Tell your father to come down here and take a week or two to unwind. Winter's hell up north."

"Tell me about it."

McNeal exhaled long and hard. He felt as if the weight of the world was on his shoulders.

"You said this was something personal. What happened?"

McNeal recounted the events that had led up to his wife's death, then the aftermath.

"Christ, son, I'm so sorry."

"We're all really torn up about it."

"You don't think this was an accident or drowning or suicide. Would I be correct in that assumption?"

"It's a possibility. We can't rule it out."

"But you don't believe it."

"No, I do not."

"What do you think happened?"

"I believe she was killed. Murdered. But I don't know by who. I intend to find out. I want some information on a certain guy."

"You've come to the right place. We specialize in *certain guys*. I need to know, though, that you're not going to use that information to cause harm to a person."

"My only interest is in finding out more about him. If I find out anything untoward, it will be passed on to law enforcement."

"That's all I need to know, son."

"It's got to be done very quietly. No trace back to me."

"Whatever we talk about, it's confidential. Very discreet. No comeback on you. End of story. What do you need?"

"I want to know everything you can get your hands on about a guy called Henry Graff."

"G-r-a-f-f?"

"Two *f*s, that's right. I believe he's based in and around DC. Heard he might have links with a security company. His wife overdosed in DC three years ago."

"In the name of God."

"I believe he's also old friends with the President."

O'Brien cleared his throat. "Interesting. My firm is very thorough. When do you need this?"

"As soon as you can. Whatever it costs."

"That won't be necessary, Jack. I knew you when you were knee-high. What's the best way to contact you?"

McNeal gave him his private email address.

"Henry Graff . . . Name doesn't ring a bell. I'll see what we can find."

McNeal knew he had crossed a line. He asked himself if he had done the right thing by reaching out to O'Brien and setting off down a path of no return.

The more he thought about it, the more he worried. What the hell was he doing? It was the kind of thing he investigated in Internal Affairs. Cops who took it upon themselves to start poking their noses into matters that didn't concern them. Crossing boundaries.

No one was above the law. That was his mantra. He was not above the law. But he was acutely aware that he was allowing his love for his wife to erode his judgment. Bit by bit, he felt himself being consumed by it all.

McNeal pushed his negative thoughts to one side. Hunger gnawed at his gut. He needed to eat. He freshened up, putting on a change of clothes before he headed down to the hotel's restaurant. He ate alone. His mind wandered. Had Caroline ever eaten here? She almost certainly had. It was a prestigious hotel in the heart of DC. She would have eaten lunch here with colleagues. Friends. He thought of her, alone, carving out a new single life in Washington, DC. It made him sad. He thought back to their wedding day. The dress she had worn. The church on Staten Island. It had been a blazing-hot day. *To honor. To love. Till death do us part.*

He remembered her friends at the wedding reception afterward. Prominent American journalists, writers, some intellectuals. His side of the family was all cops, truck drivers, and homemakers. The first dance was a Sinatra number they both loved: "Summer Wind." He remembered her smiling face, dazzling eyes. Everyone watching them. The music played. It was intoxicating.

McNeal left a twenty-dollar bill as a tip and put the check on his room tab. He headed through to the bar. He pulled up a stool and ordered a beer. Then another.

He let the emptiness return. Not in his belly this time. But in his heart.

He drank a third beer, then followed it up with a single malt. He looked around. The bar was starting to fill up. Mostly couples. A few singles. A couple of girls. Guys on business trips with colleagues. A family from the Midwest talking about visiting the Smithsonian and talking loudly about how dirty the Metro was. *They've never been on the New York subway,* he thought.

"Jack? Is that you?" A woman's voice from the other side of the bar.

McNeal snapped out of his thoughts and looked around. A stunning blonde woman wearing a tight black dress approached. "I'm sorry, do I know you?"

"Jack McNeal, right? Don't say you don't recognize me."

McNeal turned red, embarrassed. "I'm sorry. I'm not good with names."

The woman offered a manicured hand, bright-red nail polish. "Sylvia Walsh."

The name didn't mean anything to him. "Sylvia Walsh?"

"We went in Catholic school together. Staten Island? I was only there for a few weeks. But I remember you."

McNeal sensed something was wrong. He shook her hand. "I'm sorry, but I can't seem to place you. I'm pretty good with faces."

"Well, no matter. I remember you. You've barely changed at all. Mind if I sit down?"

McNeal squirmed, uncomfortable. He wanted to be alone. But it seemed rude to say he didn't want her to sit beside him. "Sure, please."

Sylvia slid into the stool next to him, her thigh brushing against his. "I can't believe it's you. I heard you had joined the force."

"You did?"

"Yeah, I bumped into a girl you dated at the time. Shirley O'Connell?"

McNeal didn't want to engage in small talk, or any kind of talk, for that matter. "Shirley? That's a blast from the past. How is she?"

"She's good. She's still working on Staten Island."

"What about you?"

"What about me?"

"Why are you in Washington?"

"I'm in town for a conference."

"What kind of conference?"

"Lingerie. I run a shop in Jersey City."

McNeal smiled. "Is there much demand for sexy lingerie in Jersey City?"

"You'd be amazed. So, what brings you to town? I can't believe I just bumped into you after all these years."

"This and that."

"Tell me about the NYPD."

"I don't talk about my job, if you don't mind."

"Sure, I understand. I see you're married."

McNeal looked at his wedding ring. "I was married."

"I'm sorry. I didn't know. That was insensitive."

"You couldn't have known. My wife died recently. Very sudden."

"Oh my God, and here's me, blabbering on. I'm so sorry to hear that, Jack." She reached out and held his hand, squeezing it softly. "I know what it's like."

"To lose a spouse?"

Sylvia nodded. "Husband knocked down and killed by a careless driver in the Village. He was leaving the Blue Note jazz club just after one in the morning."

"I live on that same street."

McNeal sensed something was off. He questioned what the odds were. He had bumped into a girl who claimed she had gone to the same school. And her husband was knocked down and killed on the street where he lived.

"Are you kidding me?" she scoffed.

"Scout's honor."

"So, there was an Uber driver from Romania or Rwanda, or something. He was on his cell phone at the time. Ran into my husband. Dead on arrival."

"That's tough. I'm sorry."

"It was a couple years back, but the pain is always there. I know that better than anyone."

McNeal felt it in his bones. He could tell she was playing him. He wondered if she was a grifter. He imagined she made a lot of money picking up men in bars. But if she was a pickup artist, how did she know so much about him? Something was definitely off. No doubt about it. She hadn't gone to his school. He would remember her.

As the evening wore on, he played along with her. She was good company. They enjoyed a few drinks, and conversation was easy. Maybe too easy. She was a Yankees season ticket holder. She liked the President. She was thinking about relocating to Nevada for the weather and low taxes. Her easy manner grated on McNeal. He tried to figure it all out as they chatted.

"Look, I've got an early start tomorrow," McNeal said. "I've really got to call it a night."

"You wanna join me? I've got a nice room. No ties. No obligations. Just a couple of New Yorkers with a few hours to kill."

McNeal's mind was suddenly racing. His senses were switched on. He definitely couldn't remember who she was from back in school. But she seemed to know a hell of a lot about him. Her story didn't add up. So, why had she approached him? Had someone sent her? "I don't want to impose."

"Just a nightcap, what do you say?"

"One drink," he said, "and then I've got to go."

"You got a deal."

McNeal and the woman took the elevator to her room on the seventh floor. She swiped her room card, and he followed her inside.

"Make yourself at home," she said. "You mind fixing me a vodka martini? And have whatever you want. It's all in the minibar."

The woman went into the bathroom. "I'm just going to freshen up for a few moments."

McNeal needed to keep his wits about him. He fixed her a drink and poured a shot of Talisker single malt for himself. He looked around the room. Spotless. Tasteful. The woman's handbag on the writing desk.

"I'll just be a couple more minutes," she shouted from the bathroom. "You got the drinks ready?"

"Almost."

McNeal's senses kicked into high gear. His cop background made him naturally suspicious. He thought there was something scripted and unsettling about her hyperconfident manner. The way she had seemed to insert herself into his life. He really couldn't place her face, and it bothered him.

He walked over to the writing desk and began to rifle through the contents of her handbag.

"I like a strong drink," she shouted.

McNeal opened her wallet. He pulled out credit cards and a Florida driver's license. She lived in Delray Beach. Her ID showed her name as Francesca Luca. His instincts had been correct. She was an imposter. He put the cards and wallet back in the purse, zipped it up again.

What the hell was going on?

A few moments later the woman stepped out of the bathroom. She wore coral-pink lingerie. Panties and bra.

"What do you think of the new fall collection?"

McNeal smiled at her. "Very nice." He stepped forward and pressed his gun to her head. "Who the fuck are you? And who sent you?"

The woman began to blink away tears. "Whoa, Jack. What's this?"

"Answer my fucking questions. Who are you? Who sent you?"

"I don't know what the hell you're talking about. I thought you wanted to relax. Have a drink. Have some fun. I didn't mean to offend you."

"Francesca, is that your name?"

The woman shut her eyes tight and shook her head.

"Long way from Florida. I want answers. Or I'll be calling the cops to find out who you really are. You want that?"

The woman sniffled quietly.

"Last chance or it's 9-1-1 time. DC police, in my experience, don't fuck around."

"What do you want to know?"

"Who paid you?"

"I don't know. I got paid in cash."

"How much?"

The woman shook her head.

McNeal pressed the gun tight to her temple. "You will answer me, so help me God. How much were you paid?"

"Five thousand bucks up front."

"Are you kidding me?"

"No. They wanted me to sleep with you."

"And then?"

"Then drug your drink. Then take pictures of you. Then blackmail you."

McNeal's blood ran cold. He puzzled over who the hell had set this up.

"Ten thousand bucks on delivery."

"Fifteen thousand dollars for a night's work? Nice way to earn a buck."

"It's a living."

"Yeah, whatever. So, where's the money?"

"In my car."

"I want a name. Who gave you the money?"

"A woman."

"A name?"

"She didn't give me her name. It's all in cash. Look, don't tell the cops. I'll lose my kids. Do you understand?"

"Tell me about the backstory you made up."

"The woman gave me a few pointers about who she wanted me to be. Staten Island was important. She showed me some pictures of you. Stuff to mention."

McNeal's mind raced as he struggled to take it all in. "Where did you meet this woman?"

"My house. Someone gave her my name. That's what I do. It's a job."

McNeal put away his gun. "So, you're a grifter. And you're a prostitute."

"I provide a service."

"Bullshit. Put your clothes on and get out of here. You have ten minutes to grab your things before I call the cops."

He strode out of her room, barely breathing until he reached his own door.

Twenty-Seven

McNeal caught his breath, shaken up. He sobered up quick. He got back to his room and called Peter.

"Are you fucking kidding me?" Peter said. "That just happened?"

"Yeah."

"How do you feel?"

"Like I dodged a bullet. It was a close call."

"Damn right it was. So, what are we talking?"

"Quite an elaborate honey trap if you ask me. Why go to those lengths, though? She said she was going to take photos of me. You believe that?"

"These are serious people you're dealing with."

"Yeah, I figured that."

"Someone has something to hide. And they want to neutralize you. Threaten to leak photos of you. Why? To silence you. What Internal Affairs cop would want lurid photos plastered all over the front of the *New York Post*? Your credibility would be shot to pieces."

McNeal could see as clear as day the danger if he pursued this inquiry further. He wondered if this should be the wake-up call he needed to call a halt to his investigation. Conversely, the honey trap was a sign of how much they wanted to end his prying. He was clearly getting under someone's skin. Maybe they were on edge, knowing he was asking questions. Reaching out to the Feds. Maybe he was getting to them.

"She was pretty convincing. I could see how she would have ensnared a lot of men."

"When did you figure it out?"

"The single girl in a bar in DC, approaches a stranger, says she's from Staten Island. I mean, come on. Seriously? It seemed strange from the outset. But I went along with it. I didn't know for sure. What are the chances that she had gone to the same school on Staten Island? At first I thought it was just another coincidence. But the longer we talked, the more it wasn't adding up. Then I rifled in her purse and saw the ID. That's when it all became crystal clear."

"Jesus. So, you suckered her into thinking you were playing along?"

"Yeah, she got down to her lingerie."

Peter laughed. "Are you kidding me?"

"Nope."

"You sly old fox."

"Gimme a break."

"Classic honey trap, alright. So, they would blackmail you to forget any investigation, and the photos wouldn't be released, right?"

"Can you imagine how the Internal Affairs Bureau would view that?"

"They'd be investigating you, that's for sure," Peter said. "Someone would release it to the press. You'd be fired, face charges, and your career and reputation would be in ruins."

"At the very least, my position within IA would not be tenable."

"My advice, Jack?"

"What?"

"If what Caroline unearthed got her killed, and she had suspicions about the death of this Sophie Meyer lady, don't you think they're going to turn their sights on you now?"

"I think they already have. I'm wondering how they knew I was here. I'm also wondering if there are any more surprises in store for me."

"Pull up the drawbridge and forget all this. They could have people inside the hotel. Ready to do God-knows-what. I'm not kidding."

McNeal knew that what his brother was saying was right. But the death of his wife and now a sophisticated attempt to snare him in a honey trap had stirred an anger deep within him. A resentment was beginning to gnaw away at his insides. "I would've thought you'd want me to pursue this."

"I'm having second thoughts. I don't want you getting hurt."

"I can deal with this."

"Maybe you can. Listen, this whole thing is fucked up. And I'm not afraid to admit it, Jack. I'm scared."

"Scared of what?"

"Scared my brother is going to wind up dead."

Twenty-Eight

The following morning, before it was even light, and after a fitful sleep, McNeal had sweated out the booze in the hotel gym. He swam thirty laps in the pool and sweated some more in the steam room. He showered, put on a fresh change of clothes, drank a half-gallon of mineral water, and ate breakfast in his room: pancakes, bacon, and scrambled eggs with freshly squeezed orange juice and two strong coffees.

His cell phone rang, and he recognized the number. He checked his watch. Just after seven.

"Jack?" The rasping voice of O'Brien.

"Yeah, speaking, Finn."

"I have what you want."

"That's terrific."

"I'm just about to send it using end-to-end encryption. But to ensure only you can open it, you need to answer a question. You and your family know the answer."

"Send it."

A few moments later McNeal's email pinged. He was asked for a password. And the hint was the place in Ireland O'Brien hailed from.

McNeal smiled. He tapped in C-O-N-N-A-C-H-T. The email downloaded with the report on Henry Graff. "Mr. O'Brien, I owe you one."

"You owe me nothing, son. We're good. We look after each other in this life. Remember that."

"Very much appreciate that."

The line went quiet. "You okay, son? You sound a bit stressed."

"Had a bit of a situation last night."

"What kind of situation?"

McNeal told him about the honey trap and Francesca Luca's ID.

"That is not good."

"Not good at all."

"I'll tell you what I'll do. How about I check out that name?"

"If you don't mind."

"Word to the wise. I'm sure you know this now. But just so we're clear, you're messing with dangerous people, son."

"Tell me about it."

"I'll get something on this girl."

McNeal was grateful to be able to reach out to O'Brien. It was good to know his digital footprint wouldn't be getting picked up if he or Peter did a search. He picked up his iPad and sat down at the writing desk.

McNeal started to scroll through the dossier on the man his wife believed to have been responsible in some way for Sophie Meyer's death.

Henry Graff had been born in Jefferson, Maryland. He was fifty-six years old, a former West Point graduate who joined the Rangers, then was assigned to a CIA unit. He was a Medal of Honor recipient, earned a Purple Heart during years working behind enemy lines in Afghanistan. He lived and breathed Kabul, according to those who knew him. He enjoyed the shadowy life, cultivating sources across the Afghan government. Tribal elders.

Military intelligence officers posted in the city. Graff had also been accused by a soldier under his command of carrying out extrajudicial executions of captured Taliban fighters.

No one else had spoken out. Graff had an air of invincibility, according to the fiercely loyal men who served with him. They remained devoted to Graff. Special Operations, meanwhile, grew concerned that he seemed to have gone rogue. Operating with his own agenda. More and more bodies were unearthed in villages he and his men had taken over.

It was believed, by CIA psychiatrists, that Graff was psychotic. Borderline personality disorder. Still, no one wanted to pull him out of the country. Superiors who visited Graff and his men in the farthest flung corners of Afghanistan, occasionally crossing into Pakistan, spoke of being in awe of the man. They talked of his "impenetrable silences," interspersed with quotes, softly spoken, from *The Art of War*. Graff, they said, occasionally spoke in Dari and Pashto, highlighting how he had "gone native." He schooled his men in the Afghan languages. Talked to them about Afghan customs. He and some of his men also cultivated poppy, and Graff became, for a while, an opium addict. It was alleged he smuggled opium back into the States. Military sources said Graff was the "point man" for the CIA, funneling opium for production in Pakistan into heroin. And the profits—believed to be in the tens of millions—bought greater covert funding as the war wore on.

Eventually, a four-star general had been tasked with relieving Graff of his duties. He concluded in a classified report that Graff was a "bad seed and psychologically flawed." That meant Graff was a perfect fit for the continuing "covert and nefarious" operations. New orders from the general's superiors at the Pentagon got handed to Graff. New electronic equipment and supplies were dropped into the mountains.

The shadowy operations intensified. Graff and his men, high up in the Safed Koh, stealthily approached hundreds of Taliban foreign fighters before battles would begin. A relentless war of attrition developed. Proxies for Pakistan and the Saudis were the enemy. Atrocities on both sides.

Graff grew to love the isolated mountain ranges. He lived with villagers for weeks, sharing their food, learning their stories. He would provide small luxuries. Cigarettes, gold coins, and dollars for information. He drank poppy seed tea with village elders. He smoked opium.

The villagers gave him information on the foreign fighters in their midst: the Chechens, Egyptians, Libyans, Uzbeks. Graff built a picture and passed it through encrypted codes back to CENTCOM in Tampa, Florida. Sometimes it was sent to the forward headquarters in Qatar.

From there, it wound its way to Langley and the CIA.

The Agency could see how a man like Graff, a man who had no compunction about killing, a man who seemed at home deep in the heart of enemy territory, a man who had built up a forensic knowledge of black operations, was a major asset. Graff excelled in false flag operations. He existed in a shadowy world.

A mixture of fascination and trepidation grew as McNeal read on. He wondered whether this was indeed the guy who had killed his wife. Was Graff responsible for killing his own wife, Sophie Meyer? Taking a human life certainly wasn't a problem for this guy.

The more he learned, the more fucked up it all sounded. McNeal read about Graff's own father, a Korean War veteran who had become CIA station chief in El Salvador during the 1980s. He got exposed by Amnesty International for his part in tipping off the El Salvador death squads to the whereabouts of a dozen American priests and nuns who were working with the poorest in the country. Some were decapitated. Years later, by then an old man, Edward

Henry Graff was found guilty of being an accessory to murder by a military court. He was jailed for exactly one year, then released, never to be seen or heard from again.

That was Graff's bloodline.

McNeal gulped the rest of his coffee and leaned back in his seat, contemplating Graff, the man. He was, in many ways, the best and worst of America. The warrior, the brave soldier, the risk taker. McNeal admired that greatly. He read on, transfixed by the near-mythical figure of this man. He studied the field reports claiming Graff suffered from "psychotic episodes." The warrior's descent began high up in the mountains of Afghanistan, Graff and his men, for months at a time, fighting the enemy. Being watched by the enemy. Blending into the villages. It took raw courage. But it also came at a terrible price. Graff's own psychological breakdown. Blood was shed. Atrocities. Innocent people were killed, or they disappeared.

Internal CIA memos spoke of the same sorts of tactics Graff's father had advocated as an advisor in El Salvador.

McNeal knew war was a dirty business. Peter had served in Iraq during a one-year tour of duty. His brother had returned haunted. Eyes dead. Crazed. His brother had turned himself around and found his home in the NYPD. Another kind of war. A war on the streets. Day by day, month in, month out.

McNeal knew how cops like himself reached breaking point. He had investigated hundreds of bad cops. One event could be the trigger to a total loss of control. A cheating wife. Then alcoholism, followed by violent mood swings. All leading to the shooting of a suspect who was mouthing off after getting caught stealing from a bodega. A street thug who spat on an officer already at the end of his rope. In a way, McNeal had more than a little sympathy for guys he investigated. Even guys like Graff. Men who did the dirty work, employed by the American government to do their bidding.

Then, when they returned fucking crazy, the man, not those who sent him there, took the rap.

The dossier O'Brien had supplied was a glimpse into a world most people never saw. Which was probably just as well.

McNeal read on. Graff's work within the CIA continued. His work in the field was over. But his knowledge as an "advisor" was invaluable. He moved around. Countries like Somalia, Iraq, Afghanistan, Turkey, and the interventions in and invasions of Libya and Syria. A bewildering array of conflicts. Graff was there, in the shadows.

Eventually, Graff returned to America. He started his own business—Graff & Associates, based in Arlington, Virginia. He picked up a lot of government contracts. He became a multimillionaire. He married well-known socialite Sophie Meyer. Clippings from *Vogue* and *Tatler* reported the "private" family wedding. The ceremony had been held at Meyer's father's home in Southampton, Long Island. A handful of guests, including a member of the British royal family and a billionaire hedge fund recluse.

No pictures of the wedding were available. That wasn't to say none were taken. But it had clearly been a very, very private affair, unusual for a woman like Meyer. A woman who would turn up for the opening of a new store on Fifth Avenue. A woman who was seen at the most achingly hip clubs in West Hollywood or the West Village. A deluxe hotel opening in Las Vegas? She was there. She added a sprinkling of glamor. She knew people. And they turned up too.

The dossier contained a handful of photos of Meyer at parties, occasionally draped on the arm of a man. One black-and-white long-range photo taken by a Washington, DC, freelance photographer appeared to show Henry Graff in the back of a limousine, approaching his offices in Arlington.

McNeal built a fascinating picture of Henry Graff, a man whose wife had died in mysterious circumstances. He stared at the photo of Graff in the back of the vehicle. Eyes hooded. Clean-shaven. Graff was a man to be feared. For sure.

McNeal was still reading the dossier on Graff when his cell phone rang.

"Jack, you okay to talk?" The voice of O'Brien.

"I'm good, thanks. Still digging through the background information on Graff. Fascinating stuff."

"Not half as interesting as the girl who came on to you last night."

"The lovely Francesca Luca?"

O'Brien cleared his throat. "One interesting chick, let me tell you."

"Yeah, no kidding. Spit it out."

"Numerous arrests for prostitution. Said it was to put herself through college. But she's been bailed out numerous times. Here's the kicker: it's always the same person."

"Who bails her out?"

"Same woman. Karen Simon. I did a bit of digging. Simon is her maiden name. So, this Karen Simon is bailing out this Francesca chick. But she's not using her married name. She hasn't been called Karen Simon for at least fifteen years. She's married but separated. Husband lives in Switzerland, I think."

"What's her name now?"

"Karen Feinstein. I checked out Francesca's phone records. She made two calls recently to a cell phone owned by Feinstein. I'll send over the dossier later."

"Who does Feinstein work for?"

"She's the founder of Fein Solutions."

McNeal's interest was piqued. "Never heard of them."

"Not many people have. Geo-strategy firm. Intelligence operatives."

"You kidding me?"

"It gets better, kid. Karen Feinstein used to work for—"

"The CIA?"

"Bingo again! Know what else? You're going to really like this."

"We've got a connection with Graff?"

"Got it in one guess. Both worked within the Parwan Detention Facility at Bagram Air Base, Afghanistan. High-level detainees were their specialty, including breaking them. Both their names were mentioned in a partially redacted report from the Red Cross."

McNeal got up from his seat and stared out over downtown DC. "I can see how that would work. Graff uses Feinstein to do work for his clients. His hands are clean. Or a lot cleaner than if he had taken direct involvement."

"Keeps the heat off his company and his clients. And if the shit hits the fan, Feinstein or her operatives will take the rap."

"And Feinstein is using people like Francesca Luca as your classic honey trap?"

"Pretty much."

"Close call, let me tell you. Finn, please bill me for this work. I feel bad for taking up your time without paying. I prefer to keep things aboveboard. You understand?"

"I understand. But I don't want a paper trail. This is a personal favor for you and your father. You need people you can trust at times like this, son. But think long and hard before you go after this guy."

Twenty-Nine

Andrew Forbes approached a small village in the eastern foothills of the Blue Ridge Mountains when his cell phone buzzed to life. He was seventy miles west of Washington, DC.

A man's voice told him, "You're getting closer."

"Thank God for that. I thought I was never going to get there."

"Drive on for two more miles."

Forbes did as he was told. He saw the sign marked Old Rag Mountain.

"You'll get on the Old Rag Mountain trail up ahead."

"Old Rag—"

"Then get out of your vehicle and hike on the dirt path."

"Got it."

"One final thing: remember, take the battery out of your cell phone."

"Why do you want me to do that?"

"So, we know you're alone and not being followed. Do you copy?"

"I understand. Sorry, copy that, yes."

"Don't be late."

Forbes's mouth went dry. He considered what the hell he was doing out in the middle of nowhere. He drove until he saw the sign and parked. He got out of the vehicle. He pulled on his backpack that contained water, a compass, and some cereal bars. He carefully took the battery out of his cell phone and placed it in a side pocket. He followed the dirt path into the woods. He hiked on for a mile through a forest, heading higher into the wild. Shoulder-high ferns brushed his skin. He flicked away the flies buzzing his face. "Fuck!"

He trudged through single-track trails and ankle-deep streams until he came to a clearing. Two men stood, wearing camouflage, shades, and masks, each holding semi-automatics, blocking his path.

The smaller of the two stepped forward. "Spread 'em! Hands on your head!"

Forbes complied as the guy frisked the insides of his legs, waist, and chest. The backpack was ripped off his back.

"We'll hold on to this for safekeeping."

"I need my cell phone."

"Not where you're going."

"Where to now?"

The smaller of the two pointed to a narrow opening in the trees. "Follow that route. Ten minutes due south, up the trail. You'll arrive at a log cabin. She'll be waiting outside for you." The man cocked his head in the direction of the trail. "Go on, get!"

Forbes took the hint and moved on, quickening his pace. He hadn't expected such a welcome party. His shirt clung to his sweaty back. He hiked hard, wishing he had his backpack to take a drink of water. Eventually he came to a clearing, and the log cabin, and the woman.

Standing, hands on her hips, was Karen Feinstein.

"What took you so long?"

Forbes wiped his brow with the back of his hands. "I got lost somewhere around God knows where." He walked up to her and hugged her tight. "What's with the goons half a mile back?"

"Don't worry, they're my guys. They're just not house-trained."

"They need to lighten up."

"That is them lightened up."

"What's this all about?"

"Loose ends. I wanted to give you an update in person. Things are getting trickier than we anticipated."

"What the hell does that mean?"

"We had a situation last night. We thought we would nip this McNeal character in the bud."

"I thought this was supposed to be a slam dunk. Send in the girl and blackmail him. What happened?"

"Jack McNeal is way more dogged than we anticipated. He's smart. And I'm worried about him."

Forbes shrugged. "What do you mean? What the fuck happened?"

"Apparently McNeal pulled a gun on our girl. A fucking gun. She's done it a hundred times before. Best in class. But this time . . . this time, she got her comeuppance."

"So, hang on, this Internal Affairs cop, McNeal. He's got the story?"

"Not exactly. He's got a version of the story. Francesca told McNeal who had paid her. Said it was a woman. But it might be only a matter of time before McNeal figures out that it's me."

"Fuck."

"This is not good."

"Yeah, no kidding." Forbes wiped the sweat from his brow.

"We paid her in cash. So, that's gone."

"The money is the least of our problems."

"We have to deal with this. And that's why I wanted to tell you face-to-face."

Forbes struggled to keep up. "What if someone starts digging into Francesca? I mean really digging into how you two go way back."

"Then we've got a major problem."

"Where is she?"

"We brought her here."

Forbes looked at her face, half-expecting this to be a joke. But there was no punchline. No laughing. No smiles. "Here? What do you mean, here? Are you fucking with me?"

Feinstein shook her head. "She's two hundred yards from here. We're going to ensure she doesn't talk anymore."

"Have you lost your mind?"

"What would you suggest? Leave her to her own devices? Allow McNeal or the cops to pressure her into talking?"

"You're going to kill her?"

Feinstein shook her head. "No, you are."

"I don't do stuff like that. That's why we hired you guys."

"I've got skin in the game. So does Henry. What about you, Andrew?"

Forbes swooned, light-headed, then fell to his knees and was sick.

"That's okay, perfectly natural."

"This isn't how it's supposed to work."

"Things change. Circumstances change. You have to go with the flow."

"I've never killed anyone."

"Not directly. But you are involved. Deeply involved. By the way, I admire that. You're a patriot."

"Isn't there anyone else who can do it?"

"I've chosen you. I want to see that you have blood on your hands too. It bonds us together."

Forbes began to pace the clearing in the woods beside the cabin. "I work for the fucking President."

"We dug the grave. No one will know. The gun was bought in Slovakia from a gun dealer for cash. Untraceable. Serial number filed off."

Forbes closed his eyes for a moment. He thought of his father. He was so proud of his son's position at the White House. His boss had been his father's closest friend since college, and now he was the President. "I'm not doing it. Absolutely not. Go to hell."

"It's going to happen. If not, my guys are under strict orders to put a bullet in your head. And you'll get thrown in the pit too."

"Go to hell."

A masked man emerged from the cabin. He walked up to Forbes and pressed a gun to his head.

Forbes felt the cold steel on his warm forehead. "Are you serious?"

"You better believe it."

The masked man took a step back, gun still in hand.

"I'm not going to do this."

"That's where you're wrong. You are not a stupid person. You're pragmatic. You understand."

Forbes closed his eyes for a moment.

"I think it would be in everyone's interests to show us how committed you are."

"I'm not going to do it. Fuck you! And fuck him!"

"Then you'll be killed."

Forbes stared at her, blinking away tears. "I don't believe what I'm hearing. You're bullshitting me."

"You need to believe it. This is as real as it gets. So, you need to answer some questions. How far are you really prepared to go? Are you prepared to put your neck on the line? You choose. Kill or be killed."

Forbes fell quiet.

"It's the easiest thing in the world to get faceless men to do the dirty work. The nasty work. You don't want to just pull the strings, huh? When I look into your eyes, you know what I see, Andrew?"

"What?"

"A rich boy who has never had to get his hands dirty in his life. Do you believe in what we're doing, or are you content to let others do your wet work?"

"I haven't fired a gun since I was a kid."

"You're a man now. Do you have what it takes? I mean, do you really have what it takes? How much can I trust you?"

Forbes closed his eyes. His heart began to race.

"Think of the big picture. Who the fuck is she anyway? A skanky little whore. She's been turning tricks for ten years. We need to make sure she doesn't talk. Andrew, you can do this."

Forbes nodded. "Where is she?"

Feinstein cocked her head in the direction of a dirt trail.

"I'm scared. This isn't me."

Feinstein smiled. "I think it is. I just think you're too scared to know what you're capable of."

"I don't want to do it."

"No way back. When this is done, it's done. We can all move on. It's a loose end. Let's tie it up, and we can all go home."

"What do I have to do?"

Feinstein cocked her head. "Follow me."

Forbes traipsed behind her for a couple hundred yards until they reached a clearing. Writhing on the ground, hog-tied, a skinny young woman sobbed beside a shallow grave.

Four guys in camouflage surrounded her, handguns drawn.

One stepped forward and handed Forbes a gun. "Sir?"

Forbes took the Glock in his right hand and aimed it at the terrified young woman.

"Do it!" Feinstein ordered.

Forbes stared down at the wretched woman, who wept, defenseless. He squeezed the trigger. Her brains exploded, blood spattering across long grass, branches, and twigs. The sound echoed through the woods. Birds scattered from the trees, high into the pristine blue sky.

The camouflage guy took back his gun. "Good job," he said.

Forbes lurched, his body in shock. He turned and walked away, realizing now there was no going back.

Thirty

McNeal paced in his hotel room, piecing together what the hell he should do next. The dossier on Graff was dynamite. He had no proof the ex-CIA agent had killed Caroline or played a part in her death, but McNeal wanted to speak to him all the same. The honey trap organized by Karen Feinstein—also ex-CIA and an acquaintance of Graff's—pointed to a highly sophisticated operation.

What had really happened to his wife? The problem was that if he reached out to speak to Graff, it might signal the beginning of the end. He was a cop who played by the book. Graff was a man who killed with his bare hands.

No one knew where it would end. Back and forth his mind raced.

He felt himself starting to slip, to lose touch with reality. It was the same way he had felt five years ago. The way he had suffered when he lost Patrick. He felt himself being pulled into the ground. Under the ground.

McNeal closed his eyes and took out the photo from his wallet. The photo of his son—his dead son. The photo showed them on Compo Beach. It had been taken six months before Patrick's death. He touched the photo.

He was hitting a wall again and going to a dark, dark place. A place he didn't ever want to go back to. Grim thoughts swirled in his head. His gaze tracked to his gun on the dresser. The cold steel. But he didn't pick it up.

He reached for his cell phone instead and called Belinda Katz.

McNeal's throat tightened. Tears streamed down his face. "I'd like to talk."

"Jack McNeal?"

"That's right. I need someone to talk to. I want to talk about my son."

"Give me a moment. I'm so glad you called. Talk to me. Tell me about your son."

"I'm involved in a situation. A lot of memories are getting stirred up. I'm starting to think about him again. So much it hurts."

"What are you feeling?"

"I don't know. I feel . . . nothing. That's the problem. I feel numb. It's like it was five years ago. But this feels . . . I don't . . ."

"I'm listening, Jack."

Anxiety and rage coursed through his veins. "I feel like I'm going down a road that I don't want to go down. But I have no option. Caroline is dead. And I don't believe it was a suicide. That's the official version. And I'm starting to think about my son, goddammit."

"Let's talk about that, then. Tell me about your son."

"Is it possible to live after your son dies?"

"Yes. Most certainly yes. But it's hard. Very, very hard. The grieving process. You haven't processed that in any way. You've buried it."

McNeal closed his eyes tight. The memories burned again in his mind. The pain.

"Talk to me. Why did you bury all your thoughts about that night?"

"I had to. I didn't want to talk about it. I still don't, really."

"It happened five years ago. I read the file. Talk to me about Patrick."

McNeal cleared his throat. "Patrick was our son. He was six years old. He was our pride and joy."

"I'm listening."

"Seems like yesterday when we brought him back home. I can see him now. I can still smell his milky breath. I want him back."

"What happened, Jack? Take me back to that night."

McNeal scrunched up his face at the painful memory. "I don't know if it was fate that he was supposed to be there. Maybe."

"The price you paid is taking its toll. I'm worried for you."

"It never goes away. My wife was never the same after that. We were never the same. Our son's death drove a wedge between us."

"How did that manifest itself?"

"I buried myself in my work. She did the same. We stopped talking like a couple. All I could think about was Patrick. He wasn't around me anymore. My flesh and blood."

"This is a difficult thing. Painful. But can you tell me a little about the circumstances of his death?"

McNeal recalled the painful, awful scene from five years ago on Staten Island.

"It was my idea to go to the barbecue. It was my fault. Caroline didn't want to go. She said my partner, Juan, was fucked up in the head. She was right. And I didn't listen."

"Jack, that night . . . we need to address these issues from that night. The grief you feel for your son has gone unresolved. I believe you have suffered traumatic grief. And this has festered for years. You have terrible feelings of guilt. But you are not to blame. We need to talk about that. Talk about Patrick. And talk about your late wife."

McNeal threw up a wall of silence.

"You loved them both, didn't you, Jack?"

"With all my heart, I loved them both. But now . . . I don't know. I feel adrift."

"What you're experiencing can be resolved. With time, space, and help."

McNeal sighed. "I can't turn back the clock."

"No, you can't. We have only a finite time on this earth. We must cherish the time that we have together. I think it's important to explore the great points in your life with Patrick and Caroline."

"All I feel is an emptiness. I want Patrick back. But I know I can never see him when I come home from work. See him coming home from school. He didn't want to go to the barbecue. He wanted to play with his friends."

"Here's something that you might find useful to hold on to at this time."

"What's that?"

"The love you had—still have—you will have forever. He loved you. You loved him. Do you ever dream of him? Being back with him?"

"When I dream, I dream in slow motion. I dream of him looking at me after he had been shot. A split second, him gazing up at me, tears in his eyes, as if asking why this is happening to him. Why did I allow this to happen to him? I was powerless to help him. I'm powerless now. I just want to hold him again. But also . . ."

"Yes, what is it, Jack?"

"There's also an anger I can't explain. I feel trapped. Like I'm going to explode."

"I'm going to ask you a very difficult question. I hope you can answer it honestly."

"What is it?"

"Do you have, or have you ever had, suicidal thoughts?"

"There are some days I don't want to go on. Some days I don't want to get up. And some days I just want to curl up and die."

"But you go on, don't you?"

"I think I've reached the end of my rope."

"I want to help you. I want very much to help you. But you need to trust me and listen to what I say."

"I'm going to go now. Thank you for listening." He ended the call.

McNeal stared out over the city, breathing hard, still processing the conversation with Katz. The deepest thoughts and fears seemed to spill out of him. His cell phone rang. It was his father.

"Jack, you okay to talk?"

McNeal exhaled slowly, wiping his eyes. "Sure, Dad. What's going on?"

"I was going to ask you the same thing. Peter told me about what happened last night."

McNeal sighed. "It's a bit embarrassing, actually."

"Son, listen to me. I'm proud of you. Easiest thing in the world to succumb to something like that. But that's not what we are. The McNeals are loyal. And true."

"I pointed a gun at her head, Dad."

"Good for you. I just wanted you to know that I love you and respect you so much, son."

McNeal closed his eyes tight. It was so unlike his father to talk about such things.

"Your mother, God rest her soul, would have turned in her grave if you had fallen for that woman's charms."

"I know she would."

"Damn right she would have. But she raised you good."

"I don't want you bothering yourself with this. This is not your problem."

"Damn right it is. You're my son. And I'll always be there for you. And Peter. Love you both. Drive me fucking crazy, but I still love you."

McNeal smiled. His father had a propensity for industrial language. His years on the force and growing up hand-to-mouth in a big family meant rough language was par for the course. He said what had to be said. He told it like it was.

"Peter been bending your ear about this?" McNeal asked.

"You know Peter. Heart on his sleeve. His gut reaction is to go after people with a gun and not stop until it's over. But not in this case."

"He's got a family. That's understandable. I don't have a family anymore."

"You have us. I wouldn't blame you for getting back to your job. You're very good at it. And it's what you are. What you wanted."

"You think I'm conflicted?"

"I think you're trying to figure out how to pursue a line of investigation into what happened to your wife without compromising your ethics. By that I mean breaking the law."

"I have no intention of breaking the law."

"I know you don't. But sometimes . . ."

"Sometimes what?"

"Sometimes, in life, you face challenges. Challenges you've never faced before. And you will be defined by how you respond to those challenges. Life's tough. Sometimes there are no easy choices."

"You mean sometimes you've got to cross the line?"

"That's exactly what I mean."

McNeal relaxed, speaking to his father. He seemed a long way from home. He felt increasingly detached, as if he were being pulled by forces outside of his control. But he wasn't quite ready to cross the line. At least not yet. "Dad, Peter might've mentioned it, but I talked to Finn O'Brien."

"Was he helpful?"

"More than helpful."

"Glad to hear it. He's salt of the earth. He won't let you down. But keep your wits about you when dealing with Finn. He knows a lot of people. Be careful."

"I understand."

"I'm worried about you, Jack."

"What would you do?"

"I don't know. My head would say leave it. My heart? Who the hell knows?"

McNeal stared over toward the White House and sighed. "I feel sick."

"I understand. I would be too. If I was you, I'd come back home. Give yourself time to get over this."

"There's a guy I want to talk to, a guy I think knows what happened."

"Jack, don't start something unless you know how it's going to end."

"I need to do this. I'll come home. But I need to talk to this guy first."

"Who?"

"The guy whose wife overdosed three years ago."

Thirty-One

It was a short drive from DC to Arlington, Virginia. A matter of minutes.

McNeal was apprehensive as he pulled up outside an anonymous-looking glass-fronted building. He wanted Graff to know that he was on to him. He wanted to shake him up. Show him he was not afraid. Maybe make him respond. Rile him up. But it was mostly to apply some psychological pressure.

He walked through the revolving doors and into a spacious lobby adorned on all sides by modern art.

A woman sat behind the granite counter. She smiled as he approached. He checked the names of the companies that were based in the building. He spotted the name of Graff & Associates on the sixth floor.

"I'm here to see Henry Graff," he said.

"Is Mr. Graff expecting you?"

McNeal knew how he was going to play it. "I don't believe he is. But it's a matter of some importance."

"I'm sorry, but Mr. Graff only allows meetings strictly by appointment."

"Of course. I understand. Can you please let Mr. Graff know I'm here?"

The woman gave a pained smile. "I'm so sorry, sir, but that's just not possible."

"Is he in today?"

"He's a very, very busy man."

"I'm sure he is. Tell you what I'll do, I'm going to sit and wait over there until he comes down."

"That is not possible, sir. That area is only for people who have appointments with one of the companies based in this building."

McNeal smiled and leaned on the counter. "Give him a quick call and say I'd like to talk to him. He'll know who I am."

"Sir," she said, her tone growing slightly annoyed, "that is not possible, regrettably. If you want to leave your name, I will try and arrange an appointment that will suit you both."

"Not possible. My name is Jack McNeal. If you can let Mr. Graff know I'm in the building, that would be very helpful."

McNeal sat down on one of the mustard-colored sofas and checked his messages. A few emails from colleagues at the Internal Affairs Bureau. A nice one from his boss, Bob Buckley, telling him to take as much time as he needed before returning to work. The truth was that the days had flown by. He didn't really even know what day it was anymore.

He looked up and watched a camera scan the lobby.

The receptionist's face had turned to stone.

"A quick visit, that's all," McNeal said, putting on his best smile.

She picked up her phone and whispered, "Sorry to bother you. There's a gentleman here to see Mr. Graff. His name is McNeal. I told him Mr. Graff wasn't available. But he is quite insistent." The receptionist nodded her head a few times. "I'll hold, sure."

McNeal pretended to nonchalantly scan his cell phone.

"Hi," the receptionist said. Then, "That's not a problem." She ended the call and looked across at McNeal. "Sir, Mr. Graff has a spare slot. Quite rare, in my experience." She pointed to the elevators. "Get off at floor six."

"Thank you so much." McNeal headed to the elevator.

He rode the elevator to the sixth floor before he stepped out into a carpeted lobby. Another receptionist, this one behind a glass desk, stood up.

"Follow me, Mr. McNeal," she instructed. He followed her down a series of corridors before reaching an outer office. She pressed her thumb against the digital reader on the wall, and the glass doors slid open. "Go right in. He's waiting for you."

McNeal walked through the door into a sprawling corner office with views of downtown Arlington. At the far end of the office, a man sat behind a huge walnut desk, leaning back in his seat.

"That'll be all," he called across the room.

The door was closed quietly behind McNeal.

The man smiled at McNeal. "I don't think we've met. Henry Graff."

"Appreciate your time."

The man shrugged. He exuded a quiet menace. He didn't stand up to greet him. But that was fine. "And you are Mr. Jack McNeal? Where are you from, Jack?"

"New York."

"You've come a long way. Can I get you a coffee? A drink of any kind?"

McNeal shook his head.

"How can I help? It's something that couldn't wait, right?"

McNeal pulled up a chair. "You mind?"

"Not at all. What's this all about? It's unusual for clients or potential clients to turn up without a prior appointment."

McNeal looked around the minimalistic office, with its floor-to-ceiling windows. "I'm not a potential client . . . you probably know who I am."

"As I said, I don't believe we've met. Certainly your name's not one I'm familiar with. To be fair, I have a long list of clients and prospective clients."

"You'll get to know my name."

Graff sat up in his seat and gave a tight smile. "Are you here on business, Mr. McNeal?"

"I'm here to talk about the death of your wife, Mr. Graff."

Graff shifted forward. "I'm sorry, who are you?"

"My name is Jack McNeal. We've got something in common. Both our wives died in DC."

Graff was quiet for a few moments, his face impassive. "I'm sorry to hear that. How did your wife die?"

"She drowned in the Potomac, apparently."

"I'm so sorry. Can you tell me more about her?"

"My wife was Caroline McNeal. She worked for the *Washington Post.*"

"That was your wife?"

McNeal nodded. "That was my wife."

"I read about that. I'm with you now. She drowned?"

"Floating in the Potomac. Three years after your wife's death."

"You seem to know a lot about this. Do you mind if I call you Jack?"

"Jack is fine."

"This is all a bit sudden and out of the blue. Beyond the manner of their deaths, I'm not sure I can see the connection."

"My late wife was, by all accounts, rather interested in your late wife. And how she died."

Graff steepled his fingers. "Why would she be interested in my wife's tragic death? That strikes me as rather bizarre. Cruel, even."

"She was a journalist. Her joy was to pursue stories."

"Real or imagined?"

"Caroline believed your wife's death was suspicious."

"Journalists, from my experience, live in a fantasy world most of the time. Barely credible, many of them. Live off the scraps given by sources, sometimes real, sometimes imagined."

McNeal smiled, feeling himself burrowing underneath Graff's skin.

Graff cleared his throat. "What exactly is the purpose of your visit?"

"Just to introduce myself and explain some background. I was hoping you might be able to provide me with some answers about either my wife's death or your wife's death."

"You're wearing my patience very thin, Mr. McNeal." His tone became slightly sinister. "What do you know about my wife?"

"I know your wife was very well known in Washington social circles. I remember there was a private memorial service that the President attended very recently on the third anniversary of her death. You're well connected. As was your wife."

Graff sighed, as if disappointed by a recalcitrant child. "Mr. McNeal, without wishing to appear rude, my wife's death has nothing to do with you. It was a deeply personal and private tragedy for my family. I'm at a loss to understand why you have come here at all."

"With respect, Mr. Graff, I have to disagree. My wife was investigating your wife's death."

Graff stared at McNeal for what seemed an eternity, as if letting the words sink in. "We seem to be going around in circles, Mr. McNeal."

"Do we?"

"What's your background, Mr. McNeal?"

"I grew up on Staten Island."

"No, I mean, what do you do for a living?"

"Internal Affairs Bureau, NYPD."

Graff summoned a wry smile. "So, you investigate corrupt cops, right?"

"Among other things."

"How fascinating. Does the NYPD know that you are conducting a personal investigation way down here in DC?"

"I'm on bereavement leave, and this is not a personal investigation."

"Is that so? I would've thought, Mr. McNeal, you would have preferred to spend your time more constructively during this very sad time for you."

McNeal thought Graff's words were tinged with sarcasm. "I would've preferred to spend this time more constructively too. But my wife unearthed some documents. It looks like there were two different autopsies carried out on your late wife. Rather bizarre, I thought."

Graff went tight-lipped. Then, quietly, "Finally you get to the point."

"Would you like me to show them to you?"

"Have you lost your mind?"

"The autopsies show inconsistencies. Did you know about this?"

Graff's skin seemed to drain of color. Bone white. "Listen here, Mr. McNeal. Just so you know, I have no idea what kind of conspiracy theory you are trying to prove. Frankly, I don't care about such matters. My wife suffered from bipolar disorder. She was either manic or suicidal. She died after taking a massive overdose. That's what the medical examiner found."

McNeal sat quietly, wanting Graff to keep on talking.

"I have given you time to talk about whatever it was you wanted to talk about, but I believe you have now overstayed your welcome. I would ask you, respectfully, to leave the premises, or you'll be escorted out."

"Your late wife was by all accounts a very popular lady. In social circles. Life and soul of the party. A wide circle of male admirers."

Graff stared at McNeal. "Ordinarily, I would have had you thrown out for such scurrilous suggestions. But you have lost a wife, too, so I understand the pain and poor judgment it causes."

McNeal nodded. He allowed the silence to linger. It was an interview technique he used in Internal Affairs.

"What exactly do you want, Mr. McNeal?"

"Some answers."

"If I'm not able to furnish you with answers, what then?"

"I'll have to go elsewhere and ask questions. I'm like that."

"Jack, I know loss. And I know what it's like. I know what you're going through. Could I have done more? Why wasn't I there for her?"

McNeal nodded.

"You know that my wife was very fond of parties. And had a very active social life. Just so you know, we had drifted apart, years earlier. We weren't living together when she died. I work abroad a lot. I understand your insinuations. I know what people said about her. Her reckless lifestyle. The liaisons with other men. I heard it all. But I was devastated when she died, as I'm sure you are about your wife."

McNeal nodded. He knew Graff wasn't going to confess to killing his own wife or McNeal's. He turned his attention to the window, suddenly contemplative. "I wonder what it was about your wife's death that intrigued my wife. Did Sophie know too much? Was that it?"

"My wife was a charitable soul. She raised hundreds of millions of dollars for worthwhile charities across the world. Starving children, cancer charities, educational charities—the list went on and on. Her death was a tragedy."

What he wanted to do was put Graff on notice, and he'd accomplished that and more. "Nice to finally meet you, Mr. Graff. I'll let myself out."

Graff sighed. "A little bit of advice to you before you go. Sometimes you just need to let go. Death comes to us all. And we just have to accept it."

Thirty-Two

It was nearly midnight when Graff's office door opened. He saw Karen Feinstein's reflection in the window while he stared out at the near-deserted parking lot, watching a pair of security guys with flashlights and a dog patrol the area. He turned around.

Feinstein pulled up a seat, ashen-faced.

Graff stared daggers. "So, Karen, do you want to explain how this is possible? How some Internal Affairs guy from NYPD comes to my office. Do you have any idea what this means for me? For our cover story? The whole thing has been blown to shit. Complete mess."

"Henry, if you just sit down, I'll try and explain."

Graff remained standing, hands on hips. "Don't tell me what to do. When I was in New York, you told me this was all under control. Did you or did you not?"

"We're working on this."

"This is you working on this? Karen, you're going to have to do better than that. Don't you see what the fuck is happening? Can't you see it? This fucker is toying with me."

"We will deal with him, trust me."

"I paid your firm over a million dollars for your work on this contract. And there are bonuses on top that could work out to two million."

"I work night and day for you, Henry."

"Listen to me. You either fix this, or I will rip up the goddamn contract, do you hear me?"

"That won't be necessary."

"That fuck was here in my office! I'm being grilled in my office? Me! A cop? What the fuck? I'm dying here! Who is this crazy fuck?"

"That's why I'm here. We are facing a challenge. But I've got this."

"I want answers! How is this happening?"

"My NSA guy has scraped telephone records from Jack McNeal. He has been in contact with a private eye down in Florida, Finn O'Brien. Old-school New York cop. Friend of McNeal's father. And O'Brien has been feeding information back to McNeal."

"This isn't making me feel any better, Karen."

"The searches carried out by O'Brien's company were initially focused on you, Henry. Then they turned their attention to Francesca Luca."

"The hooker? Tell me you're fucking kidding. Really?"

"The honey trap girl. That's right."

"Fuck."

"That, in turn, has flagged my maiden name. O'Brien did some searching about me. A deep dive of myriad records, court records, government and otherwise. Public records. Confidential IRS tax returns might have been accessed, perhaps by hackers, for the right price. Perhaps they did a forensic financial audit of my company. And it would show that your company has done work for me, Henry, just like I've done work for you. And you are the widower of Sophie Meyer. Can you see how they could be putting this together? It's cute."

Graff sighed. "You think this is all because Jack McNeal got the real identity of the honey trap girl?"

"It all stemmed from there."

"How could that bitch have been so stupid? Carrying her real ID?"

"Let's forget about that for a moment."

"Forget about it? How the hell can I forget about it? The fucker, McNeal, turns up in the lobby, wanting to speak to me. I'll guarantee he knows about my past too. The bastard was sitting where you are now, cool as a cucumber."

"Why didn't you call security?"

"Don't you understand? It doesn't matter if I got him thrown off the premises or called the cops, that by itself would have opened up further problems."

Feinstein nodded. "I understand."

"So what the fuck do we do now? He told me that his wife had found documents pertaining to two autopsies."

"That's impossible."

Graff shook his head.

Feinstein implored, "We need to stay calm. He wants you to lash out. We need to remain focused."

"What a mess."

"We are where we are."

"Well, that's just great. Let's be philosophical. That'll fix everything."

Feinstein flushed, seeming embarrassed. "I mean we need to draw a line in the sand and work this problem."

"How about another strategy? How about we neutralize Jack McNeal?"

"I think that would be desirable."

Graff turned back to the window. "Good. I'm feeling better already."

"We need to get into his life. Who is he?"

Graff balled his fist. "Everyone has a tipping point. What is he prepared to put up with? Is he prepared to walk away if his world becomes threatened? Things that matter to him? His job? Family?"

"His wife's dead. But he has family. A father. A brother."

"What about reaching out to our sources within the NYPD?"

Feinstein cracked a smile. "I'm already on that side of things. But this guy has friends. He knows people. So does his cop brother."

Graff pointed at her. "Figure it out. No more surprises. Let's turn the screw on this fucker. I want him out of my life for good."

Thirty-Three

McNeal's visit to Graff wouldn't go unnoticed. He knew that. He had crossed the line. They would now try and get into his life. But he had found Graff fascinating—cold but fascinating. He had put himself firmly on Graff's radar. It might have been foolish. It might have been reckless. But it would provoke a response.

He thought again about what Caroline had said to the psychologist. She was being stalked. There was a prowler. She had to have reported it to the cops. He needed to know more—a lot more. Ideally he could have reached out to people he knew and trusted. But his position within the Internal Affairs Bureau meant he had to be cleaner than clean.

He thought about whether he should reach out to Sam Daniels again. But what he wanted meant Sam having to access DC police databases. If Sam didn't have a good reason, he could easily be suspended or fired.

McNeal knew better than anyone that cops who crossed that line by trying to access confidential police databases about ex-wives or partners were routinely disciplined. Sometimes fired. He had investigated scores of such cases in the past couple of years.

McNeal knew one person who might be able to help. He pulled up O'Brien's name from his cell phone. It rang five times before the familiar, gruff voice answered.

"Hello, Jack."

McNeal explained the latest twist in his investigation. "So, I need another favor."

"Call in as many as you like, son. It's not a problem."

"I've got a delicate situation I need handling."

"I'm listening."

"I need a cop in DC to access a police database. It's risky."

"I know people. What exactly do you want?"

"I want someone to access the Metropolitan Police Department of the District of Columbia files. I want to know what they have on the prowler incidents around the home of my late wife."

"I know someone in Robbery there. A nephew of a friend."

"I don't want your guy to get collared for this."

"You know as well as I do there are risks in everything. I pay well. Cops do this sort of stuff all the time. It's only a problem if there's an audit. Millions of inquiries every day through local and state databases, in addition to the FBI's National Crime and Information Center."

"I don't want you trying to access the Fed stuff."

"I understand."

"I'm looking to see if the police had any reports of a prowler, and if so, what did they find out? I want a name."

When McNeal had packed his bag once again, about to drive back north, he remembered that he meant to stop by Caroline's house in the city. He had forgotten all about that in the craziness since her death. He could decide later what he was going to do with it.

McNeal had keys to the property. He had the four-digit access code to deactivate the alarm. He decided to head on over to what was now his Georgetown townhouse.

He left his hotel and walked the six blocks. He stood admiring the beautiful old colonial row house sitting in the oldest part of the city. It had existed since before DC even existed.

He stared at the black front door. He thought of how many times Caroline would have opened the door after a long day covering politics on Capitol Hill.

He took out the key and unlocked the door. He headed inside. A pile of mail lay strewn behind the door.

A few beeps warned him that he had just a few seconds before the alarm went off.

McNeal punched in the four-digit code to deactivate the alarm. He walked down the polished corridor and into the kitchen. Everything neat and clean, as she would have left it. It felt strange to be in her home. It wasn't *their* home. It was *hers*. At least that's how he thought of it.

He was humbled and so sad that she had left it to him. It was no use to him without her.

McNeal had too much on his mind to worry about owning such a prestigious property. He headed into the bedroom. There, he saw photos of himself and Caroline on their wedding day. Three small stones on top of each other, beside her bed. He ran his fingers over them, assuming they were stones from Compo Beach. Caroline had loved rock balancing with Patrick. He was touched that she had taken a small piece of the beach to her new home. Maybe as a reminder of what had been.

He opened the closets. Wall-to-wall nice clothes. The faint citrus scent of her. The French perfume she loved to wear. He looked down and saw the neat rows of shoes. Caroline loved shoes.

He made his way into the living room. It looked like a house owned by a leading American journalist. Floor-to-ceiling bookcases. Biographies of Kissinger, Nixon, Clinton, Bush, and Lincoln alongside mostly American classics like Henry James's *Washington Square* and John Steinbeck's *Of Mice and Men*. He noticed a few copies of her books were on the shelves. He remembered her writing them on rare visits home to Westport. Sitting in the upstairs study, tapping away maniacally at her MacBook, a beautiful view over Compo Beach.

He headed through to the kitchen again. Yellow Post-it notes and scribbled reminders pinned to a cork board. A postcard from Seville. He unpinned it. It was from her colleague at the *Post*, Arlene Cortez.

> *Having a great time, honey. Wish you were here. Arlene. xxx*

In the center of the board was a color picture of Caroline and Jack enjoying a glass of wine in the Bar Room at the Beekman in downtown Manhattan. The photo had been taken by Peter's wife. They had been celebrating their tenth anniversary. Eighteen months later and she would be gone from their marriage. The shocking death of their son had driven them apart. Maybe she just wanted a change of scenery. Maybe she had grown tired of his mundane job, or his mundane lifestyle. He wasn't one for visiting museums or galleries. He grumbled about going to dinner parties.

He went back to the living room and noticed a landline he hadn't known about. He picked up the bills on the table. He saw one for Verizon and opened the envelope.

The home number was printed there.

But it also showed itemized calls. Three were to the psychologist. Eighteen to the *Washington Post*.

McNeal wondered what she had wanted. Had she been looking for help? Advice? Was she reaching out, scared?

McNeal's cell phone rang, snapping him out of his reverie. He saw the caller ID and recognized it immediately. "Jack McNeal speaking."

A long sigh came down the line. "Jack, it's Robert Buckley."

"Sir?"

"Jack, we need to talk."

"What about, Bob?"

"Are you still in DC?"

"For a little while longer."

"Get yourself back to New York, Jack. I think you've got a problem."

Thirty-Four

McNeal drove back from DC and headed straight for his apartment in New York. He dropped off his bags and took the short walk to Internal Affairs on Hudson. He knew what was coming. Was he interfering with police or FBI investigations? Maybe both.

McNeal was shown into Bob Buckley's huge corner office on the third floor, overlooking the Hudson.

Buckley had dark shadows under his eyes. He stood up and shook McNeal's hand before motioning for Jack to sit down. He leafed through some papers on his desk. "I just want to say once again how sorry I am about Caroline's death. I think I speak for the whole department when I say that we are all mourning for not only her but you. I can only imagine what you're going through."

"Thank you. Means a lot."

"Secondly, you and I go back a good few years, and it would be remiss of me not to speak frankly. I hope you understand that."

McNeal shrugged. "Bob, I'd expect nothing less."

"This is not official, and there is going to be no note of this, whatever our goddamn rules say."

McNeal nodded.

"There are rules and there are rules, right?"

McNeal listened patiently.

"Jack, you are a great detective. You're as straight and as honest a cop as I've ever met. You're one of the good guys. I know you and I haven't seen eye to eye in the last year or two. Basically, I know you're pissed that we've had to put some bad seeds into dismissal probation. And I know what you think about keeping bad cops in their jobs, as long as they keep their noses clean for a year. I get that, and I sympathize with you."

McNeal waited to see where his boss was going with this.

"I understand where you're coming from. There are issues, no question. Serious issues that we need to work harder to address."

"When you've got a cop—I'm talking Mulligan, who battered his wife unconscious—and he ends up on dismissal probation, then yeah, I guess I have a problem with that."

"The rules are the rules. And I know you've written numerous memos about wanting to change those rules. Jack, that ain't gonna happen. You know it. I know it. It's politics. You know how it is. He was dealing with his son's alcoholism."

McNeal nodded. "That's not why you called me here, though, is it?"

Buckley sighed and leaned back in his seat. "You're on bereavement leave now, right?"

"I'm thinking about coming back next week."

"Jack, you know it's not my style to be a ballbuster, least of all when it comes to you. But do you know who called me?"

McNeal shrugged. He had a good idea.

"FBI Assistant Director John Gutierrez threatened to have you arrested with intent to interfere or impede an FBI investigation regarding the death of someone named Sophie Meyer."

"Are you serious?"

"Do you have any idea how pissed he was? I'm telling you, this guy was citing every goddamn law up to national security."

"Did Gutierrez say who the complaint originated from? I took documents to the FBI in Bridgeport. When I called back, the guy had been transferred to DC. I brought that all to them, then I ran into a brick wall."

"That's not how they're reading it."

"You want to know the real story? I handed over documents that my late wife's lawyer passed to me. An investigation she was working on, into the death of Sophie Meyer. And I'm the bad guy?"

"Christ almighty. I know you're grieving, God knows I do, but I have no idea what this is about. When the FBI calls my number, at home, it bothers me."

McNeal knew he wasn't going to win this particular argument. Best to just sit quiet and listen. He also knew that Buckley's political ambitions required him to run a tight ship. He couldn't be seen having rogue detectives carrying out private investigations. It didn't look good.

"From what I know about this Sophie Meyer—party girl, socialite, and all the rest—it was a simple overdose. That was three goddamn years ago. But now I hear that you turn up and start hassling the bereaved husband? Are you nuts? You're out of line."

"I just wanted some answers."

"That's not the way to go about it. Grief does terrible things to a man. Now I have the fucking FBI on to me, busting my balls about you poking around about Sophie Meyer."

"Did they tell you I was a person of interest for Caroline's death for a day or two?"

Buckley closed his eyes, as if not wanting to hear any more. "From what I've been told, this Sophie Meyer was having affairs with a senator on the Intelligence Committee, among others."

"Among others. Did you know that someone set a honey trap for me?"

"What?"

"I'm surprised the FBI left that out."

"What are you talking about?"

McNeal told the story of how he had nearly been snared by Francesca Luca. "She's a hooker. She's been bailed out multiple times by a woman called Feinstein. An associate of Henry Graff, the guy I visited, former husband to Sophie Meyer. A friend of the President, apparently!"

"What the fuck has the President got to do with this, Jack? Are you having a breakdown? That's why we referred you to the psychologist in the first place."

"Yeah, thanks for that."

"Snap out of it! You're at a crossroads. Believe me when I tell you, when you've got the FBI and Secret Service breathing down your neck, it's not nice. Not nice at all. If you continue down this path . . ."

"What?"

Buckley sighed. "Christ, this shouldn't have gotten to this stage."

"Do you want to tell me what's going on?"

"Well, if having the Feds breathing down my neck isn't bad enough, I spoke to the police commissioner just over an hour ago. He says that if your conduct continues, you will be suspended, then fired and stripped of your pension if found guilty. Do you understand?"

McNeal detached, as if Buckley was talking to someone else. He didn't know where he would be without his job. It defined him.

"Do you understand?"

"Yes, I understand."

"Will you give me your word this crazy behavior is at an end? Can I tell the Commissioner that?"

"Tell him it's over. I've been under immense stress." It was the sort of thing McNeal heard time and time again from bad cops. "It won't happen again."

"That's what I wanted to hear. Take some time off. Go fishing. Get some rest. And sleep. Let's forget all about this bullshit."

Thirty-Five

The sky darkened as McNeal pulled up to his home in Westport. Inside the house, the lights were on. Upstairs and downstairs.

McNeal got out of his car and steeled himself for a trashed house. He opened the front door and realized right away the alarm had been deactivated. He always set the alarm. And he always turned the lights off.

He locked the front door behind him, took out his gun, and went from room to room. Every closet. Even the attic. But he found nothing.

The house was exactly as he'd left it, except the lights were on and the alarm deactivated.

"What the fuck?" He holstered his gun.

McNeal couldn't understand it. It looked like nothing had been taken. He questioned if he had simply forgotten. But that wasn't like him. He was sure he had turned all the lights off and set the alarm. McNeal always made sure everything was turned off. Someone had been inside. But who? If it had been a thief, the place would have been ransacked. Or at least shown evidence that people had been there.

He pushed those thoughts aside as he began to doubt himself.

McNeal headed upstairs, showered, and changed into fresh clothes. He poured himself a strong whiskey and slumped into an easy chair, switched on the TV. Fox News. A reporter was covering a gang shooting in Los Angeles. Three dead, including a thirteen-year-old boy. Bad news only made good news.

He sipped the whiskey and stared at the screen, the volume down low. The liquor warmed his belly. It took the edge off. He finished the rest of the drink, put down his glass, and sighed.

McNeal closed his eyes. He drifted off to sleep. Suddenly he floated down a river, peering up at the night sky. Billions of stars overhead. The sound of garbled whispers. Incessant. Ominous voices bearing down on him.

The sound of ringing startled McNeal, and he awoke to his cell phone vibrating on the side table.

McNeal gathered his thoughts. He didn't recognize the caller ID.

"Hi, I'm looking to speak to Jack McNeal." The voice of Henry Graff.

McNeal sat up, phone pressed tight to his ear. "Mr. Graff, how can I help you?"

"Is it an okay time to talk?"

"Sure."

"Jack, I hope you don't mind me calling to say I'm sorry."

"Sorry for what?"

"I think we got off on the wrong foot. What you said, turning up out of the blue, and telling me all those things . . . it startled me. I was insensitive to your feelings. I want to apologize if I came across as unfeeling. To be honest, I was shocked to the core by what you said."

McNeal wondered about the purpose of the call. Was it to fuck with him? Was Graff trying to ingratiate himself? Maybe throw him off the scent? Was this part of his mind games? Jack knew about

Graff's links with Feinstein. But did Graff know that McNeal knew? He assumed a guy like Graff would.

He considered how he should play it. Tell Graff what he knew? Maybe it would be better to conceal his knowledge. All these thoughts careened around his head.

"Are you still there, Jack?"

"Yeah, I'm still here."

"I want to say again, and I mean this, that I'm so sorry for your loss. I can see clearly now how devastating that must have been for you. I appreciate your willingness to be open and share what you know. I'm sorry if I came across as slightly unfeeling. Uncaring. Angry, even."

McNeal let him talk.

"I'm still grieving my wife. The news of her death was like a bolt from out of nowhere. So much regret. So much pain, wondering what if."

McNeal sighed. Was this the same Graff who was the killing machine he had read about in the dossier? Or maybe it was just Graff trying to pull at his heartstrings, appear as if he was hurting, casting himself as the victim. McNeal had encountered more than his fair share of psychopathic cops, the sort of malignant individuals who used emotional influence for selfish reasons. The sort of people who could manipulate, turn things around, make you feel sorry for them.

"Anyway, it's true I've had my share of trials and tribulations in life. Losing people that are dear to me. Close friends. But I thought it important to speak to you man-to-man about this . . . Are you still there, Jack?"

"I'm still here."

"The other thing I wanted to talk to you about was the autopsy. You mentioned there were two."

"Sure."

"That really upset me. Probably more than I realized. But I checked with the medical examiner whose name appears on her death certificate. He gave me a letter outlining his findings, and it mirrors his original findings exactly. He couldn't explain the second autopsy."

"I believe the second one was carried out by a medical examiner from the UK."

"Thankfully I can clarify that. I checked on that too. The guy's name is Dr. Malcolm Robertson. But he has written to me confirming he knows nothing about this. He said he didn't carry out a second autopsy on my wife. So, it's all very upsetting and bizarre. I can't for the life of me figure out how this confusion came about."

"I know my wife was a meticulous journalist. She had many high-level sources. I trust that what she unearthed was true."

Silence. Then, "I very much admire your loyalty to your late wife. It must be a terrible burden, especially when you're under investigation by the NYPD and the FBI."

McNeal's gut clenched tight. He hated being patronized by fucks like Graff. He could see he was being tested. He wondered if Graff disclosed his knowledge of the investigations as a means to unsettle him. He suspected every aspect of his life was under the microscope. Was Graff going to leak the information to the media? Was he recording the conversation? Nothing would surprise him.

Graff added, "What would worry me would be the loss of my pension rights."

McNeal was dumbstruck. It was clear that Graff already knew about the conversation between Buckley and the NYPD commissioner about stripping McNeal of his police pension. Graff was showing how far his influence and connections extended. It was unnerving, to say the least.

"Anyway, I thought it only right to bring this to your attention."

"Very good of you, Mr. Graff."

"I hope you take this time to grieve properly. A time to reflect. Space to contemplate what you had together."

"Thanks for the call, Mr. Graff."

"Don't hesitate to contact me if there's anything you want to know. My door is always open."

Thirty-Six

McNeal called his brother and relayed details of the surreal conversation with Graff.

"Are you fucking kidding me?" Peter said. "That's what Graff told you?"

"That's what he said."

"Why didn't you tell him that you know about his links to Feinstein?"

"He probably knows that I know already."

"Why didn't you sock it to him?"

"For what purpose? I'm on sticky ground. I had the riot act read to me by my boss." McNeal quickly outlined the conversation he'd had with Buckley.

"Bob Buckley said your pension might be at risk? Seriously?"

"I need to be careful."

Peter sighed. "I think you do too."

"Forgot to say, there was something else. When I got back here, the alarm had been deactivated and all the lights were on. Nothing taken. No sign of a break-in. I was starting to doubt myself. Maybe I forgot to put the alarm on and turn off the lights."

"Easily done."

"I'm fucking careful about stuff like that."

"What do you think happened?"

McNeal sighed. "I've been thinking about that."

"And?"

"Someone is fucking with me. Playing mind games with me. They've got me starting to doubt myself."

"Who exactly are you talking about?"

"Graff. Feinstein. I don't know. People that work for them, more likely. Then the weird call from Graff."

"This is starting to sound like a bit of a stretch."

"You don't believe me?"

"I believe you. I'll always believe you. You're my brother. But why would they do that? For what purpose?"

"Psychological warfare. Think about it. They want me to think that I'm not in control. That I'm losing it. They're fucking with my head."

"Slow down, man."

"Don't you get it? They're doing this so I react, and by reacting, they hope I'll make a bad decision."

"You're making it sound like a low-level war of attrition."

"That's exactly what it is. They want to unsettle me. Want me to know that they can get to me. It's subtle. What am I going to do? Call the police and say someone has broken in and done this? No. Why? Because the police would think I'm nuts. By doing nothing, they exert pressure on me. Quietly."

"Sounds like goddamn KGB tactics."

"More like the CIA. Straight out of their playbook, right? That's exactly where Graff or Feinstein comes in."

"I've got to say, I'm worried about you, man."

"Do you think I'm losing my mind?"

"No, I don't. I'm just worried about you. I care about you."

"Remember I told you about the break-in at Caroline's psychologist's office? And the prowler outside Caroline's house in DC? Now this. It's a pattern."

"It ain't good, I know that. I'm going to come up and spend a few days with you, if that's okay."

McNeal picked up his empty glass, swished around the melted ice. "Look, I'll get through this. I'll deal with this."

"I know you will. But I want to be there for you now. I want to talk."

"What about?"

"About how we're going to deal with this."

Thirty-Seven

The following morning, after a restless sleep, McNeal got a text from Peter saying he was on his way. He got up, showered, put on a fresh shirt and jeans, and headed downstairs. It wasn't long before Peter rolled up in his Ford with his Labrador, Charlie, in the front seat.

McNeal hugged his brother tight. It felt good to have Peter with him.

"You okay with the dog?"

"Not a problem. Put him in the backyard. Plenty of space for him to run around."

McNeal poured them each a fresh cup of coffee and served pancakes with maple syrup. He headed out to the backyard and put some dog food in a bowl.

McNeal and his brother walked down onto the deserted sand of Compo Beach.

Peter spoke first, collar up against the chill, hands in pockets. "You look like you've lost weight. You're stressed, man. I can tell. You used to get like that when you were studying for your goddamn finals. Sitting up half the night studying, calling me the following day. You were driving me out of my mind."

McNeal laughed. "I was kinda driven."

Peter wrapped a huge arm around him. "Nothing wrong with that."

McNeal walked on as the sand continued to get whipped up by the wind. He relished the cold breeze off Long Island Sound. "I miss this. The space. The water. The sense of calm. You don't get that in Manhattan, that's for sure."

"Especially in that tiny little apartment you've got."

Jack loved having his brother beside him. It had been years since they'd had time to talk and shoot the breeze, just them. No one else. Not wives. No kids. No dad. Just them.

"I've been having flashbacks again."

"I didn't realize."

Jack nodded. "I haven't had them for a couple of years. All of a sudden, they're back in the last few days. With a vengeance. Having nightmares too. Don't know what's going on with me." The memories were still there. He still saw his son, dead, in Caroline's arms. And then his partner lying dead in a pool of blood, gunned down by him.

"I'm guessing being under such acute stress is bringing all those things back to the surface."

"Maybe."

"Know what you need?"

"What?"

"A few drinks to forget things for a few hours. How does that sound?"

"Is that a good idea?"

"Can you think of a better one?"

McNeal smiled.

"Any good bars around here?"

"Sure. You've just got to know where to look."

They headed back to the house, put the dog inside, and took a cab to Rothbard's.

Jack got the first few rounds, tequila shots and beers, before they moved over to single malts. They talked baseball, in particular how shitty the Yankees were this season, but also highs and lows of life and memories of growing up on Staten Island.

"You think Dad'll ever leave?" Peter asked.

"Staten Island?"

"I mean, I've asked him if he wants to move in with me."

"What did he say?"

"'Are you nuts?' That's what he said. Said he loved Staten Island. 'Why the hell would I move to Jersey?'"

"Old habits die hard."

"Better believe it. He's old-school. He likes what he likes."

McNeal smiled as his gaze wandered around the gastropub. A lot of well-heeled Westporters enjoying kicking back for a few hours.

"Nice place, by the way."

"Yeah, Caroline liked it a lot. We had a lot of great Saturday afternoons in here. I was away from New York, she was away from Washington, and it was just us. It was like she could switch off here."

"You think you're going to stay here in Westport?"

"I don't know. The commute is a pain in the ass."

"I hear you."

The bonhomie and good cheer continued for a few good-natured hours. The brothers had a few more drinks before they called it a night. They caught a cab back to the house on Compo Beach.

As they approached the gravel drive, McNeal again spotted lights on upstairs.

"Are you fucking kidding me?"

Peter said, "You definitely turned off all the lights. I saw you."

"I know I did."

McNeal paid the cabdriver, who drove off. He drew his gun, as did his brother, before they headed inside. The alarm had again been deactivated. He switched on the hallway lights. It was all just as they had left it.

McNeal headed upstairs, his brother covering him. He saw the bathroom door slightly ajar. He pushed back the door with his gun.

"Oh my God!" Peter screamed.

His beautiful dog was on the bathroom floor in a pool of his own vomit, eyes open. Charlie was dead.

Thirty-Eight

A cotton candy dawn bathed the dark waters of Long Island Sound.

Jack McNeal stood over the newly dug grave at the edge of his backyard as Peter carefully lowered Charlie down into the hole. After a few words from Peter about how much his dog meant to him and his family, he helped his brother fill in the grave with shovelfuls of earth, patting it down with the back of his spade.

His tough-guy brother broke down sobbing.

"I'm sorry this happened, Peter. Truly sorry."

"Who kills a fucking dog?"

"The same people who killed Caroline."

"But why? It's a dog."

McNeal nodded.

"Why would they do that, Jack?"

Peter wiped away the tears with the back of his sleeve.

McNeal explained, "They're sending a not-so-subtle message. 'We can get you any time we like.' Remember what I said? They're fucking with us."

"What do I tell the kids?"

"Tell them the truth. You found him dead."

"What do we do now?"

McNeal knew it was important not to have a gut reaction. He needed time to think. But Peter wanted answers, and he wanted to crack some heads. "We take stock."

"Then what? What the hell is really going on? Are they watching us?"

"Maybe. We might be under surveillance. Maybe electronic."

"We need to get new phones."

McNeal nodded.

"The question is, do we just sit here and wait?"

"There is no 'we.' This is not about us."

"That's where you're wrong, Jack. They killed my dog. My brother is in their sights. I can't just sit back and take this."

McNeal stood, hands on hips, cursing the mound of earth. "Motherfucker!"

"They're not going to divide us."

"I need more time to figure this out."

McNeal's cell phone interrupted the conversation.

"Sorry for taking so long to get back to you, son." The gruff voice of O'Brien bled through. "You okay to talk?"

"Not a problem. You find out anything from the police files?"

"It makes interesting reading."

"How so?"

"Your late wife reported a prowler to the DC police. This was noted. Police arrested a guy a couple hundred yards from her home matching the description."

"You got a name?"

"Frank Nicoletti. He was released after he was questioned. Pled the Fifth. I've been doing some digging. He's onetime CIA."

"What else?"

"He's also a close associate of Henry Graff."

Thirty-Nine

McNeal ended the call and relayed the news to his brother.

"I think the time has come," McNeal decided.

"For what?"

"You need to get back home to your family."

"What about you?"

"Gimme your cell phone?"

"What?"

"Do it."

Peter handed over his LG phone.

McNeal took out the battery, then did the same for his own Samsung as well.

"Let's assume they have a roving bug on us."

"Possibility," Peter acknowledged.

"First things first. The documents belonging to Caroline. All that information that we copied for the Feds."

"It's inside the family safe deposit box," Peter said.

"We both have access, right? It's got everything?"

"Everything. And I also made copies of it all, just on the million-to-one chance something happens to us."

"Where did you put that?"

"Gave it to my lawyer."

McNeal cocked his head. "You've got a lawyer?"

"He's a former cop. Has a practice in Jersey City. It's in his safe. Only to be opened in the event of my death."

McNeal nodded. "Extreme situations require extreme measures."

"You got it. So, what now? You going to disappear?"

McNeal shook his head. "On the contrary. I want them to know where I am. Put the batteries back in ten minutes from now. Then we split. If they want to follow me, they can follow me. They've been tracking me from the start. Let's use that to our advantage."

"This is all too fucking crazy. You're Internal Affairs. You investigate bad cops. Don't jeopardize everything you have."

"What the hell do I have? I have nothing. I've lost everything. My wife. My son. They have me in their crosshairs. I'm not going to hang around like a sitting duck to see how it plays out."

"So, what's the plan? You want them to come to you? Make the next move, right? Like as bait? Is that it?"

McNeal nodded. "That's exactly it."

"You're going after Graff?"

"I want him to think that I'm coming for him. And see where it leads me."

"You're going down a dark road, Jack."

McNeal took his handgun out of his waistband and stared long and hard at it. "I don't see any other way."

Forty

The brothers went their separate ways.

McNeal watched Peter reverse down his driveway, turn, and begin the long drive south on I-95 to New Jersey. His brother faced at least a two-and-a-half-hour journey, returning home without the family pet.

McNeal realized that his home in Westport was no longer safe. There could be cameras in the house. He could get an expert to look the place over. But that could be done another time. He had business to attend to first.

His gaze locked on a photo of him and his son. He crumpled under a heaviness in his heart. He had beaten himself up for years over his son's death.

McNeal knew he had changed since his son's death. He had kept the pain and the hurt inside. He hadn't wanted to communicate with anyone. Caroline had wanted to talk about it. He couldn't. He just couldn't.

He would walk on the beach, always alone, with his thoughts and grief. Only when he was out of sight would he allow himself to break down. He prayed some days that he wouldn't wake up. His wife hadn't been able to live with him anymore. He just worked, slept, and grieved. On and on, a vicious cycle. Eventually she left.

But his wife's sudden death had resurrected all the old feelings. He began to think more and more about his son. He wanted more than anything to expunge the rage. A black rage.

McNeal had never really gotten over his son's senseless death. It was all too much to bear. The pain—a sickening pain—had never really subsided in his heart. He just thought it had. He took his son's photo off the wall and kissed it. He stared at a boy fixed in time. A boy who would never grow old. A boy who would never become a man. "If I could bring you back, I would. I want you back. But Daddy will see you one day, I promise."

McNeal put the photo back on the wall and looked around the living room. It might be the last time he saw the place. He quickly filled a backpack with a change of clothes, some bottles of water, and snacks. He had three hundred dollars in cash, a wallet with three credit cards, and his two guns—his NYPD-issued Sig Sauer for when he was on duty and his Glock, his personal firearm.

McNeal placed the Sig Sauer and the ammo into a locked box in the trunk of his car. The Glock he tucked, locked and loaded, into his shoulder holster.

He headed back into the house and sat down on the sofa, watching TV, channel surfing for an hour or so, clearing his head.

He challenged himself to think about how far he was really prepared to go with this. Was he prepared to take the fight to *them*? The problem was that all he had was circumstantial evidence. It all pointed to Graff. But there was no proof that he was involved in the break-in. Even the CIA links to Feinstein didn't prove that Graff had authorized or was involved in the operation to discredit him. But McNeal knew Graff was behind it.

The problem was proving it.

McNeal picked up his cell phone and called Belinda Katz.

"Jack, I was going to call you later. I haven't heard from you for a couple of days. I was worried."

McNeal's breath sped up. His heart raced.

"Talk to me. What is it? This is what I'm here for."

"I haven't got much time."

"What do you mean?"

"I . . . I wanted you to know something before I embarked on a particular course of action."

"Jack, I'm concerned. I hope you won't do anything rash."

McNeal closed his eyes.

"What is it?"

"I found out my wife was murdered."

"What?"

"I believe it was organized by a man called Henry Graff."

"Why are you telling me this? Have you told the police?"

"Can you write that name down? And no, I haven't told the police. I don't know who I can trust. Henry Graff murdered my wife. If something happens to me, I want you to know that. And take it to the cops, do you understand? NYPD. Not the Feds."

"Where are you now?"

"Westport."

"I'll come up and see you."

"Not now. I have things to do."

"Like what?"

"Personal business."

"Jack, I sense you're in a very dark place. This man, Henry Graff . . . I would caution you against taking the law into your own hands. I would urge you to get treatment. We can resolve some of these feelings. We can find a path forward."

"I think I'm at the end of my rope."

"Please don't talk like that."

"Belinda, thanks for your time and help."

McNeal ended the call and realized he was shaking. A few moments later, his cell phone rang again, snapping him out of his thoughts.

"It's Peter."

McNeal's head was swimming. He checked his watch. His brother had been gone nearly an hour. "You must have nearly hit the city by now."

"Not far. Listen, I've been doing some thinking. We're going to do this together."

"This is my fight. I'll deal with it."

"I'm going to head home, freshen up, and we can meet up and talk things through. I have a couple of things I need to pick up on my way home."

"Peter, I love you, but you've got a family. Stay in New Jersey. I'll deal with this."

"I thought about this. It's not an easy decision. But you're my family too. I'm guessing you might be heading to DC?"

McNeal sighed. That was exactly what he had in mind. "I am going to head south."

"And do what?"

"Whatever it takes. That's what."

"You want to meet up later tonight? Midnight snack?"

"The truck stop diner?"

"That's the one."

"You got it. See you then."

"Take care, bro."

Forty-One

It was just after midnight on the long drive south.

McNeal spotted the neon sign for the Deepwater Diner at a truck stop a few minutes from the Delaware Memorial Bridge. He walked in, past a couple tables of truckers, and sat down at a booth away from the front window. He had arrived before his brother. He scanned the menu and ordered crab cakes and fries with a coffee. Within ten minutes he had been served and had finished eating.

He was on his third refill of black coffee when his brother arrived, backpack slung over his shoulder.

"Sorry I'm late, had to make a slight detour," Peter said as he sat. He put the backpack on the floor at his feet.

"You eat?"

Peter nodded. "Yeah, I'm fine." He indicated for the waitress to come over. "Strong black coffee, thank you."

A few moments later, they were both nursing coffees, the diner all but deserted after the truckers had drifted out.

Satisfied there was no one in earshot, Peter leaned closer and spoke in a whisper. "I think we got company," he said.

"Outside?"

Peter nodded. "When I pulled up, I waited for five minutes. An SUV with tinted windows pulled up. Virginia plates."

"That's not a crime."

"They were tailing me for forty miles, maybe more. But then they pulled away without getting out."

"Interesting. Could just be some guys headed down 95."

"I know what I saw. They were tailing me. I'll bet they pick up that tail when we leave here. Perhaps in another vehicle."

McNeal took a gulp of the hot coffee, feeling the jolt from the caffeine. "Here's where I'm at. If we head to Graff's tomorrow morning, he might just have his security goons throw us out."

"We could turn up to his house in Arlington?"

"I thought of that. He'll have cameras everywhere. And what will it look like? Two desperado cops, brothers, harassing him. He wins, we lose. And we're fucked."

Peter nodded. "So, what's the plan?"

"I've got two plans."

"What's the first one?"

"We keep driving and driving. We want Graff, if he and his crazy gang are monitoring our movements, to assume we're going after him. But he might think we're headed to the FBI."

"They might ambush you."

"I'm expecting them to. And if they do, on a major highway, they're increasing the odds that they'll get caught. These people operate in the shadows."

"It's a high-risk strategy."

"It's a provocation. They tried it with us, and they're getting a response. But my actions might very well initiate an overreaction."

"You don't know the end game."

"The beauty of this is that neither do they. They *will* respond. I guarantee it. But plans have a way of unraveling."

"You said you had two plans. What's the second?"

"I've got Feinstein's cell phone number. I have Graff's cell phone number."

"Okay . . ."

"This is a more proactive plan as opposed to the first, which is strictly reactive."

"What is it?"

"You heard of SMS spoofing?"

"Like text messages?"

"Exactly. The plan is I send a message as if it's coming from Feinstein, and I tell Graff that she wants to meet him somewhere. She has something for him."

"I'm with you. Whereabouts?"

"Graff was born and raised in Maryland. I think I could send a spoof text from Feinstein telling Graff Jack McNeal's been intercepted in Maryland after he got off the freeway."

"What if he doesn't take the bait?"

"Then we go with the first plan."

Peter pushed the backpack to Jack's feet. "Since it's high risk . . . thought you might like that."

"What is it?"

"Don't take it out here. This is going to go bad at some point. You're going to make contact with Graff, or whoever the fuck Graff has tasked with this."

"Possibly."

"Inside the backpack is an untraceable 9mm Glock."

"I've got a Glock."

"What happens if you have to use your gun? Do you really want to try and explain to Internal Affairs how a registered personal handgun, or even worse, your NYPD gun, killed someone, and you weren't in New York? This one is untraceable. No serial number. My militia guy also gave me an earpiece so I can communicate with you. State-of-the-art two-way radio, in case of bad cell phone reception. I've also got a sniper rifle."

"What for?"

"I'm going to cover your ass. If you manage to get Graff or one of his guys in your sights, I'll have him in my sights too. I'll cover you. I can take the fucker out, if need be. It's a backup."

McNeal shook his head. "Holy fuck."

Peter made a fist. "This is not going to end well." He looked at his watch. "I've got to get back to Jersey."

"Work?"

"Took a week's vacation time I'm owed. Doing renovations."

"What about the wife and kids?"

"With her mother. Until this blows over, I don't want them anywhere near the situation. Anyway, I might be able to take the heat off you by heading north, but I'll double back when I can. Where you planning for this to go down? Just so I know."

"Just outside Frederick. The Frederick Diner, three miles south of the town."

"I'll find it."

"Don't worry about me."

"You run into problems, you just need to holler." Peter got up from his seat. "Take care, bro."

McNeal watched his brother leave the diner. He sat alone for fifteen minutes. He left a twenty-dollar tip. Then he gathered up the backpack, got back in his car, and headed south in the dead of night.

Forty-Two

Graff was prowling his Arlington penthouse, unable to sleep, when his cell phone rang. He had been told that McNeal was headed south on I-95. It looked like the cop was going to take matters into his own hands. McNeal knew too much. And he posed a huge threat to Graff and the whole operation.

He let the cell ring.

The provocation of killing the dog had worked. The question was, what was the guy planning? Was McNeal going to try and ambush him? Kidnap him and take him to the cops? Maybe he just wanted to stay away from Westport, aware now that he was being watched? Maybe he was on his way to the Hoover Building with the information he had.

The cell phone kept on ringing. Eventually he answered, thinking it would be Feinstein with an update. "Yeah."

"Henry?" It was Nico, his most trusted lieutenant. A man he'd known since the invasion of Iraq. The black sites in Poland, Romania, Iraq—they had been in the same places.

"I thought you were going to call in the morning."

"I was. But something's coming up. Something that requires your attention."

"I'm listening."

"You asked me to keep an eye on Karen."

Graff anticipated what Nico was going to say. "I need to know if I can really trust her."

"Well, that's for you to judge."

"What do you mean?"

"I'm sorry to be the bearer of bad news. But you've got a problem with her."

Graff swallowed hard, a sickness deep in his stomach. His head swam, and now he felt nauseous. He had pictured Feinstein as his wife. She fit the bill, and he had long admired her. But he had started having feelings for her. Feelings that had grown since his wife's death.

Feinstein was that rare find—a woman as cold as ice who he enjoyed being with. A woman who understood him. A woman he found bearable. But he remembered what his father always said: *Trust no one. Friends are enemies in waiting. Love is death.*

"She's playing you, Henry," Nico said.

"In what way?"

Graff trusted Nicoletti implicitly to be a man who held secrets, but he was also a natural-born sadist. Nico loved waterboarding prisoners, watching them scream in pain. He loved getting in their heads. He loved watching the men and women being stripped naked and filmed. The guy was a grade-A psychopath. And he was perfect for his job. If Nico was telling Graff he had a problem with Feinstein, Graff had to listen. This man was the number-one person in his operation he trusted, to the exclusion of all others.

"I don't feel comfortable even talking to you about such matters. Do you mind if I send you the surveillance photos?"

Graff's heart sank. His worst fears were coming to life. A fear of betrayal.

"Send what you have."

Graff ended the call. He experienced a terrible emptiness in his gut. He sensed that something was going badly wrong.

A ping sounded from his encrypted email.

Graff double-clicked on the email. Eight photos opened up. They all showed Karen Feinstein *in flagrante* with Andrew Forbes, a man whose father Graff had served with. The father was Special Forces, CIA, before he formed his own billion-dollar management consultancy in DC. The son was part of the jigsaw. The first piece in the jigsaw. But he had never imagined the son, and certainly not Feinstein, betraying his trust.

His mind flashed back to the photos of his wife Karen had shown him. The compromised, sickening photos he couldn't erase from his memory. The photos with a movie star half her age. That one had hurt the most.

It was happening again.

The more he thought about all the betrayals, the more detached he became. Graff absorbed a numbness, his way of dealing with such situations. The years and years of blood, filth, and corpses had filled his soul with a darkness he was unable to expunge, a cancer devouring his very being.

There was nothing left. No love. Just duty.

A duty to protect. To serve. To sacrifice.

Graff stared out his windows across the floodlit monuments. He began to feel a sense of his own mortality. Whatever strength he had slowly ebbed away.

He called Nico.

"I'm sorry, Henry," he said. "How do you want it to play out?"

"I'll figure something out. In the meantime, we need to get McNeal out of the way. We take him out first and then we can focus on her and that little fucker."

Graff ended the call as he sensed he was losing his bearings. All of a sudden, the world of intrigue he had inhabited and immersed himself in for so long was collapsing around him. The people within the intelligence community he trusted were gone, and alliances he had built over the years, were crumbling.

His mind flashed images of Feinstein with Forbes, the preppy kid. The confident, smart, risk-taking young man, not too unlike himself. But whereas Forbes had contented himself with being the President's bag carrier, sashaying around the Hamptons with his Ivy League friends, skiing in Europe in the winter, Graff had joined the American military. He had learned to kill. He had a higher calling. Maybe Forbes had once had what it took to become Special Forces like his father. But Graff believed that time had come and gone. Andrew Forbes had gotten soft. He didn't know about sacrifice. Real sacrifice. He would never sacrifice himself for the greater good.

A few minutes later Graff's cell phone rang.

"Henry, it's Karen."

A mixture of grief, anger, and jealousy ran through his veins. But he detected an iciness still running through his blood. "Nice to hear from you," he said. Graff was good at concealing his true feelings. "Got the latest?"

"We've got a team in place. We can deal with this situation before it reaches DC."

"Method?"

"Cop car. Drug stop. Drugs found. Shot. It's going to look like McNeal went bad."

Graff was quiet for a few moments. "I like it. Very elegant."

"Do we have the green light? I'm talking McNeal neutralized. Problem solved."

Graff sighed long and hard. He closed his eyes and could see that Karen's next target could be him. He could see it with startling clarity. McNeal's investigation might be ended with the Internal Affairs cop being killed. But what about the files and documents

McNeal would have stored? The Feds might have ignored the evidence. What if that changed?

He knew too much. He knew it all. He knew it went all the way to the top. He also knew Karen would have no compunction about saving her own skin. He would have to be sacrificed. At some stage. Maybe not tonight. Maybe not for a while. He had no way to know for sure how it would end. But eventually, they would come for him. He too would die.

"Henry? Are you there?"

"We're sure he's headed for DC?"

"One hundred percent."

"You think he's headed for me?"

"It's a real possibility. He's either headed for you or to the FBI. Going straight there with evidence. And then what?"

"I'd considered that as well."

"Either way, we have to deal with him. The stalling has only gotten us so far. Are we good to go?"

Graff squinted, tears in his eyes, thinking suddenly of his father, an unloving, brutal, sadistic bastard who he had worshipped. The type of man he himself had become. And for what? He had operated in the shadows for so long that he was immune to pain. Or at least he thought he was. Her treachery was something he hadn't imagined. Not by a long shot. She seemed to calm his soul. He loved Feinstein's high intelligence as much as her high cheekbones. But the reality was he had been played.

The hunter had become the hunted.

It was at that moment that Graff himself realized the fate that awaited him. It wouldn't stop at just Jack McNeal. Or Caroline McNeal. He knew the story. He saw in staggering detail how it was going to play out.

Graff might have reached the end of his usefulness. He sensed he would eventually become a liability. He knew how Karen operated.

Why the hell hadn't he seen it before now? He was expendable. Just like all the rest. For the first time, he was expendable. He closed his eyes for a few moments as he mused on that point.

"Henry, you got quiet on me. Are you okay? Are you conflicted about this?"

"Where is the stop?"

"We're going to flag him down just outside Calverton. We have a place in mind."

"Double tap to the head?"

"What else."

Graff sighed.

"Is this a go?"

"What's the ETA to when he hits Calverton?"

"Ninety minutes, give or take. The team is in place."

"Go green. I repeat, it's a green."

Forty-Three

McNeal drove twenty miles north of Baltimore, anticipating when his GPS would be pinged. His cell phone rang in the cupholder. He expected it to be Peter. But it wasn't. It was Graff.

"Jack, I'm sorry to bother you so late."

McNeal knew at that moment he was not only in mortal danger, but that his plan had kicked in. He needed to roll with it now, come what may. "What's on your mind?"

"I've found out quite a bit about you. The thing is, I don't know what you know about me, Mr. McNeal. But I suspect you know a lot more than you're telling me."

"Go on."

"And I'm guessing you harbor negative feelings toward me. Would I be correct?"

McNeal let the silence linger.

"I suspect you want to kill me. I suspect you believe I may have been involved in the death of my wife."

"You want to get to the point, Mr. Graff?"

"I know you're headed down I-95. Maybe you're headed south to the Carolina beaches. But maybe not."

McNeal glanced in his rearview mirror. A motorbike was in sight behind him. He assessed whether he was being followed, possibly all the way down from Westport. "Now we're getting somewhere."

"I'm trying to figure it out. You're either heading my way or you're going to the Feds. Which one is it?"

"A man is free to do what he wants in this country. At least the last time I checked."

"Thank God for that, I say."

"What's on your mind, Graff?"

"I want to meet up."

McNeal was caught off guard. He hadn't expected that. He had expected a set-up. But maybe this was it. Was this a trap? Almost certainly. Had to be. "And why would you want to meet up? You gonna confess your sins?"

Graff sighed. "You're not a million miles from the truth, what you said. I have sinned."

"I'm not a fucking priest. You want to talk?"

"I want to talk. I want you to know some things."

"What kind of things?"

"I'll get to that. There's a lot you need to know. Plans that are in place."

"I'm surprised at you, Graff."

"In what way?"

"I expected a more dramatic way to intercept me."

Graff was quiet for a few moments. "I can help you."

"Is that right? How?"

"Jack, right now I am the only person who can help you stay alive."

Forty-Four

McNeal passed a sign telling him he was approaching Baltimore. "I don't know what you're trying to pull, Graff."

"I don't blame you for thinking I might have ulterior motives. But I'll say it again: I can keep you alive."

McNeal stayed quiet.

"If you don't listen to me, there's a very good chance you'll be dead before dawn."

McNeal drove on, glancing in his rearview mirror. He changed lanes. He spotted the motorbike four cars back from his, keeping in his slipstream. Just as it had been for the last ten miles.

"Are you still there, McNeal?"

"I'm still here."

"I give you my word. This is not a trap. I want to help you *avoid* a trap. If you keep driving down that highway, you are dead. Do what I say, and you can live. I just want to meet up and explain a few things. You deserve to have some answers."

McNeal had to make a snap decision. He suspected it was indeed a trap. But if it was, why would Graff give him a heads-up? He decided to go with it. He had a location in mind.

"You name the place. Where do you want to meet?"

"You need to get onto the Baltimore Beltway."

"I'm not far away," Graff said.

"Then take I-70 west until you hit Frederick."

"I know it well."

McNeal checked the map on his phone. "After Frederick, get off at Exit 52 and take 15 south toward Jefferson. A town in Maryland. There's an old gas station three miles past the town."

"I grew up around there."

"So, you're on home turf. One final thing, Graff."

"What's that?"

"Don't bring any friends. I'll be watching you."

McNeal drove on until he pulled into a truck stop just off the highway in the crummy O'Donnell Heights neighborhood of Baltimore. He scanned the area. The place was crawling with junkies. He got out of his car, making sure it was securely locked. He slung his backpack over his shoulder, the unlicensed Glock hidden in the back of his waistband. He headed to the restroom, splashed some cold water on his face. He gathered his thoughts for a few moments. His heart was racing.

McNeal headed back outside to the parking lot.

A panhandler on the ground called up to him, "Hey, man, you got a spare buck? I'm starving."

McNeal handed him a five-dollar bill. "Get yourself some soup."

"Bless you, sir."

McNeal walked on. He knew the guy with rotting teeth was more likely to get a bag of meth.

"Hey, Jack, hold on!" A shout from behind.

McNeal spun round and saw his brother. "Peter, what's going on?"

"Sorry to spook you."

"What the hell, man?"

"I've been tailing you."

"That was you?"

"I lost the tail, so I ditched the battery from my phone and turned around and headed south. I've been with you the last few miles."

"Goddamn."

Peter sighed as his gaze took in the derelicts. "Nice place to hang out, Jack."

"I got a call."

"From who?"

"Graff."

"What?"

"He wants to meet up."

"Henry Graff? No fucking way."

McNeal nodded. "Says he wants to talk."

"It's a trap."

"Maybe. But I don't think so."

"How come?"

"The best-laid plans you don't see coming. This, I see."

"It could still be a trap."

"I sense it's not."

"You sense? What the hell does that mean? What's wrong with you?"

McNeal nodded. "Think about it. Would a guy like that do something as crude as 'let's meet up'? Besides, I've told him where we should meet up. The diner I told you about near Frederick."

"I don't know. The guy sounds nuts. And dangerous."

"He's dangerous, alright. There was something about his tone of voice and the fact that he called me that tells me something has changed. Otherwise, why would he tell me I was going to be killed if I continued driving south?"

"It could still be an elaborate plan."

"It would be overly elaborate. The best plans rely on simplicity."

"Could be playing a double game. I don't know."

McNeal closed his eyes for a moment, his heart racing.

"Jack, it's not too late to head home. You don't have to do this. You have nothing to prove."

"I'm going to see him."

"If you do, it won't end well."

"Maybe."

"I'm telling you, if you go there, he will take you out. Guaranteed. You need to be prepared. The guy's a trained killer."

"I can take care of this."

"I know you can. But I'm going with you."

"I said it was just me and him."

"So, you lied. Since I'm here, let me go scout the place. Eyes and ears for you in case it *is* a trap. I'll watch him from afar with the sniper rifle."

"That wasn't the deal I made with him."

"We'll both go. He's not the only one who's a trained killer."

Forty-Five

McNeal drove back onto the highway. His mind raced, as he squinted against the oncoming headlights. He was going to meet Graff. He could be killed. Maybe Graff's crew were lying in wait. His reactive plan, his plan B, was now in play, but not in a way he had expected.

The lights of oncoming cars flashed past him. "Fuck!" It was happening fast. Unfolding like a fevered dream.

The miles rolled by. Deeper and deeper into the dark, verdant Maryland countryside. Jefferson. A place he'd never been to. He wondered just how well Graff knew the territory.

The more he thought about the situation in which he had become embroiled, a situation of his own making, the more McNeal began to ask himself what the hell was wrong with him. Was he blinded by grief? Was Belinda Katz rightly concerned for his mental state? Was he suffering a breakdown?

Was this a fucked-up mind game Graff was playing with him? It was true he wanted answers about Caroline's death, but he knew better than anyone that taking the law into one's own hands was never the smart move. Never the right choice. McNeal had let himself be led by emotion. By gut instinct. He was definitely not using his head.

He wondered if the burning rage he felt at his son's senseless death was fueling his desire for some kind of revenge. Some kind of justice. Or maybe his recklessness was just part and parcel of his personality, something he had kept hidden from most.

The more he thought about it, the more he questioned if he even wanted to live anymore. Did he have a death wish? Maybe he didn't care if he lived or died. Was that it? Had he become like his dead former partner, Juan Gomez? Did he want someone to end his life? Was that the driving force?

On and on the questions mounted, with no answers in sight.

McNeal had investigated hundreds of cops who had embarked on similarly hotheaded adventures, all ending in terrible mistakes. Cops stalking estranged wives. Psychotic cops roaming the streets in the dead of night, screaming and hollering at anyone that would listen. Suicidal cops who wanted their partners to put them out of their misery.

McNeal knew that if all his layers were peeled back, the one constant was the loss of his son. He had never gotten over that. Never would. He should have tried to come to terms with it. He should have done the therapy sessions. But he hadn't. Instead he kept all his emotions in check, as he had been trained to do. But the animal instincts were always there.

McNeal drove on. Headlights pierced the nighttime highway gloom. He got closer and closer. He passed a sign for Frederick.

He turned off the highway and drove into town.

The two-way radio buzzed and he pulled over. "Yeah?"

"Jack, the gas station?"

"Yeah?"

"I'm here. Up the road from it."

"Is he there yet?"

"No one's here. It's abandoned."

"What do you mean, abandoned? It's not open?"

"I mean it's an old, run-down place. There are old gas pumps still there but nothing else. The shell of what was once a diner. It's empty. The place looks like it's been like that for years, maybe decades."

"What else?"

"I see there's a restroom adjacent to the diner. A pay phone next to that."

McNeal's mind raced as he tried to figure out a plan. "You can see the pay phone clearly with your night sights?"

"Got it."

"What's the number?"

"Hang on . . . got my hunting binoculars with night vision in the trunk."

McNeal waited for a few moments as he got closer.

"Bingo! Got the number."

"Write that down. Then text me the number."

"What's the plan?"

"You wait where you are with your lights off. You let me know when he arrives. I'll text him telling him to pick up the pay phone when it rings. And then I'll call that number."

"I like it."

"It's the best we've got. I'll bounce him to a place of our choosing farther down the road. And that's where I'll be."

Forty-Six

McNeal slowed as he drove past the abandoned gas station. It was a relic from the sixties. Faded Pepsi ads peeled off the windows. He looked to his left and saw bean fields. Somewhere down there perched his brother. He checked the luminous display on his dashboard. It showed 3:23.

He drove on for about a mile.

A few moments later, his cell phone vibrated. A text from Peter.

Porsche Carrera with one male driver just pulled in.

McNeal's heart beat hard as he drove on. Up ahead, beside a telephone pole, a dirt road had been illuminated by pale moonlight. He turned there, down the bone-dry, rutted earth road. The bean field seemed to go on forever. The middle of nowhere. This was good.

He stopped and switched off his lights.

He had perfect sight to the old gas station just over a mile away, the lights of the Porsche visible.

McNeal texted Graff. *Pick up the pay phone when it rings.* He then called the number. It rang for nearly a minute before it was picked up.

"Jack?"

"Turn off your lights. Leave your keys on the passenger seat."

"Why?"

"This is how we're going to work it. You're going to walk a mile on the path adjacent to the road until you get to a dirt road marked by a telephone pole. You walk up that dirt road. I'll be waiting for you."

McNeal ended the call. A few moments later he got a text from his brother. *Our guy hung up the phone. He's walking.*

He replied, *I'm in position. Dirt road, one mile out of town. Turn into it. That's where I am. Follow with lights off. But also find a spot behind the gas station to get Graff's car out of sight soon. Keys on passenger seat.*

He took out the unlicensed Glock. There was no safety on the gun. He was locked and loaded.

Twelve minutes later, the sound of heavy footsteps approached. McNeal crouched behind his car.

A silhouetted figure came into view, slowly approaching, as if tentative.

"I'm alone." The voice of Graff.

McNeal stood up, gun aimed at Graff's head. "Nice of you to turn up."

"Easy there," he said. "Well, this is an out-of-the-way spot. I think I played in these fields as a boy."

McNeal leaned forward and expertly frisked Graff. He found a handgun and put it in his pocket. "Nothing personal, Graff. I like to know who I'm dealing with. Hands on head. Slowly." He found a cell phone in a trouser pocket. A new Nokia. Face recognition. He shoved the cell phone in front of Graff's face, and it unlocked. He tapped in a new passcode. He took a step back, gun still trained on the imposing man, both cloaked in darkness.

Graff put his hands on his head.

McNeal scrolled through the contacts. He saw Nicoletti's number. He committed it to memory. "You wanted to talk. So, talk."

Graff turned slightly. "This is not a trap."

"We'll see."

"I know you hate me. And I don't blame you for hating me. I would if I was in your shoes."

"Cut the bullshit."

"I'm here to help you stay alive but also to help you get some closure."

"Are you fucking kidding me?"

"Life comes at us in sudden, violent, unexpected ways. I wish I could turn the clock back. But that's the way of the world, I guess."

"Listen here, you bastard. Cut the psychobabble. Talk. Why are you here? Are we talking remorse? You double-crossing someone? Or are you setting me up? Which one is it?"

"There are highly trained individuals who were tasked with taking you out after stopping you on the highway if you had continued down that route."

"Who are they? And where are they now?"

"Former CIA operatives. They're in position close to Calverton. Traffic stop. I've bought you some time. But they are on their way. A two-man team."

McNeal didn't know what to believe. He couldn't trust Graff. But he sensed the man might, on this occasion, be telling the truth. Or maybe part of the truth. But it was only part of the jigsaw.

"That's what I wanted to tell you. That's why I'm here."

"Why should I believe you?"

"You have no reason to believe me. I understand that."

McNeal searched around, seeing if Graff was waiting for backup to arrive. He braced himself for an ambush. "Let's pretend that what you're saying is true. Why on God's earth are you telling me?"

"Penance . . . atonement."

"Atonement for what?"

"My sins."

McNeal thought his words sounded genuine. But then again, some people were very good at appearing to sound sincere and genuine. Like psychopaths.

"My mortal sins."

McNeal waited for Graff to make his point.

"I don't want to kill you. I thought I did. But I don't."

"What changed?"

"I thought I could trust someone. A woman. Turns out my trust was misplaced. I've been played. And I can see it all as clear as day. I don't have long before they come for me."

"Who's 'they'?"

Graff shook his head.

"I said, who's 'they'?"

"The powers that be. Forces at work which can devour people. Shadowy forces. I'm talking deep state."

"Weren't you part of the deep state?"

"I was part of it. But no one ever gets out of such operations unscathed. Psychologically. And eventually physically. There is no escape. I realize that now."

"Did you have a part in my wife's death?"

"I organized your wife's death. And my wife's death. For that, I'm sorry."

McNeal's body tensed. It was as if Graff wanted to be shot in cold blood.

"You have every reason to want to kill me. And I wouldn't blame you if you did. But this goes way beyond just me."

"Did you kill my wife?"

"I had people kill your wife."

McNeal let a black anger stir within him. "How was she killed?"

"She was drugged. And then she was placed in the Potomac."

McNeal pressed the gun tight up against Graff's forehead, which was slick with sweat.

"Go ahead, do it!" Graff barked. "Why don't you?"

"I want to know more."

"What do you want to know?"

"Why did you kill your wife? Did you give the order?"

"I gave the final go-ahead. My wife . . . my late wife often laughed at me. Flaunted her affairs. Talked about who she was having sex with, who she wanted to have sex with. She fucked pop stars. Movie stars. Businessmen. Businesswomen. Black. White. Made no difference. She fucked them all. And she fucked politicians. People with influence on Capitol Hill."

McNeal pressed the gun tighter to Graff's head.

"I worried I was going to be humiliated in the eyes of the world. She taunted me. She said she was going to tell the world what she was like. What I was like."

McNeal clenched his teeth, venom coursing through his veins.

"My wife knew secrets. About me. About my world."

"What kind of secrets?"

"The shadowy world in which I operate. The politicians who contract me. She tried to blackmail politicians. She took pictures of herself with these men. And she left them on our kitchen table. Our children saw them. The nannies saw them. She was shameless."

"So, she deserved to die?"

Graff sighed. "Yes, she did."

"For her behavior? Her treachery?"

"One of my tasks, what my company does, is to safeguard this nation and its secrets. I've abided by that principle, always. Don't you get it? It's about safeguarding this great nation of ours. And the men who lead us."

"No matter the cost?"

"No matter the cost. Precisely."

"Why are you telling me all this?"

"I'm sacrificing myself. So you know. Before you kill me."

McNeal's hand tightened on his gun.

"I know you want to kill me, Jack. I'd want to do the same thing. You know what I see when I look into your eyes?"

"What?"

"I see a man with his own secrets and ghosts from your past never far from the surface."

McNeal was taken aback for a few moments. "Don't play mind games with me; you're so full of shit. You don't know the first thing about me."

"That's where you're wrong. I know everything there is to know about Jack McNeal. Staten Island, old-school cop father; wife the supersmart political journalist who probably outgrew you, if you're honest with yourself. And your dead son."

McNeal pressed the Glock tight to the fleshy part of Graff's forehead.

"I know what happened at the party. The stray bullet ricochet. Your son died. I wouldn't have been able to hold the line like you have for so long. I wouldn't have been able to deal with that pain."

"Shut the fuck up!"

"Your cop partner did it, waving his gun around. He was an idiot. And you killed your partner after what he did. In cold blood. You did the right thing. But don't kid yourself. You have blood on your hands too, Jack."

McNeal seethed.

"I read all about it. And I began to understand you better. You're not just a great cop; you're fearless. Without fear or favor. That partner was an Iraq veteran with a wife and three kids, but you had the nerve to take the fucker down. I admire that. Your NYPD partner was suicidal. He'd seen too much. He wanted suicide by cop. Very selfish, if you ask me. But not just any cop. He wanted *you* to kill him."

McNeal's mind flashed back to that hot night. A night he had killed someone. He realized now that Graff too wanted to be killed. He was trying to provoke him. Suicide by cop. He could see it all now.

"I'll tell you why he did it, Jack. He was jealous of you. And he wanted you to be put through the NYPD wringer. Internal Affairs would be crawling all over the case. He wrote it all down, didn't he? How he wanted to be more like you. He was a lost soul, he said. He wanted to be a hero cop. But he realized that would never happen. He was jealous that you were on the fast track. You were smart. You arrested more perps than anyone. You were a superstar. He couldn't stand it anymore. He wanted to be put out of his misery. I understand those very same feelings. Does that surprise you?"

"It doesn't interest me."

"You say that . . . but that's not true. That's why you turned up. You were intrigued. I pressed a button. And you came to me."

"Wrong. You came to me."

"Fact is, you're an ice-cold killer. You pretend you're not like me. But you are. You're so like me, it hurts. You're me twenty years ago. Idealistic. Tough. Uncompromised. A lot of water has gone under the bridge in my life. Now the same thing is happening to you."

McNeal motioned with the gun for Graff to get down. "On your knees, hands on your head."

Graff complied, bones creaking. "Are you going to kill me? Here? In a fucking bean field."

"Not before I know the full story. I'm not leaving here until I know the truth."

Graff let loose a guttural laugh. "Gimme a fucking break, McNeal. What is the truth? There is no such goddamn thing."

"You're protecting someone. Not just our country, but an individual, aren't you, Graff?"

"You're a very perceptive man. Smartest detective in Internal Affairs."

McNeal's finger tightened on the trigger.

"I think you're wasted there. A man of principle. Stoic. A man like you can make enemies. Was that why you transferred to Internal Affairs? The locker room talk of cops not to your liking?"

"I'm asking the questions. You're protecting an individual. A powerful individual. You going to tell me? Or are you going to take that to the grave?"

Graff shook his head. "I wish I'd gotten to know you before. I like you."

"Go to hell."

"Speaking of which, are you going to kill me?"

"I might. Is that what you really want? For me to blow your head off? Is that what you're counting on? You want to neutralize me by making me the triggerman? And I would be implicated in my wife's murder."

"Very perceptive. Actually, yes, that is exactly what I was counting on."

McNeal had thought as much.

"Just kill me!" Graff shouted.

"Who are you protecting? Was it someone fucking your wife? Who was it? A friend of yours? Someone important?"

Graff bowed his head like a lame dog.

"Give me a name. Who? Who are you protecting? Who was fucking your wife?"

"Oh for fuck's sake, kill me now!"

"Not before you tell me the truth. You sent Nicoletti to kill my wife, didn't you?"

"I had to, Jack. She knew the story. The whole goddamn story."

"Who are you protecting?"

"They'll come for you. I see it now. They will come for you. You'll be set up too. The trail will land at your door. You will take the fall. Can't you see that?"

"Did someone order you to kill my wife?"

"I am a dutiful soldier."

"Whatever the fuck that means."

"People like you will never know about sacrifice. Real sacrifice. How necessary it is. Do you think this country would be as great as it is without sacrifice? Without lives lost?"

McNeal pressed the gun even tighter to Graff's skull. "You will answer me, you sick fuck, so help me God."

"I have sacrificed. Lord knows I've sacrificed. For my country. All for America. I've sacrificed relationships, my marriage, and my sanity, and for what? Don't you get it?"

"Get what?"

"I'm protecting the quarterback."

"We're talking in analogies now, huh?"

"The guy who makes the plays. Makes the calls. And takes the hits."

McNeal stared down at the shaking, tragic figure on his knees. His insides grew cold. His brain was getting the signal. He could see now what this was all about.

"I was approached by people. They showed me a picture of my wife in . . . compromising positions."

"With who?"

"So many people. But there was one in particular."

McNeal wanted him to say it.

"I did it all to protect him."

"Say it! Say his name!"

"The President of the United States, that's who! He was fucking my wife."

McNeal froze in horror.

"Now do you understand what you're dealing with?"

"The President? The President was fucking your wife?"

"Yes."

"What else?"

"The people who approached me said it was mutually beneficial. My wife wouldn't cause me or the President any further embarrassment. But you need to know one thing: killing your wife wasn't my idea. I swear."

McNeal's thoughts careened around his head. He thought of his wife's last moments. Her final moments before she drowned. He pulled out his cell phone, turned the flash on. He started to record, gun trained on Graff. "Henry Graff, who ordered the murder of your wife and my late wife, Caroline McNeal?"

Graff shook his head, eyes closed. "Someone close to the President."

"Who? Give me a name?"

"I don't have a name. The person approached Nico, who in turn spoke to me. Inside track. That's how it started. He passed on the photos of my wife and the President. Nico acted as the link between them and me."

"Where does he live?"

"Nico? He's from Warwick, New York. He has a place there. Actually, I have an address."

Graff kept one hand on his head and used the other to reach into the back of his shirt collar.

McNeal saw the glint of steel.

Graff lunged forward, arms outstretched, penknife in hand.

Time stood still.

McNeal's mind flashed back to when he had killed his partner. The night his son died. A split second. Then he squeezed the trigger. The shot rang out. The blood and brains erupted out of a small hole in Graff's forehead, his body collapsing into a heap on the dirt road.

Forty-Seven

The seconds that followed were a sickening blur for McNeal. He stared down long and hard at the body of the man who had organized his wife's murder, watching blood pooling around Graff's head in the near darkness. Time stood still. He became aware that someone had started speaking to him.

"Jack!"

McNeal snapped back to reality as his brother ran up to him.

"What the holy fuck, Jack?"

"He went for my gun. The guy had a death wish. He wanted to die. He had a knife."

"Holy mother of God."

"He knew about my partner. About how I killed him. And he taunted me. He wanted to die the same way. He wanted me to take him down. Fuck!"

"We'll figure this out. We can deal with this."

McNeal shook his head. "This is not your fight, Peter. Get the hell out of here."

"Jack, you're holding the gun I gave you."

The blood seeped toward his shoes. McNeal took a step back.

"Know what he said? He said his wife was having an affair with the President. His wife was fucking the President."

"What?"

"That's what he said. Sophie Meyer was fucking the President. He had pictures. And he was approached to do something about it. That's how this all started. Now he's sacrificing himself. He said he thought he'd be next. He saved me too. Said there was an ambush waiting for me."

"Listen to me—"

"The guy wanted to die. This was his way of putting me in the picture. He said he wanted to save me, but what he really wanted was to embroil me in the whole shitshow. He also wanted me to kill him. The bastard lunged at me with the knife. He knew I would have to take him down."

Peter shook his head. "You can explain to the cops how it all got out of hand. Here's the evidence you had pointing to Graff being involved in your wife's death. We can salvage this."

"Not possible. That's not how this is going to play out."

"We'll get a great lawyer. We'll own up to it."

"You think a jury would be sympathetic? Think about it. I killed my NYPD partner. Now I've killed this former army hero in cold blood. A courtroom will bury me."

"For the love of God, you need to think straight."

Jack grabbed Peter by the arm. "Listen to me. There's another way. It might work. But we need to get lucky. I'll get rid of the body."

"Have you lost your fucking mind? You're going to dispose of the body? We're cops. We need to face up to this."

It was about self-preservation. Pure and simple. That was McNeal's rationale. But it was the same bullshit rationale he listened to day in and day out from bad cops.

"He pulled a knife on you, so you had to kill him. How about we plant a gun? Drop the Glock on the scene. It's a suicide."

"Not an option."

"You're the smart one. Don't do this. We could drive off now."

"I'm going to be arrested and face some serious time in jail. I'm not prepared for that. Besides, there's too much evidence linking me to Graff. That's why I need to get rid of this fucking body."

Peter rubbed his face hard, shaking his head. "In the name of God. Jack, let's drop the gun. It's a simple suicide. It'll work."

"I'm not going to take the fall for the man who killed my wife. I don't regret killing him. He deserved it."

"This is not you talking."

"If a body is found, they'll start piecing it together. Slowly. It might look like suicide, but the cops wouldn't leave it at that. Forensics would say that, from the angle of the bullet entry wound, it couldn't have been suicide."

"Fuck."

"You see what I'm saying. We need to move the body."

"In that case, I'm going to help you."

"This is not your fight."

"Shut the fuck up. It is now."

McNeal's mind raced.

"Let's think about this. There's no crime without a body. It would just be a missing person."

McNeal bowed his head, realizing the chain of events had spiraled out of control. He'd lost his goddamn mind. That's what had happened. He'd gone insane. Would that be how the court would see it? He was mad. Disordered thinking? Was that it? But the truth was he thought cogently. Rationally. He had killed without compunction. Maybe he did have something in common with Graff. Maybe his own grief had consumed him.

The body had to be moved. And it would be best to have some help. Another line being crossed.

"Jack!" Peter snapped. "Your car!"

"What?"

"We'll use your car to get the body out of here. The trunk of your car."

"Has to be." McNeal's insides had been ripped to shreds. "What the fuck am I doing? I should be calling this in, but I don't want to serve out my days in a state penitentiary because of that fucker."

"The time for second thoughts has come and gone."

Jack nodded. "Let's get rid of the fucker."

He took a few moments to take some deep breaths and gather his thoughts. The smell of earth and swine manure carried across the stifling night air. He popped open his trunk.

Peter reversed his car and pulled up beside Jack. He also popped open his trunk. He took out the shovel and two bags of rock salt. He opened the first bag and poured out the contents over the spilled blood. He poured the second bag on top. And he shoveled dirt on that, covering it up.

Jack shone the flashlight on the mound of rust-colored dirt and salt grit. "I can't see any visible signs of blood."

"It wouldn't pass the luminol test." Peter put his shovel and empty bags of rock salt in the trunk.

Jack cleared his dry throat. "We need to move quick. We need to wrap up the body. But we also need to think how we can dispose of it."

"What about the old-school method?"

McNeal bent over, sick. He knew what his brother was saying. "Where are we going to get what we need at this time of night?"

"I've been renovating our house, remember. I've got stuff in the trunk. DIY stuff. Builders' equipment. Tools. It's all in the trunk of my car."

Peter reached inside the trunk and hauled out polyethylene waterproof sheeting, rolls of duct tape, a five-gallon bucket, two large bottles of water, and a large bag of quick-drying cement.

Jack McNeal retched.

"You know what I'm saying?"

McNeal had worked a case a few years back when a gang member had washed up several years after being killed in New York. The cement shoes method of body disposal. "We're really doing this?"

"Yes or no, are you in?" Peter said.

McNeal shook his head at his pig-headed, stubborn, and fiercely loyal younger brother. "Fuck it. Let's do this."

Peter stared down at the body. "Grab the feet."

McNeal taped up the body and tied Graff's hands behind his back as Peter tied the feet together. Peter poured the cement into the bucket, then the water.

Peter stirred the contents of the bucket with a stick as it thickened. "We need to do this right. Slowly."

McNeal reached under Graff's arms as his brother took the feet. He held the dead body upright as his brother carefully placed the feet into the bucket. "Nice and easy. It needs time to set."

The sound of their breathing and the smell of gun smoke lingered in the dank air. Forty-five long minutes later, they stood in the middle of a soy field as the cement had solidly encased Graff's feet and shoes.

The brothers wrapped more sheeting around Graff's upright body, like he was a mummy. Then they duct taped it all up.

Jack was breathing hard. "You okay?" Peter asked.

"I'm fine."

The brothers lifted the weighty Graff and the extra cement into the trunk carefully.

Jack slammed the trunk shut. "Let's move."

They both checked over the road again, the flashlight showing what looked like a pile of dirt and salt. It would be dry in a few hours. The wind would blow it all out of sight.

"Did you get Graff's car out of the way?"

"Like you asked, I put it behind the gas station. I found an old tarp and covered it up."

"It will be discovered eventually."

"Not for weeks, months . . . who knows."

"Which should hopefully have degraded any fingerprints or DNA trace."

"We've got to take the chance."

"Agreed." Jack decided: "We need to get this fucking shitshow on the road." Jack hugged his brother. "I didn't mean for any of this to happen."

"Shit happens. We'll deal with it."

Jack got into his car, the body wrapped up in the trunk. He took out his cell phone and checked for any major lakes nearby. He saw there was a major reservoir about forty-five minutes away, Liberty Reservoir. The average depth was fifty-nine feet. He checked Google Maps. He put down his window and Peter did the same. "We head back east and then head up to Liberty Reservoir."

"There?"

"You got any better suggestions?"

"Are you sure?"

"No, but we need to act. Let's head there. There's a bridge over the reservoir, according to the map. And there's a road that crosses it. We stop, as if we've broken down, and dump the body."

Peter reached out his window and handed him what looked like a fob. "Remove the cigarette lighter in the car and plug this GPS blocker into the power socket."

"You're crazier than I thought."

Forty-Eight

The red taillights of Peter's car pierced the darkness on the road up ahead.

Jack stared at the lights as his dark thoughts and fears ricocheted around his head. They could be stopped at any moment, and the body in his trunk would be found.

He wondered if it could all have been different. Maybe he should have engaged the services of an attorney to investigate his wife's death. Instead, he had plunged into the depths of depravity. He had succumbed.

He tried to rationalize his actions. Graff had engaged him in a fight to the death. He needed to kill or be killed. To bring him to that point, the bastards had been toying with him. Lights on and off. The dead dog. The blowback for reaching out to Bone at the FBI.

The more he thought about it, the more amazed he was at the lengths Graff and his people were prepared to go. He thought it telling that an FBI agent had gotten transferred back to the Hoover Building after he handed over damning documents. And then, when McNeal reached out again to Bone, he had been met by a wall of silence. Maybe Graff knew the documents would never see the light of day. Maybe his reach extended to the upper echelons of the FBI.

The questions kept on coming. The cover-up was wide-ranging, perhaps encompassing elements within the FBI, the CIA, other players within the American government.

McNeal thought back to what Graff had said. The former CIA operative had been approached by Nico, a wet work specialist, who had been contacted by someone close to the President. It was all too much to take in. He searched his memory to try and determine if Graff was lying. Maybe the crazy bastard wanted to throw him off the scent. But something about Graff speaking those words with a gun pointed at his head made McNeal believe that Graff was telling the truth. It was a gut instinct, that's all.

What did the President know about the death of Graff's wife? Was someone shielding him? Was Graff's killing a vow of silence too? Had he told McNeal all he knew?

McNeal's head was going to explode. He checked his rearview mirror. A light appeared. It was closing in. A single light. A motorbike. Jack's gut tightened. The light edged closer. He gathered his strength and focused, in case this was it. Was this the end game? He slowed down. The light was still there. The same distance, as if whoever it was didn't want to get too close. He picked up the two-way radio. "Peter, motorbike in my rearview."

"What?"

"The last mile."

"Slow down."

"I have. They did the same."

"Fuck!"

"Keep moving, Peter. I'm going to pull over."

"Jack, for Christ's sake. Think!"

"This car is not going to outrun them."

"You got your gun?"

"Yup. Keep on going, Peter. Take care of yourself."

Jack pulled over and flicked on his hazard lights. He pulled out his gun. The cold metal on his warm fingers. The beam of the headlight washed over his car. He was in their crosshairs. The seconds seemed like hours. The motorbike was closing. A matter of yards now. Then the motorbike accelerated hard past him, the driver and a hanger-on both clad in black.

His heart skipped several beats. "Motherfucker."

Suddenly, the two-way radio on the passenger seat crackled into life.

"You okay, Jack?"

McNeal put down the gun and got back on the road. "I'm okay. Graff said it was a two-man team coming for me. I swear to God, there were two people on the bike."

"Jesus Christ, seriously?"

"So, why didn't they open fire?"

"I have no idea."

"We're not out of the woods yet."

"What do you mean?"

"Jack, up ahead, we've got single-lane traffic. Some truck crashed. Cops and paramedics everywhere. The traffic is slowing."

McNeal's heart nearly stopped. This was exactly what he had feared. "Fuck." He questioned whether this was an elaborate trap. Were the two people on the bike part of this?

"Let's just go with it."

"Nothing else we can do. Let's sit tight and be cool."

"Exactly."

"If I get pulled over, Peter, I just want to say I love you. But you need to look after number one."

"No one's going to get pulled over."

McNeal slowed down until he saw the red lights in the distance. The traffic slowed to a crawl. Cops with nightsticks and high-visibility vests directed the cars to keep moving. He knew they would see his out-of-state plates and wonder what the fuck he was doing in the dead of night in the Middle-of-Nowhere, Maryland. At least that's what he would think.

McNeal began to disassociate. He disconnected from his thoughts. His identity. Even his consciousness.

His mind drifted. He saw a time when he and Caroline were together. Before she left him. Before she was by herself, without him to protect her.

He grappled with a sickness that spiraled to the very depths of his soul. He had become everything that was immoral in man. The beast within had raised its head. McNeal wanted to close his eyes and see his son again. He wanted his son back in his arms. He remembered the day his son was born and the days that followed. He was working, and when he returned home, there was his baby son, sound asleep in Caroline's arms.

The sound of police shouting for traffic to slow down snapped McNeal back to reality. It was single-line traffic as they passed the smoking wreckage. He stared straight ahead as he drove on.

McNeal tightened his grip on the steering wheel. He drifted into a fugue state. He mentally fled his own body. He could hear his heart beating. But a strange calm washed over him.

The faces of the cops were bathed in red and blue lights. Waxy. Slow-motion blur. Nightsticks pointing the way.

McNeal edged slowly forward. He drove on. Past the cops. Without even a glance.

Eventually, McNeal was in the clear.

The road ahead opened up before him. He eased his foot on the gas, putting distance between himself and the cops in his rearview mirror.

McNeal drove hard. The taillights up ahead in the darkness illuminated the way to the reservoir.

The two-way radio crackled into life. "You okay, Jack?"

"No, not really."

"Let's focus. Just checking the GPS, the reservoir is three miles away. We're looking for Nicodemus Road, just outside Reisterstown. Do you copy?"

"Copy that." Jack put down the radio and drove on, the headlights bathing the woods all around and illuminating a sign for Reisterstown.

McNeal turned off onto a winding rural country road. He slowed around a sharp bend shrouded by trees and foliage, then saw the bridge in the distance. His heart hammered like a pneumatic drill.

Peter had clicked on his red hazard lights. He emerged from his car carrying his flashlight, indicating for McNeal to pull up beside him.

McNeal glanced in the rearview mirror. Just darkness. No other cars on this isolated stretch of road.

He pulled up, got out of his car, popped open the trunk.

McNeal grabbed the head, his brother the feet. They were both breathing hard. "Let's do it," McNeal instructed.

They lifted the body from the trunk, eased it onto the small concrete wall and rolled it into the water below. A heavy splash. Ripples of water.

Peter shone the flashlight down onto the dark waters. "It's gone. It's done."

"You sure?"

"It's over. Let's get out of here."

Forty-Nine

The first glimmers of pale morning light flickered through the blinds of Andrew Forbes's office in the West Wing. He was drinking a strong coffee, watching Fox News, when the President appeared in the doorway. The big guy was smiling this morning, sporting a bespoke navy suit.

Forbes got to his feet. "Morning, Mr. President."

"So, what do you think, Andrew?"

Forbes took a few moments to admire the beautiful cut and fit. "It's truly fantastic. When did it arrive?"

"Last night. Flown in from London. Appreciate the heads-up on the tailor."

"Got to love a great suit, Mr. President."

An aide passed in the corridor and handed the President a mug of coffee. The President smiled and took a couple of gulps.

"Mr. President, do you mind if I have a quick word?"

The President shrugged and walked into Forbes's office, shutting the door behind him. He sat down in a desk chair and took in the room. "This is nice. Cozy. Got a nice ambience." His eyes fixed on a photo of Forbes with his dad and mom. "Lovely family you've got, Andrew. Cherish that."

"I hear you."

"Is there a lucky girl in your life?"

Forbes blushed. "There's a girl I'm seeing. She's talking about getting married. She's a lot of fun."

"A lot of fun, huh? Let me tell you, I've met girls who are a lot of fun, which is fine, but has she met your mother?"

"Not yet. I'm taking it slow."

"Slow is always good. It pays to take your time." The President looked at his watch. "I've got a CIA briefing in an hour, and I need to read the report again. So, if you don't mind."

"Of course, Mr. President. A friend of mine works at the *Post*."

The President nodded.

"I was asking her in passing about any other reporters interested in the death of Sophie Meyer."

"Very sad, her passing."

"Indeed. Well, my source at the *Post*—and this person is involved at the highest level editorially—reassured me that this is not an area of interest. No reporter is pursuing this. So, the matter is closed. They are satisfied it was a tragic accident."

The President got to his feet. "Which it was. Appreciate the heads-up. A million things going on in the world, Andrew. The death of a rich socialite taking her life while high is a personal tragedy. But the world moves on. Anything else?"

"No, Mr. President. Is there any way I can be of assistance?"

The President smiled. "How about a beer tonight. *Monday Night Football*?"

"Love to, sir."

The President winked at him and walked out, shutting the door quietly as he left.

Fifty

The dawn of a new day. McNeal and his brother pulled into a diner on the outskirts of Trenton, New Jersey. They carefully washed their hands in the men's room before sitting down to plates full of pancakes with maple syrup and black coffee. They ate in silence for a few minutes.

Peter wiped the syrup from the corners of his mouth. Then he leaned forward, his voice a whisper. "Couple of things we have to go over."

"The car. My car."

"I've been thinking about that. I know a guy. Five miles from here. Old friend of mine. He won't ask questions."

"Who is he?"

"You don't need to know. He runs a breaker's yard. We put your car in. Pulp it. End of story."

Jack realized he had slipped into murder and criminality with surprising ease. He wondered why he didn't feel much. Maybe he was in shock. Maybe it was his way of dealing with it. "I want to talk about Nicoletti, the prowler."

Peter sipped his coffee. "What about him?"

"I want to know what he knows. Graff said that Nicoletti was the link man."

"Link man to who?"

"Someone close to the President. I want to know who that is."

"Are you out of your fucking mind? Are you going to kill him too?"

"Maybe."

Peter was quiet for a few minutes. His gaze skipped around the diner, as if seeking divine intervention.

"Please walk away," McNeal begged.

"No can do. I'm not leaving your side until this is done. What do you want to do?"

McNeal took out Graff's cell phone. It was using a virtual private network to preserve anonymity, and the location showed as Mexico, which clearly wasn't the case. He scrolled through the contacts. He saw Nicoletti's number. "I want to speak to this Nico. He's the fucker who killed Caroline. He's the one who was contacted by some serious people."

"Do you realize this isn't going to end well?"

"I'm way beyond caring."

Peter bowed his head and sighed.

"We kill this guy, the chances of getting caught rise exponentially."

Jack shook his head. He had already made up his mind. He was going to find the man who killed his wife. And find out exactly who was giving the orders. Where did it lead?

Peter leaned closer. "You're going to send him a message pretending to be Graff?"

McNeal realized he was smiling. "That's exactly what I'm going to do. He lives in a place you might remember."

"Where?"

"Warwick."

"Warwick, New York?"

"Got it."

Peter nodded. They both knew the town. They had visited their grandmother, who lived there. They had played in the fields outside the town.

"Think back."

"I am."

"Remember the place where we used to play?"

"I see where you're going with this."

McNeal could see his brother knew the very location he had in mind. "No one will ever find him there. It's the perfect place to kill this guy."

Fifty-One

It was past midday when Andrew Forbes got called into the office of White House Chief of Staff Blane Skinner. He knocked twice and walked in, shutting the door quietly behind him.

"Pull up a seat, Andrew."

Skinner sat behind a huge desk, neat piles of paper in front of him.

Forbes had been in there just once before, on his first day. He knew Skinner only by reputation. He was feared by nearly all staff at the White House. He shouted at staffers, interns. On occasion, even shouted at the Secret Service for standing too close to the President or getting in his way. He was known to harbor grudges that lasted months, sometimes years. He never forgot people who slighted him, or those who disappointed him in some way. Sometimes people were dismissed simply for giving off weird vibes, but the people who crossed him were invariably coldly dispatched. Skinner was supremely fit. He prided himself on working out three times a day, wherever in the world he was. Even on Air Force One, Skinner took up yoga positions. The guy was a machine. A maniac.

Forbes shrank in his seat. His gaze fixed on the chief of staff's lifeless gray eyes. They seemed to match Skinner's pallor.

Skinner adjusted the knot of his red silk tie. "How long have you been in this job, Andrew?"

"Three years, three months, and five days, sir."

Skinner grimaced. "That's a long time. The President is a demanding man. I know that better than most. It takes its toll, right?"

"I find him to be good company, sir."

"He is good company; I'll give you that." Skinner picked up an envelope from his desk and handed it to Forbes. "You want to have a look inside?"

Forbes took the envelope. "What is it, sir?"

"Have a look for yourself."

Forbes opened the envelope and rifled inside, pulling out some color photos. He took a few moments to digest what he was seeing. All of a sudden, he felt as if his world had imploded. Intimate pictures of him with Karen Feinstein. He looked through the five photos.

"She looks like good company too. Do you know how I got those photos?"

Forbes gripped the chair, as if the room had started to sway. He felt light-headed. But instead of answering, he just sat, mute, lost in a bad dream.

"These photos were couriered from the national security desk of the *New York Times*. They received these from an unknown email address in Oman. Clearly not where they came from. Can you explain how these came to be? And who is this woman?"

Forbes's gut reaction was to leave the room and call his father. His father always sorted things out for him. His father had instilled in him that, above duty to country and president, family was everything. He ran through his mental list of evasions, whether he should try and bluster his way out of the situation. Maybe he should just take the Fifth.

"Are you refusing to answer? Is that it, Andrew? You won't be leaving here until I have an idea of what the hell is going on. Who is the woman? Why is the *New York Times* getting photos of you and her? How have you been compromised? Because if you have been compromised, this reflects on the President's judgment. Do you understand?"

"Yes, sir."

"I can make this easy. I can make this go away, but you have to be up-front with me, son."

Forbes steeled himself, like a freight train was careering in his head. "I understand, sir."

"You see, there is one other thing I have to consider. Actually, it's the obvious thing."

"What's that, sir?"

"That this is a honey trap. And you have been sharing information. Classified information with this woman. Do you understand that this means you are prime blackmail material with these photos? Was she a Russian spy? Was she working for the Chinese? A million and one possible explanations. Maybe she has a different agenda. I don't know."

Forbes nodded, as if reflecting on what he'd been told. He thought about who had set him up. The photos had been taken in a hotel room. Had the room been bugged? Who would spy on him?

His mind flashed back to how he had gotten involved with Feinstein in the first place. It began with a meeting with the President. The Commander in Chief had just been elected and was finding his feet. Three months in, late one night, the President visited Andrew in his office. He confided in Andrew how stressful the job was, how much pressure he was under, day and night. He spoke of the long-standing affair with his mistress, Sophie Meyer. She had grown increasingly erratic, threatening to go to the press. It was causing him problems. *I trust you, Andrew.* That's what he had said. *I know people, Andrew. But they can't make this go away. I might have to resign. Can you reach out to your father? He's a man I trust.* Andrew said he would speak face-to-face with his father. He met up with his father at his club on the Upper East Side and told him everything. His father made a call and told him to return to Washington and await instructions. Twenty-four hours later, a friend of his father's—Jason Iverson, a New York attorney—took Andrew for lunch at a fancy restaurant on Capitol Hill and handed him a card for the services of Fein Solutions. A personal referral to Karen Feinstein. Her firm dealt with such matters.

"Do you understand the severity of this?" The voice of Skinner snapped him back to the harsh reality of the present.

Forbes nodded, struggling to wrap his head around it.

"We'll find out who she is. Might take an hour. Maybe a day. And then we'll piece this thing together. You either come clean now, or we start making inquiries. Things can get messy."

Forbes squirmed. His gaze fixed on the framed photo on the desk: Skinner with the President.

"We serve, Andrew. It's an honor to serve your country and your president."

"I love my country. And I will do anything to serve the President."

"I know that's true; I'm sure you'll make the right call."

"Does anyone at the White House know about this? Does the President?"

Skinner solemnly shook his head. "I thought you had a girlfriend, Andrew."

Forbes nodded. "I do."

"Jenny Sinclair, if my memory serves me right. Are you serious about her?"

"We're taking it slow."

"I'm guessing her father wouldn't be too happy if he saw such uncensored pictures on Twitter? Or if such photos were mentioned in certain salacious tabloid magazines. You know the type I'm talking about?"

"Indeed, sir."

"The Sinclairs are a very wealthy, very powerful family. Like your own. This event could tarnish you forever. So, you see, it's vital you come clean about this woman and what exactly happened."

Forbes needed to speak to Jason Iverson. The lawyer's number was on his cell phone. Should he just walk out of the office and make the call? Then again, maybe he should just sit tight and play for time.

"Now there's two ways this could play out. The dumb way or the smart way. The dumb way involves you dragging this out and refusing to cooperate. Your name will be confirmed. The smart way, you tell me who the hell she is, and we manage this situation."

Forbes nodded as he stared at the mug of steaming hot coffee on Skinner's desk.

"We will not confirm your name as being the guy in these photos, which you clearly are. We will put pressure on the reporter, insinuating that her newspaper will lose any contact with official sources within the White House, effectively shutting down their political coverage. We will give them nothing."

"I understand."

"We will stand by you, but only if you tell us who the fuck she is. And, before you ask, no. You can't call a lawyer. Deal with it like a man, or face humiliation. Think of the humiliation to your father. The family. Your mother."

Forbes closed his eyes.

"Do you think Jenny's parents will allow this relationship to proceed when they read about your activities with another woman? What if they see the photos? 'Can he really have feelings for our lovely daughter,' the Sinclairs will say, 'if he's fucking this other woman?' I don't fucking think so, son. Now, either wise up or face the music. That's your choice."

Forbes nodded but didn't say a word.

"You will be asked to leave, and you will be given glowing references, of course. The best and most loyal body man a president has ever had. And you know what, I'm good friends with several guys at the networks. Studios. Producers. You want to make a name in Hollywood, right?"

"At some point, yes."

"Well, you're in luck. I can help you. But I can also crush your dreams. Believe me when I say that. Just ask my ex-wife." Skinner smiled tightly, as if afraid to show his teeth.

Forbes felt his throat tighten. "This is difficult for me, sir."

"How so?"

"I don't believe in betraying trust."

"I'm asking you a simple fucking question, Andrew."

Forbes experienced a stabbing pain in his right knee and winced. He stared at the coffee. An idea slowly began to form in his head.

"You okay?"

"Just my knee injury."

Skinner nodded empathetically. "It's a bitch. Had the same sort of deal after an accident in Aspen three years ago."

"Slow recovery, but I'm getting there."

"I imagine jogging with the President doesn't help?"

"It's fine, just needs time to heal."

Skinner's cell phone rang. He checked the ID display. He held up a finger. "Never a fucking break. Two minutes, Andrew. Don't move." The chief of staff left the office, shutting the door softly behind him.

Forbes sat motionless. His breath grew faster. He didn't have much time. He needed to do it now.

He took out a small plastic bottle from his jacket pocket, unscrewed the rubber dropper. He leaned across the desk and dropped six minuscule shots of oxycodone in Skinner's coffee.

He sat back down, screwed on the dropper, and carefully put the bottle back in the inside pocket of his jacket.

Forbes reached into his other pocket, pulled out a pen, and stirred Skinner's coffee for a few seconds.

His heart pounded like it was going to explode.

What the fuck had he done? Was he losing his mind?

Forbes took a few deep breaths, trying to calm himself down. He leaned forward, careful to pick up the correct coffee cup. He sat with the untainted coffee. He took a large gulp.

Time dragged. The caffeine and adrenaline coursed through his system.

The door opened.

Skinner was smiling as he shut the door quietly behind him. He sat back down and placed his cell phone on his blotting pad. "I'm sorry about that interruption, Andrew. If it's not one thing, it's something else, right?"

Forbes sipped his coffee. "Not a problem. I really appreciate you being up-front with me. I very much respect where you're coming from and also for giving me a chance to wrap my head around this."

"I'm glad you understand my position, Andrew. It's not easy. But I know you can see the benefit of talking this out."

"Absolutely, sir." Forbes was willing Skinner to drink the coffee.

Skinner ran his tongue over the front of his teeth.

Forbes wondered if the fucker was ever going to drink the damn coffee. He exhaled as Skinner picked up his mug and took a couple of large gulps.

"Listen, I set aside the next few hours to get this situation resolved, okay?"

Forbes shrugged.

"But we've got a change of plan. We're headed down on Air Force One to Florida. Leaving in forty-five minutes."

"I'm going, I assume."

"That's right. So, we'll have to reschedule this chat to this evening, when we return. Ten o'clock?"

"Works for me."

"You need to heed this advice. Leave, and we can deal with this situation."

Forbes nodded. "I think you're right."

Skinner drank the rest of the coffee, licking his lips. "Nothing personal, kid."

Forbes smiled. "It's business, right?"

"That's all it is, son. It's just the way of the world."

Fifty-Two

The breaker's yard was located on contaminated wasteland in New Jersey. It was run by two Hells Angels. But it was owned by Peter's childhood friend, now capo of a New York Mafia family, Luigi Bonafessi. He was a twenty-first-century John Gotti. He also had a penchant for designer suits and flashy gold jewelry. But both Mafia men shared the same fearsome reputation.

Bonafessi had climbed the ranks quickly. He started as a street thug. His notoriety for beatings and killings grew. He came to the attention of the head of the family. He became an associate. Then he was initiated, and became a *made* man. A Mafia "soldier." A few years later, he was a capo. Head of the crew.

McNeal had heard of the guy. Peter, by contrast, knew the mobster well. He had hung out with Bonafessi throughout elementary school on Staten Island. Schoolyard fights, him and his friends. Italians versus Irish. Italians and Irish versus Blacks. Then they had gone their separate ways.

Bonafessi had turned to crime when he was a kid. But throughout everything, he and Peter had kept in touch, off and on, over the years.

Jack McNeal squirmed, deeply uncomfortable hanging around with such people. He knew they were animals and would kill you as soon as look at you. But, in his current predicament, turning a blind eye was the only option. He knew the favor would be called in some time down the line. That was a given.

He and Peter watched as the car got picked up by a crane and dropped into a steel crushing machine. It was a matter of minutes before it was pulped and ready for scrap.

Luigi shook Peter's hand and then Jack's. "Nice to meet you, Jack. I've heard a lot about you. Good things."

Jack forced a smile.

"Listen, don't worry. It's done. We'll bury it. None of this happened."

Peter said, "I owe you one, Luigi."

"I don't call in favors unless I need to. Buy me a nice drink when we meet up, huh?"

Luigi turned his gaze on Jack. "Stuff happens. I respect you for reaching out to us. We all need a helping hand from time to time. I try and help out people in my neighborhood." He patted Jack on the shoulder. "You don't have to have sleepless nights about this. I wish you well."

"Appreciate that," Jack said.

Peter smiled. "Tell your dad I hope he gets better soon."

"He's a tough old dog," Luigi said. "He's like your own father. He'll never leave Staten Island unless it's in a fucking box."

Peter smiled again. "We've got to go, Luigi. I owe you that drink."

Luigi cocked his head in the direction of the pulped metal. "Luigi can make anything disappear. You just need to ask nicely." The Mafia guy laughed as two of his men stood watching from a distance.

The brothers took the short walk back to Peter's car. Jack was lost in his thoughts as they drove back to Manhattan. He and his brother were killers. No better than Luigi and his crazy family.

They parked around the corner from Jack's tiny apartment on West Third Street.

Jack showered as Peter bagged his dirty clothes and put them down the garbage chute.

Jack put on a fresh set of clothes. He had always wondered why people like cops, who were supposed to uphold the law, went bad. Now he knew. Stuff happens. Life is messy. People are fucked up.

He needed time to decompress. Time to think about what had happened.

McNeal's mind flashed images of Graff lying dead in the bean field, bullet in his head. He knew that if push came to shove, he would kill Nicoletti. The bastard had murdered Caroline, a woman who had single-handedly unearthed Graff's involvement in killing his wife, Sophie Meyer. And Caroline had paid the price.

He remembered what Graff had said. About the ambush waiting for him. Was Graff behind that, or was it Feinstein's people? What would they be thinking now that they couldn't contact Henry Graff? No sign of him. At least no visible sign of him.

He imagined they wouldn't go to the cops to report a missing person. Then he started thinking about Nicoletti. Would he try and contact Graff? Would Feinstein try and contact Nicoletti?

The more he learned, the more he wanted to expose the whole fucked-up operation.

The brothers walked to a nearby diner. Jack ordered a burger and fries while Peter ordered a pastrami sandwich.

They ate in silence. When they were finished, and on their third cup of coffee, Jack asked, "You think we can trust Luigi?"

Peter leaned forward and whispered, "I don't trust many people, but I trust him. I use him as an informant. Very, very useful. I've gotten his father a couple of breaks over the years."

"Jesus Christ."

"Sometimes you have to get your hands dirty. The father is a big shot, as you know. But he also has dirt on other big shots. You know how it works."

McNeal hunched over his coffee. "What a mess."

"You're right. But we roll with it. You still want to get that creep, Nico?"

"I'm all in."

"So am I. Fuck it."

McNeal grinned. "Fuck it."

"We almost certainly left a trail. But that's in the past. We move on."

"We've done our best to minimize it, including the digital trail through cell phone towers."

"Nothing is foolproof. But without a body, they have nothing."

"I want to talk to Nicoletti. We need to get to him before Feinstein or any of her crew try and reach out to him or silence him."

Peter tossed his napkin onto the table and leaned back. "You know how it's going to play out if you do find him?"

Jack nodded.

Fifty-Three

Andrew Forbes ate pretzels on Air Force One, trying to appear nonchalant as he watched the President floss his teeth. The Commander in Chief was due to speak to the press corps at the back of the plane. The President was fanatical about his oral hygiene. But Forbes's thoughts were mostly on Skinner, who sat farther back.

Skinner was barking instructions to some poor PR sap who was being berated for taking a call from the mayor of Washington, DC. *I mean, who the fuck is she, anyway? Some self-important social worker. Wanting to save the world. She could start by losing fifty pounds off her ass, right? And you're seriously going to waste the President's time putting that on the agenda? Really? Get a fucking grip, son!*

Forbes vibrated, a mixture of excitement and blind terror about what would soon unfold on the plane. He'd had no particular problem with Skinner until an hour ago. But the fucker was blackmailing him with compromising photos. It begged the question who had sent them in the first place. Who had even taken the photos? It sure as hell wasn't him. It couldn't be Feinstein. How would she benefit from this? Was it someone Feinstein worked with? He knew no newspaper would publish the photo. They couldn't possibly authenticate that the photo hadn't been digitally manipulated. Besides, he would sue their asses for millions, citing libel and invasion of privacy. He would say the photos were fake and a politically motivated hatchet job. But if the photos were leaked by someone in the *New York Times* to a political blogger, or maybe to a reporter at the *National Enquirer*, it would cause him a lot of trouble.

The more he thought about it, the less he understood. He wondered if they had been under surveillance all along. If so, by whom?

His blood ran cold. If Nicoletti was running a surveillance operation for Henry Graff, then they all had serious problems.

The President took a deep breath, his tongue moving slowly across his gleaming white teeth. "What do you think?"

"You look great, Mr. President. Fresh. Vital."

The President handed over the used piece of dental floss, slivers of pizza still attached and dripping with presidential saliva.

Forbes remained impassive. He folded the dirty dental floss in a tissue and tossed it in a trash can. He straightened the President's tie. "Hermès. You got to love a proper silk tie."

"Andrew, what would I do without you?"

Forbes smiled. "Flounder?"

The President threw back his head, laughing. "You're a riot; I love it."

Out of the corner of his eye, he saw Skinner slumping across his paper-strewn table. He turned and saw that the chief of staff had gone pale, sweaty, head lolling, a pile of briefing papers in front of him.

The President noticed. He stared across at his chief of staff. "What the hell is wrong with Skinner? Is he drunk?"

"Maybe tired," Forbes said, trying to appear empathetic.

"Tired? If anyone should be tired, it's yours truly. I've been up since four."

Forbes leaned over and looked at Skinner, who was now drooling at the mouth. "Mr. President, he's not well."

The President touched Skinner's forehead. "He's cold. He's completely cold."

Forbes called for the doctor aboard. The doctor got up from his seat and checked Skinner's pulse. He signaled over to a table of Secret Service agents playing cards. "I need help. We need to get Mr. Skinner to the medical suite! Now!"

The agents carried Skinner through to the medical suite. "Make way, please! Emergency!"

Forbes watched the whole thing play out. He struggled not to laugh as Skinner disappeared into the medical suite adjacent to the President's office. He tried to put on his best concerned expression. He turned to the President. "Sir, is there anything I can get you? Anyone you want me to call?"

The President shook his head as he signaled two national security advisors. "I got this, Andrew, thanks. Good thing you spotted he had taken a turn for the worse."

"Is he going to be okay, sir?"

The President sighed. "I don't know, Andrew. I just don't know."

The rest of the flight, Forbes sat on a miniature couch, exchanging gossip on Skinner's condition with a junior staffer.

"Was it something he ate?" she asked.

Forbes feigned quiet contemplation for a few moments. "Maybe. I'm surprised. He's such a robust guy most of the time. He works longer hours than anyone I know, apart from the President. Tremendous work ethic."

"I heard he has a heart condition."

"Is that right?" Forbes said. "I hadn't heard that. I know an uncle of mine who was a workaholic got heart palpitations and ultimately had to be put on beta blockers or something, and he also had stents inserted after a blockage. Chief of staff is a tough, tough gig. No letup."

The minutes passed as it was decided to continue the flight to Orlando.

"Fifteen minutes to touchdown, people," a Secret Service suit bellowed. "Can we buckle up? We need to get the chief of staff off without any delays."

"Is he alive?" Forbes asked.

"Barely."

Forbes shook his head. "How awful. What's wrong with him?"

The agent had already turned and walked away.

Forbes stared out the window as the descent began. His ears began to pop. He closed his eyes as he smiled to himself, giddy at what he'd done.

Fifty-Four

The McNeal brothers sat in silence on most of the hour-long journey as they headed through the Lincoln Tunnel, westbound through New Jersey and back north across the state line into New York. Jack was getting progressively more nervous as they drove down the highway. He sensed he was being pulled, inexorably, toward his fate. Maybe it was always meant to be this way, next to his brother. His blood.

He checked the location of Nicoletti's phone using a GPS tracking app. Graff's henchman was fifteen miles from Warwick. "He's at home."

Peter headed down a back road. He pulled up one mile from the site, off the road and out of sight from anyone passing by. "There are no guarantees this will work, Jack. No guarantees at all. No guarantees this fuck will show up."

"I think he will."

Jack turned on Graff's cell phone when they were in the middle of nowhere. He scrolled through the contacts and sent a brief message to Nicoletti.

We need to talk, face-to-face. Super urgent. Got a job for you. One hour. Not far from you. Head down Cascade Road and onto dirt road through woods. Then ten minutes on foot before the old entrance. A friend of mine will show you down the dirt path. H.

Jack took the battery and SIM card out of the cell phone.

"You think that'll work?"

Jack shrugged. "Who the hell knows?"

"I've got my flashlight. And my gun."

"And I've got the Glock I used on Graff. Let's get a move on and get in place."

Peter edged slowly along Cascade Road. He turned onto the dirt road leading through the woods.

"Seems like a thousand years ago we were here," Jack noted. "But it's all so familiar."

Peter nodded. The place they had played in when they were kids. Exploring the caves. Carrying flashlights.

He drove on for a mile until they got to a clearing.

Jack put on a Knicks hat from the back seat. They both got out of the car and hugged tight.

"You okay, Jack? You got this?"

Jack was consumed by doubt, but he wasn't going to show it. They were both in over their heads, and there was no turning back. "I got this."

"No fucking around. This guy is a killer."

Jack stared at his brother. "That makes two of us."

Time dragged as Jack waited. He didn't know if Nicoletti would show up. Even if he did, would he come alone or bring a crew? Maybe the fucker would shoot him on sight.

The more McNeal thought about it, the more a strange sense of calm seemed to wash over him. He had one advantage. Nicoletti probably wouldn't recognize Jack or Peter. He would have known what Caroline looked like if he was stalking her, but not her estranged husband. Then again, maybe Graff had already circulated a photo of Jack to Nicoletti.

McNeal needed to bear that in mind. He envisioned Caroline's last conscious moments. Had she seen her killer's face? Had Nicoletti killed her near the Potomac before dumping her body in the water?

The black, putrid thoughts filled his head. A virus filled his soul. Bastards like that had no compunction about killing. But then again, neither did he—not anymore. He hadn't hesitated to kill Graff. He had calmly watched as his brother had poured the cement into the bucket, then they had both dropped the trussed-up dead weight into the dark waters of the reservoir. One day, local fishermen could drag up the body, or parts of the body. It might be weeks. Nothing would tie what remained of Graff to either McNeal or his brother. No forensic evidence. Maybe circumstantial. Maybe a surveillance camera out in the middle of nowhere would catch them traveling down the highway. Maybe their luck would run out.

Jack wondered if, one day, when he thought this was all in the past, it would catch up to him. Then again, like a lot of cases, maybe not. Maybe Mother Nature would do her work. The fish in the reservoir could chew the meat off of Graff's bones, leaving only a skeleton, its feet in concrete.

McNeal thought back to his first session with the psychologist. She had been concerned for his well-being. She was right to be concerned. His wife's death had plunged him into a darkness from which he might never emerge. The hours since had been a living nightmare. And it was all still playing out. He would die in jail, haunted by the memories of what he had become. But, as it stood, a free man had become a hunter. He didn't give a damn.

He thought of his son. His poor, dead son. The pain was too much to bear. Maybe dying would be a respite for McNeal. A beautiful release.

The sound of crunching footsteps snapped him back to the present.

"Henry?" A man's voice. "You here?"

"This way," Jack said.

A lone figure approached wearing a combat jacket, jeans, and heavy boots.

McNeal brushed against the cold metal of the Glock in his pocket as he scanned the man's craggy features. It had to be Nicoletti.

Fifty-Five

Jack stepped forward and waved the gun at Nicoletti. He approached just close enough to get a whiff of strong cologne. "Hands on your head, motherfucker," he ordered.

Nicoletti tilted his chin, amused. "Who are you?"

"Are you fucking deaf?"

"I don't want any trouble, man."

McNeal implemented his game plan. He fired one shot and blew out Nicoletti's kneecap. The fucker screamed, collapsing on the ground, blood gushing from his knee. The sound of the gunshot and screaming echoed through the woods, birds scattering. "Too bad."

Nicoletti shook, gripping his bloodied knee. "What the fuck, man?"

Peter ran out of the woods and kicked Nicoletti in the head. The guy passed out for a few moments.

Jack grabbed Nicoletti's right hand as Peter grabbed the left. They hauled him headfirst down the dirt path until they reached the cave entrance. Peter had already ripped off the wooden sheeting.

Nicoletti came to and began to scream.

The brothers dragged Nicoletti through the filthy ankle-deep water of the cave. The fucker's screams echoed in the dark mine.

"Hey, hey, you guys, what is this?"

Farther and farther into the abandoned mine.

"What the fuck are you doing?"

Deeper and deeper they dragged him, flashlight beams bathing the tunnel in a ghostly light. On and on they went. Hundreds of yards into the mine. Way out of sight.

Nicoletti shivered. He was bleeding in the cold, fetid water. "Sweet mother of God, what are you doing? Where is Henry? Does he know you're doing this? When he finds out, you guys are dead!"

Jack punched him twice in the jaw. The sound of bone cracking resonated in the cave.

Nicoletti began to wail, his mouth twisted.

"Just so you know, pal, we're only just getting started."

"Are you out of your goddamn minds? Do you know who I am?"

Jack bent over and pressed a gun to Nicoletti's head as Peter frisked him. He found a set of car keys and a cell phone. "Where's your weapon?"

"In the trunk of my car, man," he said with a groan.

"What's your passcode for your cell phone?"

"What?"

"You heard!"

"11131114."

Jack tapped in the numbers and unlocked the contents of the cell phone. He put the cell phone in his pocket. "11131114, you got that, bro?"

Peter nodded. "Got it."

Nicoletti shook uncontrollably, wincing in pain when he spoke. "What the fuck you guys want? You working for Henry? Did he send you?"

Peter pressed his foot onto the bleeding knee.

Nicoletti screamed again and scrunched up his eyes. "Motherfucker! What do you want?"

"You're gonna talk. And then we'll let you go."

"Man, I've done everything Henry asked me to do. What the hell is going on?"

Jack grabbed Nicoletti by the hair and pistol-whipped him. Blood spurted from his nose and mouth. The pent-up fury was starting to unfurl. "Who told you to kill Caroline McNeal?"

Nicoletti spat out blood and a broken tooth. "Henry did," he mumbled. "I don't operate without his say-so."

Jack stomped on the man's head three times. Nicoletti spat out more teeth. He screwed up his eyes in pain.

"Who are you, man?" he gasped.

"You'll find out soon enough. How did you kill her?"

"Man, what is this?"

"You talk, and you might live. Stay silent, and you will die. Your choice."

"Fine . . . I broke into her place. I waited until she came home, and I jabbed her with drugs. Huge amounts of barbiturates and a morphine solution."

"Why?"

"To make it look like suicide. And then I took her body down to the river. And that was it."

Jack's mind flashed to his wife on their wedding day. The smile on her face. He bent over and pressed the gun tight to Nicoletti's head. He needed to maintain control. At least for now. "How about Sophie Meyer?"

"A simple break-in. Sprayed some synthetic opioid into her ear. It's known on the streets as Pink. Then fentanyl in her carotid. She collapsed and died. I sprinkled some pure coke around her lips. And I dropped a variety of sleeping pills around her body."

"You did it?"

"I did. But I was only following orders."

"Whose orders?"

Nicoletti winced, as if not wishing to divulge any more. "I don't know . . ."

Jack punched him twice in the face, blood spurting onto his shirt.

"Graff! Henry Graff!"

"Graff gave you the go-ahead?"

Nicoletti spat out some more blood, one of his eyes blackened, swollen, unable to see. "Yes and . . . no."

Jack pressed his foot down onto Nicoletti's face, partially submerging it in filthy water. "Don't fuck with me!"

Nicoletti spluttered and spat out the water.

"Let's try again. What does that mean?"

"Meyer was Henry's wife, man. Don't you understand? Sophie Meyer. He was married to her."

"I know that. But he wasn't the only one that wanted her dead."

"A lot of people wanted her in the ground. She was a threat. She fucked everyone in DC if they had money and influence. A lot of people wanted her out of the way."

"What kind of people?"

"Important people!"

"People in high levels of government? Who? Give me names!"

"I don't know exactly who," he mumbled. "But that's right. Look, man, I'm just a guy that does wet work. I don't know the big picture. I'm just a foot soldier."

"Did Graff know the big picture?"

"Yeah, he did."

"Were you the first point of contact?"

"No."

"What if I said I don't believe you?"

Nicoletti was shivering uncontrollably. "Get me to a hospital, you sick motherfuckers!"

"Just as soon as you talk."

"The approach was made to a woman first. And she approached me. That's how it all began. I swear to God."

McNeal knew who he was alluding to. "A woman?"

Nicoletti nodded.

"I need a name."

"Do you work for her?"

Jack shook his head.

"I don't know her name."

McNeal aimed his gun at Nicoletti's other knee. He fired two shots. The screams echoed through the mine.

Nicoletti passed out again.

Peter slapped him repeatedly until he came to. He yanked at Nicoletti's hair, keeping his bleeding nostrils above the water. "You're not checking out on us yet, pal."

Nicoletti's eyes rolled around in his head. He began to moan and sob as new waves of pain took hold.

"I need a name. I won't stop until you give me the name."

"Feinstein! Karen Feinstein. She runs a black ops crew."

Jack looked at Peter, whose face was filled with pent-up fury.

Peter said, "Company name?"

"Fein Solutions, motherfucker!"

"Is she connected to Graff?"

"They go way back. We all go way back. Agency. Look, man, I need fucking medical help or so help me God . . ."

"So, you did the wet work required by Feinstein or Graff?"

Nicoletti scrunched up his eyes and began to scream. "Yes! Yes! Motherfucker!"

Jack took Nicoletti's cell phone out of his pocket, tapped in the eight-digit code, and pulled up all the contacts. Three contacts. He saw Graff. Feinstein. But there was a third name that caught his eye. "Tell me about Ted Outcrow?"

"I don't know."

"What do you mean you don't know?"

"I don't know the guy. Karen knew him. And she gave me his number. For emergencies."

"It's a weird last name."

Nicoletti nodded as he began to sob, shaking, bleeding.

"So, was Karen contacted by Ted Outcrow?"

"Karen was the only one who knew Ted's true identity. That's what I know. It began with Ted making the call to Karen. That's all I know, man. I didn't have any dealings with him. Nothing direct."

"This is a bullshit name, isn't it?"

"I don't know, man. I'm cold. I need to go to a doctor."

McNeal pressed his foot hard into Nicoletti's right knee as Peter did the same with the left.

Nicoletti writhed in agony.

"Tell me the truth! Who the fuck is this guy?"

"I can't say any more. Ask Karen."

"We will, don't worry. But now we're asking you."

Nicoletti shook his head wildly, as if having a fit.

Peter gave a knowing look to Jack.

Jack bent over and grabbed Nicoletti's right foot as Peter grabbed the left. They dragged him a few more yards deeper into the cave.

Nicoletti's face partially submerged in the shallow water.

The brothers got to the edge of the mineshaft. They lifted Nicoletti up over the rim, holding him headfirst, slowly lowering him down.

Nicoletti's head dangled into the darkness.

Nicoletti struggled. "What the fuck are you doing, you sick fucks?"

Jack held on tight. "I want a name. You know this person's real name."

Nicoletti writhed frantically. He began to scream, calling for his mother.

McNeal and his brother held on tight. "You're going to tell us everything you know about this guy. Or we drop you. You know how deep it is down there?"

"Motherfuckers!"

"Give me a name! Right. Fucking. Now."

"You're out of your fucking minds! Go fuck yourself!"

"Last chance, tough guy. Give me a name."

Nicoletti thrashed like crazy.

"We need a name?"

"Woodcutter! Woodcutter is the name! Now let me up!"

"What?"

"Woodcutter!"

"What the fuck are you talking about?"

"That's what Karen said he was called."

"You're saying Ted Outcrow's name is Woodcutter. Is that a nickname?"

"It's a fucking anagram."

McNeal's mind raced. He mentally pieced it together. It was an anagram of Ted Outcrow.

"Why was he known as Woodcutter?"

"He's a powerful dude. He knows powerful people. That's all I know."

"Why is he called Woodcutter? Who is he?"

"I don't know his true identity." Nicoletti wept. "Please . . . I'm scared."

"Give me more!"

"Woodcutter was the Secret Service codename for this guy. He worked in the White House!"

McNeal's mind flashed back to the Secret Service guys speaking to him in Brooklyn.

"Woodcutter!" Nicoletti screamed. "He started it all."

"Why?"

"He wanted them dead. First Sophie Meyer. And then the journalist lady."

"Why?"

"He was shielding the President."

Jack gripped Nicoletti's ankle tightly as the struggling continued. "What do you mean?"

"He was protecting the President. The affair. Sophie Meyer had been gossiping she had photos of her and the President. And she did. That's what Karen said, so help me God!"

McNeal looked at his brother. His brother nodded back. They both knew instinctively what it meant. "And Caroline McNeal? What about her?"

"The bitch knew too much. I swear to God, I swear on my daughter's life, I don't know any more."

Jack stared at his brother and nodded again. They simultaneously released their grip.

The deathly screams as Nicoletti plunged headfirst down the abandoned mine shaft echoed for what seemed like an eternity.

A few moments later, a ghostly silence took their place.

Fifty-Six

It was still dark when they arrived at Peter's cabin in the woods overlooking Greenwood Lake, New Jersey.

Jack showered as Peter gathered up their dirty clothes and burned them in a firepit in the backyard. He lent his brother a pair of jeans, shirt, sweater, socks, and old Rockports.

Afterward, Peter had a shower as Jack stood at the firepit, watching their filthy clothes turn to ash before his eyes.

Twenty minutes later, as the first light flickered through the trees, Peter came outside with some logs and kerosene. He started a fresh fire. It burned brightly, the flames bathing Peter's face in a warm orange glow.

Jack got two cold beers from the fridge and brought one to his brother. He stared into the flames. "I'm sorry I got you into this," he said.

"You didn't get me into this. I got me into this. Besides, blood is always thicker than water. You think I'm going to let my older brother deal with everything by himself?"

"I shouldn't have let it get so crazy."

"Shit happens."

Jack gulped his beer. His mind was seared with images of Nicoletti falling into the darkness. He did that. He was responsible.

"And you know what? Fuck it! We'll take this to our graves."

McNeal sighed. "Woodcutter. That's the guy's name."

Peter bowed his head. "I want you to know that I'm drawing a line in the sand. I don't want this to go on. I need to get back to my old life. I've got a wife. And I've got kids."

"I know you do."

"Jack, listen to me. You want my advice?"

McNeal said nothing.

"You need to get back to your old life too. Before it's too late."

"I will."

Peter added a log to the fire. "There's something I meant to ask you. What happens if you get a knock at the door and it's the cops? What happens if I get a knock at the door and it's the cops? Maybe the Feds. What then?"

"Do what you have to do."

"I'm going to plead the Fifth."

"It's your constitutional right."

"You think they'll come knocking?"

"I don't know. What I do know is that they could piece it together. It is possible. But without the bodies, it's all just why the hell were you driving around Maryland and Jersey at such and such times."

"What would your answer be?"

"You know how it works. They'll drill down until you incriminate yourself. Best plan? Say nothing. Without a body and forensic evidence, they have zilch."

"What about blood in the soybean field?"

"I believe that will dissolve. Erode. With wind. And rain."

"Graff's car, if it's discovered?"

"Who knows? His body is in a lake an hour away."

“There might be surveillance cameras picking up parts of our journey. There are no guarantees.”

Jack patted his brother on the back and shrugged. “I’ll give you a guarantee. Neither Graff nor Nicoletti will be telling their side of the story, that’s for sure.”

Fifty-Seven

The sky was bloodred as McNeal returned home to Westport. He had rented a car in New Jersey and driven all the way home. He waited until it got dark. Then he put on a thick coat, wrapping himself up against the cold. He headed out onto a deserted Compo Beach, moonlight bathing the sand in an icy glow.

McNeal walked and walked, hands deep in his pockets. He felt empty. He closed his eyes and smelled the salty breeze in the air. It cooled his skin. He thought he would feel a sense of closure. He wondered if he had undergone some sort of psychotic breakdown. He had enacted a retribution both brutal and shocking, even to himself. He sensed this was not the end. Maybe it was the beginning of the end. But whatever it was, he didn't believe it was over. Not by a long shot.

He knew deep down that he had left a trail, and one day it would lead cops to his door. An investigation was like a jigsaw puzzle. But McNeal also knew that circumstantial evidence could be pieced together. The problems accelerate when a suspect lies to police. Gives fake alibis. That was why pleading the Fifth was always the best option.

He was relying on his brother to stick to that policy.

However, once the Feds or cops realized Jack had a dossier on Henry Graff sent to him, he would become the number-one suspect. It was possible to prosecute a case on the circumstances. But having a file on Graff didn't point in any way to McNeal being responsible for his disappearance.

There might be pressure applied to Peter. Maybe his brother would lose his pension. Maybe he would get desperate. His brother might crack. But that was only supposition.

McNeal knew the forensic link was the best possible evidence, and that would be harder to prove. No body. No DNA. There was always the possibility of hair strands or circumstantial evidence turning up. Graff's car would be discovered eventually. But what would it show? His brother's DNA? Within days and certainly weeks, the DNA would have degraded. At least that was what he hoped.

McNeal knew one thing: Nicoletti's body wouldn't be discovered for a long time. At least not now. It might eventually. Years from now. Maybe decades, but by then there would be nothing left. Deep in the mine, rats would have eaten the flesh down to the bones. Anything left, right down to fragments of bone, would wash away in the flooded mine shafts.

He had also visited the Feds with Peter. Given them the evidence painstakingly compiled by Caroline.

Just plead the Fifth. Silence was a powerful weapon. Can't incriminate with silence. Can't dig a hole if you don't say anything.

He would say nothing. He would get the best lawyer he could afford. As it was, he could afford the best. The money Caroline left him meant he could get a great lawyer.

His cell phone rang. He recognized Peter's caller ID.

"Hey, bro. Made it back safe and sound?"

"Yeah, safe and sound. How are the wife and kids?"

"They're fine. Jack, this is over, right?"

"It is for now."

"And if the cops or Feds come calling?"

"As I said, we both take the Fifth."

"Always works for the scumbags I deal with."

"Listen closely. If the shit hits the fan, you call me. I'll get us a great lawyer. Money is not an issue now. But until then, we move on."

"You going to let it go, Jack?"

"I'm going to try. It won't be easy."

"We need to just let this nightmare go."

McNeal stopped and stood, staring out over the dark waters of Long Island Sound. He absorbed the hypnotic sound of the sea washing onto the sand. "The nightmare will always be with us. What we've done. We will have to atone. Maybe not now, but someday down the line."

"Someday down the line is fine by me."

"Me too. I love you, bro."

"Love you too. Take care."

Jack McNeal locked the door and headed upstairs to his wife's study. He sat down in her favorite easy chair. He took in her books. Her desk. The photo of them on their wedding day. Her favorite photo of their son: Jack, holding Patrick's hand, walking along the beach.

When he couldn't sleep in the middle of the night, he sometimes imagined he was back on that beach, watching Patrick skim stones into the water. Moments in time. Etched into his brain. Memories of the son he lost.

The pain had lingered, festered, and erupted in a manner he could never have foreseen. The events of that night at the backyard barbecue haunted him. He closed his eyes. The steely gaze of Graf flashed through his mind. The blood-curdling scream as Nicoletti plunged down the mineshaft into the darkness echoed in his head.

Then the demented, reddened eyes of his NYPD partner, gun in hand, wanting to be killed by a cop.

McNeal had killed three men. He was a stone-cold killer.

His mind began to play through the events at the mine. He had committed Ted Outcrow's phone number to memory before he dropped Nicoletti down the mineshaft. He had taken out the SIM card and flushed the cell phone down a storm drain. Ted Outcrow. The anagram of Woodcutter. But who exactly was that? Did he really work in the White House, as Nicoletti claimed? Did he even exist?

He slipped into a deep, dark sleep, thinking only of his son.

Fifty-Eight

Three days later, McNeal decided he was ready to face the world again. He got up before dawn. He showered; shaved; and put on a suit, a pale-blue shirt, tie, and black oxfords. He checked his reflection in the mirror, peering at the dark shadows under his eyes. But he was alive. He was still breathing.

McNeal had a big breakfast, tidied up, ran the dishwasher. He called a rental company. An SUV was dropped off, and they took away his other rental car. He drove up to the cemetery and bought flowers on the way.

He crouched down at the graveside, the names of his wife and son carved in granite. He took out the weeks-old flowers, replacing them with white lilies, his wife's favorite. He touched the carved names on the headstone and bowed his head.

"Please forgive me. That's all I ask."

McNeal said a silent prayer and headed back to the car. He sat for a few minutes in the car, contemplating his wife's fate. His one consolation was that she was back in a town she loved, at peace. He would tend to her grave, same as he did for his son's. Lying together for eternity. He would try and atone for not being there for her.

He would carry that to his own grave.

The regrets.

McNeal pushed those thoughts to one side and drove down to Manhattan. The familiar skyline quickened his pulse. He parked a block from the office and took the elevator to the third floor.

A few familiar faces.

Dave Franzen, cup of coffee in one hand, embraced him tight. "Long time no see, buddy. I've been trying to call you but got no answer."

"I thought you retired?"

"I'm still clearing out my goddamn desk. What about you?"

"Just trying to put things back together."

"I've been thinking about you. You want to go for a beer tonight?"

"I'd like that. Thanks."

"Meeting a few of the guys at Flannerys."

"Sounds good. See you there. I'm going in to see Bob."

Franzen patted McNeal on the back. "Take care, man."

McNeal knocked on Bob Buckley's door and walked into his corner office.

Buckley looked up and smiled as if he was seeing an old friend. "Christ almighty, Jack. Everyone's been trying to contact you. It's like you'd disappeared off the face of the earth."

"Just needed some time to try and get away from it all."

Buckley got up and shook his head. "So sorry for your loss. And I'm sorry for all that crap with the Diplomatic Security guys and the Feds. Christ knows what they were thinking."

"Just doing their jobs."

"Fucking insensitive pricks."

"I'm from New York. I'm surrounded by them twenty-four seven. I'm used to it."

Buckley smiled. "Take a seat, Jack. You shouldn't be back at work yet. You need time to recover and get your head straight."

McNeal settled into a chair and did a tour of Buckley's office. Photos of Buckley with the mayor, governor, and President adorned the walls. "You get around, Bob."

Buckley laughed. "They're all a pain in the ass. But hey, you need to kiss ass sometimes. Besides, the photos look good on the wall for visitors."

McNeal smiled.

"I meant to ask, how was the session with the psychologist?"

"It wasn't something I enjoyed, but I think it helped me address a lot of issues."

"I'm glad. Might want to take a vacation too."

"I'll think about it. As of now, I want to get back to my job."

"Nothing wrong with some hard work."

"So, are we good? No further inquiries from the FBI regarding my late wife?"

"That's all done."

McNeal's shoulders relaxed.

"I understand you were just trying to find out what happened to her. I get that, Jack. And I sympathize. God knows I do. But I think it put a few noses out of joint."

"I should have just let it be."

"You're a great investigator. It's what you do."

McNeal was quiet for a few moments. "If it's okay with you, I'll just get back to my desk and try and sort out my backlog."

"You okay to do that?"

"I'm perfectly fine."

"Good to have you back."

"Like I've never been away."

An hour later, McNeal sat at his desk. He sifted through the backlog of his files, prioritizing which one to focus on in the morning.

Domestic assaults by cops on their wives, kids scared of their drunken cop dads, guns pointed at civilians on the subway for shouting—an endless list of stressed-out cops at their breaking points. Now, he knew exactly how they felt.

His desk phone rang.

"McNeal speaking."

Silence.

McNeal sensed there was someone there. "Hello?"

He thought he heard breathing.

The line went dead.

Epilogue

A week later, Jack McNeal sat opposite Belinda Katz. He studied the modern art on the walls. “Are these originals?” he asked.

“Yes. They all belonged to my late husband. He was a collector. He used to drink with Willem de Kooning and all his pals. They’re pretty valuable, or so I’m told.”

McNeal’s gaze lingered on the colors, the shapes, and the lack of form. He didn’t know if it was random or if it was bullshit. “It’s nice on the white walls.”

Katz smiled. “You’re seeing beauty in art. That’s a big step forward.”

“I don’t know about art, but I know what I like.”

“Sounds like a song I once heard.”

McNeal smiled. “Quite possibly. Nice line.”

“So, tell me, Jack, that was quite a disappearing act you pulled. I seem to have lost track of time. You want to talk about that?”

“I needed space and time, as they say.”

Katz fixed her gaze on his. “You seem far more peaceful now.”

McNeal shrugged. “Maybe. Maybe I was just having a bad day when you saw me last.”

“I still have the scrap of paper you asked me to write a name on,” she said. “You remember that?”

McNeal's mind flashed back to the conversation they'd had just a few weeks earlier.

"Do you remember that?"

"Yeah."

"You gave me a name. You believed that you might be in danger. If something happened to you, the name on that piece of paper was responsible, you said."

McNeal wondered where she was going with this.

"Do you feel that anyone is out to get you today?"

"No, I don't."

Katz smiled and scribbled down a few notes. "I've been looking over your psychological profile. NYPD. Your IQ and emotional intelligence set you apart. I can see that for myself."

"What's your point, Ms. Katz?"

"I was wondering if you were having a psychotic episode when you called me. Something out of character. Perhaps some sort of mental collapse."

"I don't know. I wasn't having a good day, that's for sure."

"The thing is, in my experience, a nervous breakdown, mental collapse, psychological breakdown, psychotic episode—call it what you will—isn't usually rectified in a few days. You appear . . . reborn. More assured than when I met you at our first session."

"I've had time to evaluate my priorities. What's important in my life."

"The name of the man, Henry Graff. I wrote down the name, as I said. Do you want this as a reminder of a dark episode in your life? Perhaps to serve as a reminder of how powerful the mind is?"

McNeal saw the smile on her face. It was almost as if she knew something.

"Would you like it back?"

"That would be nice."

Katz took out the crumpled piece of paper and handed it over. He studied her handwriting. The name Henry Graff and the date and time when she had written it.

"Thank you."

"I didn't make a note of that name. I've decided that perhaps that painful episode is something for you to process."

McNeal put the scrap of paper in an inside pocket of his jacket.

"Do you mind talking to me about Mr. Graff?"

McNeal shrugged.

"I was skeptical if he even existed. Maybe, I thought, he was a figment of your imagination."

"I hadn't thought of that before. Maybe he was."

"It's something we might want to explore at a future date, when you might feel more comfortable talking about it."

"Time's a great healer."

"Psychotic reactions vary according to an individual. It could last a day, maybe a week or two. But it's often a result of a stressful event in a person's life. And you may very well have slid into that extremely dangerous state."

McNeal nodded.

"I think you've been on a little journey recently. I'm glad you're back. I hope this episode is over. Do you think it's over? Have the voices in your head been quieted?"

McNeal closed his eyes. He didn't have an answer.

Acknowledgments

I would like to thank my editor, Victoria Haslam, and everyone at Amazon Publishing for their enthusiasm, hard work, and belief in my latest book, *No Way Back*, and the Jon Reznick Thriller series. I would also like to thank my loyal readers. Thanks also to Faith Black Ross for her terrific work on this book, and Randall Klein, who looked over an early draft. Special thanks to my agent, Mitch Hoffman, of the Aaron M. Priest Literary Agency, New York.

Last but by no means least, my family and friends for their encouragement and support. None more so than my wife, Susan.

About the Author

Photo © 2013 John Need

J. B. Turner is a former journalist and the author of the Jon Reznick series of action thrillers (*Hard Road*, *Hard Kill*, *Hard Wired*, *Hard Way*, *Hard Fall*, *Hard Hit*, *Hard Shot*, and *Hard Vengeance*), the American Ghost series of black-ops thrillers (*Rogue*, *Reckoning*, and *Requiem*), and the Deborah Jones political thrillers (*Miami Requiem* and *Dark Waters*). He has a keen interest in geopolitics. He lives in Scotland with his wife and two children.

Made in the USA
Monee, IL
25 February 2023